ONLY HIM

Annie didn't feel like a little girl, not in this man's arms. He still frightened her, not because of his anger, but because of the power he had over her, even after all this time. No one else had ever made her want as much as Isaac did.

When she tried to step back, to give herself some breathing room, he stopped her, using nothing more than a gentle caress that started at her waist and moved slowly up to cup the back of her head. It dawned on her that he intended to kiss her, and she was going to let him.

Not because it was the right thing to do, but because at that moment, it was the only thing to do.

The strength of him surrounded her, making her ache and setting her very skin on fire with the pleasure of his embrace. Lord of mercy, his kiss was sweet, so very sweet. He tried to be gentle with her, coaxing her at first and then just that quickly, the kiss became so much more as he demanded as much as she could give and more.

ANNIE'S CHRISTMAS

PAT PRITCHARD

ZEBRA BOOKS
KENSINGTON PUBLISHING CORP.
http://www.kensingtonbooks.com

ZEBRA BOOKS are published by

Kensington Publishing Corp.
850 Third Avenue
New York, NY 10022

All Kensington titles, imprints and distributed lines are available at special quantity discounts for bulk purchases for sales promotion, premiums, fund-raising, educational or institutional use.

Special book excerpts or customized printings can also be created to fit specific needs. For details, write or phone the office of the Kensington Special Sales Manager: Kensington Publishing Corp., 850 Third Avenue, New York, NY 10022. Attn. Special Sales Department. Phone: 1-800-221-2647.

First Printing: October 2004
10 9 8 7 6 5 4 3 2

Printed in the United States of America

This book is dedicated to
Michelle Grajkowski, agent extraordinaire.
Thank you for all your hard work,
your unflagging support,
and the way we always laugh together.
I love having you in my corner.

12/04

CHAPTER ONE

Annie breathed on the glass and used the side of her fist to clear a spot big enough to look out. To the east, faint tinges of pink at the edge of the night sky outlined the trees in stark relief. She shivered at the sight. Only a short time ago they had been decked out in their brightest finery. Now the last vestiges of red, gold, and orange had scattered to the wind, leaving only the bare limbs to tremble in the cold. It seemed that winter had come early and settled in to stay a long while. Sighing, she turned away from the narrow window, feeling lonesome for the warm days and vivid colors of autumn.

Sometimes she thought her whole life was drawn in shades of gray. No black, no white, no color. Just pale shades of gray, leaving her bitter and cold. She pulled her shawl up closer around her shoulders and neck, not at all sure that the chill was coming from outdoors. A flicker of movement outside caught her eye. A pair of cardinals—the male bright red,

the female less so—were hunting for their breakfast. The bright spot of color they made cheered
her heart.

Her bare feet stung from the icy-cold floor once
she left the relative warmth of the braided rug. She
should have used better sense and stayed upstairs
long enough to pull on her heavy woolen socks
and slippers. But she'd been too restless and hadn't
thought about it until too late. After she added
enough wood to the stove to warm up the kitchen,
she'd scurry upstairs and get dressed before Millie
found out that she had let herself get so cold.
Annie rarely got sick, but Millie had a tendency to
fuss.

She managed to avoid the step that creaked loud
enough to wake the dead, or at least her boarders
seemed to think so. The last thing she wanted was
to have the whole bunch of them up and complaining so early in the morning. The longer they slept,
the more peace and quiet she could enjoy.

She passed the bedrooms on the second floor of
the house and kept going until she reached her own
located on the third. If anything, her bedroom was
colder than the kitchen below. Very little of the heat
from the stove would make its way up that far, but
she didn't bother to light a fire in the fireplace in
her room. There was no use in wasting wood heating a room that wouldn't be used again for hours.

The water in the pitcher on her dresser had a
thin film of ice over it. Rather than break it, she decided she'd wash up in the kitchen. The reservoir
over the stove would have hot water in it, or at least
warm. As the owner of the boardinghouse, she figured she was entitled to a few special privileges.

She shrugged out of her nightgown and into her last clean dress. Regardless of the temperature outside, she and Millie were going to have to do some laundry tomorrow.

Once she had her socks on, she picked up her shoes and started back downstairs, seeking the warmth of the kitchen. Once Millie was up and about, she would have her light a fire in the parlor and the dining room. For now, Annie needed to start the day's baking.

She checked the stove. The kindling was burning steadily, so she added a pine knot and some larger pieces of wood. Quickly the flames licked at her offering, already sending more heat through the room. She filled a basin with water from the reservoir. It was pleasantly warm and felt good to her face and hands. After drying off, she left the kitchen long enough to give her hair a good brushing. Once it was neatly braided, she reached for the bowl she kept handy for mixing up biscuits.

It didn't take her long to have two pans ready for the oven. After setting them aside, she took her coat off its peg and bundled up to go out and check the henhouse for fresh eggs. She had a few left from the day before but not enough to feed everyone. Figuring two eggs for each of her boarders as well as herself and Millie, she'd need a dozen at least. Picking up the lamp, she stepped outside on the porch.

The sky had lightened up something considerable since she'd first peeked out awhile ago. A few stars still twinkled overhead, so it appeared likely that the day would be clear and cold. That pleased her. She didn't mind the cold so much when the day was bright, a welcome change from the dreary, cloudy days they'd had so many of recently.

Holding onto the railing, she made her way down the frost-covered steps and across the small yard. She unlatched the henhouse door and stepped inside. One or two of the hens protested the blast of cold air that came with her, but most simply fluffed out their feathers for warmth and ignored her. Things got a bit trickier when her best laying hen tried to peck her when she reached into the nest. Annie didn't take it personally; the crabby old thing had a right to resent a cold hand disturbing her sleep.

The hens had been busy despite the cold weather. Her basket soon had more than enough eggs for breakfast with enough left over for a cake if she could talk Millie into baking one. Since two of her favorite boarders were leaving tomorrow for several weeks to visit family back east, she'd like to serve an extra nice dinner for them. They'd been good tenants, and she wanted to make sure they came back when the holidays were over.

She had enough money set by to do all right without their rent for a few weeks, but reliable boarders were hard to come by. Besides, the two sisters were both nice, decent women, just the kind of person she preferred to have living in her home. She'd occasionally rent to men, but only when she'd had to. On the whole, they were more trouble than they were worth, no matter what Millie said.

As she climbed the last step, the back door opened. Millie had been watching for her. From the look on her face, Annie had managed to offend her again.

"What are you doing out there?"

Millie had definite ideas which jobs were hers and which were Annie's. "I was collecting eggs."

"I can see that." She closed the door behind her with enough force to rattle the windows. "I told you last night that I'd take care of the chores this morning so you could sleep."

Annie set the egg basket down on the table and took off her coat. "I know you did, and I appreciate the thought, but I was tossing and turning. You know when I get like that, I might as well get up."

Never one to miss an opportunity, Millie launched right in on one of her favorite topics. "You'd sleep better if you had a man beside you to keep you warm. And if you can't sleep, well, there are other things you could be doing with him."

"Millie!" Annie looked up at the ceiling, as if she could see through to the room above. "If Miss Barker heard you talk like that, she'd be completely scandalized."

"A night with a man would do her some good, too." Millie got out a bowl and began breaking eggs into it.

Annie knew she should disapprove of Millie's rather earthy outlook on life, but she couldn't help but laugh. "Well, I don't want or need a man in my bed or my life. Too much trouble."

Millie wagged a finger in Annie's face. "That's because you haven't found the right man. When you do, you'll feel differently, I promise you." She beat the eggs with a fork and kept talking. "My Daniel was a good man. He wasn't perfect, mind you, but a woman doesn't mind a few faults when her man treats her right."

Annie knew that Millie meant every word. She'd

been a widow only a short time when she'd come knocking on Annie's door looking for a room to rent. The two of them had hit it off right away and had become close friends. That first year there'd been more than one night that she'd held Millie in her arms when she got to missing her late husband too much.

Annie was a widow, too, but the tears she'd cried hadn't been over her late husband. Looking back had never been her way, not when there was nothing to be gained by it. These days she didn't look forward much either for the same reason. The future stretched out before her in a dreary sameness, but she was content. Or so she kept telling herself.

The floor overhead creaked and groaned, warning the two of them that Miss Barker was stirring. The others wouldn't be far behind. Annie reached for the cast-iron skillet and set it on the stove. There'd be more time later for Millie to lecture her on any variety of subjects. For now, the two of them had a meal to prepare.

"Damn it, man, what are you thinking? It's pure foolishness and you know it. You don't even know the river."

Isaac leaned back in his chair with his legs stretched out in front of him. Rather than answer right away, he savored his cigar for another minute or two and considered his options. Finally, he set the cigar aside and straightened up. It didn't much matter what reason he gave, his friend wasn't going to like it. He appreciated Matthew's concern, but he wasn't about to be talked out of his plan.

He settled on the simplest answer. "I need the money."

Matthew pounded the table with his fist. "That's no reason at all, Isaac. You don't need money badly enough to risk everything on one more run at this time of year. You said yourself that the boiler needs work." Reaching for the bottle in the middle of the table, he poured himself another stiff drink. "Have you forgotten about the two boats that tried it last year and got iced in? If that happens, not only do you have to pay your crew, but you risk more damage to your precious boat—serious damage, I might add."

Isaac shrugged. They'd already been over the same arguments half a dozen times in the past two days. Both men knew neither one was going to change the other one's mind anytime soon. That didn't keep them from trying.

"I'll be able to make the next payment on the boat six months early."

"The bank is willing to wait that six months. I know. Remember, I'm the one who makes those decisions." He shot Isaac a triumphant look and played his ace. "We won't wait for the money, though, if the boat is on the bottom of the river somewhere between here and the Upper White."

"Then you'll have to take it out of my hide because I sure as hell don't have it sitting around in my stateroom. Besides, with one more successful run, I'll have enough money to live the rest of the winter eating beef instead of beans." Isaac smiled, proud of himself for coming up with a new point in the ongoing argument.

Matthew rolled his eyes. "Since when have you

gotten picky about what you eat? Hell, we both grew up on beans and cornbread and were grateful to have that. A few more months won't kill you." He tossed back the last of the whiskey. "But one more trip just might."

And that was the crux of the matter. Matthew worried more about keeping Isaac alive and well than Isaac did himself. He appreciated his friend's concern, but he was worse than a mother hen with just one chick.

"I know what my boat is capable of, Matthew." It was time to end the argument once and for all. "We leave in the morning."

His friend's shoulders slumped in defeat. "I wish I knew what drives you to do fool tricks like this."

Isaac would tell him the answer if he knew it himself. All he knew was that he could tolerate being on dry land for only short periods of time before the river started calling him. Out on the water, life was never dull. Each bend in the river, each shift in the water level brought a whole new set of challenges. Even when he was cussing the boilers or the gravel bar ahead, he loved every minute he spent on his boat.

And she was lovely, at least in his eyes. He knew there were other, newer steamboats plying their trade up and down the rivers that covered the heart of the country in a spider web of connected waterways. But the *Caprice* was a real beauty and as fickle as any real woman could be. When she was in the mood to be a lady, even the worst stretches of the rivers weren't a problem.

Oh, but she could be moody, making his life miserable. He loved her capricious nature and the challenge she presented. But Matthew, content to work behind a desk, wouldn't understand that Isaac was never happy unless he felt the throb of engines beneath his feet and watched the world slip past as his lady carried him upriver and down.

So come dawn tomorrow, he'd be aboard and ready to head upriver. They'd be carrying a full load of cargo as far as Willow Shoals. After taking on the last of the year's cotton, he'd turn around and wend his way back down to Hart's Ferry. Once he returned, he'd make arrangements to have the starboard boiler overhauled. If the weather stayed mild, he might even get some of the painting done that he'd been putting off.

So despite Matthew's qualms, Isaac had a solid plan of action, one that would keep him afloat financially as well as on the river. To celebrate his final decision, he reached for the bottle and poured them both one last drink. Matthew seemed reluctant to pick his up.

"Come on, Matthew. I won't be gone all that long. I'll be back in plenty of time for Christmas. After all, I promised your daughter I'd be there to watch her sing at church."

If the roof didn't fall in when he walked through the door, but he kept that thought to himself. He'd risk it for five-year-old Cynthia. She knew full well that she had her adopted Uncle Isaac wrapped around her little finger. All she had to do was stick out her lower lip in a pretty pout, and he was on his knees begging forgiveness.

"She'll not forgive you easily if you don't make it, you know."

"I'll be there." He would be, too, if he had to swim back downriver.

Matthew checked his watch. "Well, I'd better get on home. Melissa doesn't mind me being a little late getting home for dinner. But late and a bit drunk tends to make her mad." He closed his watch and slipped it back in his pocket.

Another reason Isaac hadn't tied himself down to a woman. He liked his freedom too much to want to give it up. Women who understood a man's need to live on the river were few and far between, and he had yet to find one.

For an instant, a memory long buried stirred and drifted through his mind. There had been a woman once, one who had made his blood run hot and convinced him she was in love. He'd been wrong about a lot of things, but not about that. She'd been in love all right, just not with him, and he'd been the last one to find out. One morning he'd awakened to find her, his best friend, and most of his money gone. He considered the money well spent in the long run.

Matthew interrupted his thoughts, bringing him back to the present. "What time are you leaving in the morning?"

"First light, if everything goes well."

"I'll try to be there to send you off. If I don't make it, keep your wits about you."

He held out his hand. Isaac didn't hesitate to accept the gesture. Matthew had proved himself to be a good friend over the years. Neither of them trusted easily, but they'd hit it off the minute they'd met. Despite all the changes in their lives, they kept their friendship on solid ground.

"Hug Cynthia for me and give Melissa my regards."

"I'll do that. Watch your back."

With that, Matthew walked out of the saloon, leaving Isaac alone with his thoughts. He considered his options and decided for his own sake that he'd better leave for the *Caprice* now before he was tempted into finishing off the rest of the whiskey. He rarely drank to excess, but the dark memories from the past were still stirring around in the back of his mind. Drinking them back into oblivion held some appeal, but he'd need a clear head in the morning if they were to make good time starting out.

He shoved back from the table and reached for his hat. After a second's hesitation, he reached for the bottle, too.

Isaac stepped out on deck and grimaced. For the past week, the days had been gray and gloomy. Now, when his head pounded in counterpoint to the throb of the engines below, the clouds had disappeared, leaving the day too bright and sunny. Maybe it was a good sign, but all he wanted to do was curse his own stupidity and crawl back into the shadows of his room.

"You look like hell."

Isaac managed not to wince, but he didn't argue the point. As usual, Matthew had the right of it. Hell, if he looked as bad as he felt, then it was time to call the undertaker. He'd put the bottle away as soon as he reached his room last night, but sleep had been long in coming. Tossing and turning, he'd gotten up to walk the deck for hours, finally falling asleep about the time the sun made its first appearance in the east.

"Did I ever tell you how much I hate cheery people in the morning?" He glared at his friend, but quickly forgave him for everything when Matthew held out a steaming cup of coffee. "Bless you."

The two of them stood at the railing looking down at the river below in companionable silence, as Isaac waited for the coffee to pump some life back into his veins. Finally, when he thought he could talk without moaning, he turned to his friend.

"I really didn't expect you to be here this morning."

Matthew's grin was wicked. "I didn't expect first light to be at ten o'clock either."

"Aw, hell!" Isaac looked around for the mate. He caught sight of him just coming out of the pilot-house on the deck above. "Joe!"

The man in question leaned over the railing and cupped his ear to hear what Isaac wanted to tell him.

"I left orders to cast off at first light."

He nodded and shouted back, "We were still taking on a load of wood for the boilers. It was late coming, but we're all set now."

Isaac muttered under his breath but nodded and waved. The mate disappeared behind the pilot-house, no doubt seeing to some other last-minute details.

"Well, I'd better be going before you put me to work." Matthew clapped him on the shoulder, not helping Isaac's headache at all.

"Don't worry about us. We'll do fine."

"You always do." His dark eyes still looked worried, but he didn't say anything.

Isaac walked him to the gangplank. Once Matthew reached shore, Isaac cranked the gangplank back up so they could pull away from the landing. Once he had it secured, he made a final inspection of the boat. He trusted his men to know their business, but now that he was up and about, he'd do a quick turn around each deck before signaling the pilot and engineer that it was time to head upstream.

Since they weren't carrying any passengers this trip, he was running with a smaller crew, all of them men he'd worked with for several years. It was worth the extra he paid to keep them, knowing everybody's lives, crew and passengers alike, depended on their skill.

Finally, he approached the pilothouse. Out of courtesy, he knocked on the door before going in. Although Isaac was the boat owner, Barton considered the pilothouse his personal kingdom. As hard as it was to get a good pilot, Isaac saw no reason to dissuade him from that opinion.

"Good morning, Barton."

"Captain."

"You may take her out as soon as you're ready." Isaac had the right to issue orders, but both men knew the real boss was the pilot. He was the one who knew every twist and turn of the river, each boulder, every riffle, and where the water ran deep and straight.

Barton signaled the engineer working three decks below, and they were under way. As always, Isaac's heart pounded with excitement as the gap between his boat and the land widened. Despite the cold temperatures outside, he left the pilothouse to stand out on the deck, breathing in the clean freedom of the river.

Here was his peace, his life. And if Matthew thought it a lonely life, he was wrong. The river and *Caprice* herself were all the company he needed.

"We'll miss you and Millie, Annie. If our brother and his wife weren't expecting a new addition to the family, we wouldn't leave you alone for the holidays. But, you see, his wife Josephine had a difficult time with her last child and needs our help." Kate, the elder of the two sisters, gave Annie a quick hug.

"If everything goes as planned, we'll be back right after the first of the year." Patience waited for her turn to embrace Annie. "Christmas won't be the same without you and the others." Her voice dropped to a whisper. "We left some gifts for each of you in my room."

Annie felt an instant mix of pleasure and guilt. Unexpected gifts had been rare in her life, but she hadn't thought to get at least a small token of some kind for the two women. After all, Thanksgiving had passed only a few days ago. She hadn't thought far enough ahead to plan for Christmas yet.

On the other hand, she had a basket of food all packed and ready for Kate and Patience to take on the stage with them. Once they reached St. Louis, they would continue their trip by train. But at least for the first leg of the journey, they'd eat well. Millie was just coming out of the front door with the basket on her arm.

"Here you go, ladies. Don't let the other passengers talk you out of one crumb of your food." Millie softened her stern warning with a smile. "With care, this should last you all the way to St. Louis." She handed the basket to Kate and accepted a hug from her with an ease that Annie always envied.

"You two shouldn't have gone to all the trouble." Despite her words, it was obvious that both sisters were pleased.

"Thank Annie. It was her idea."

Annie almost bolted for the door, sure that Millie's comment would set off another round of hugs. She was relieved to see the hired carriage pull up in front of the house at that moment. Everyone hurried to stow the substantial amount of luggage and boxes in the back while Kate and Patience climbed up in the seat.

With a final flurry of good-byes, Annie and Millie watched the carriage pull away, taking away their favorite boarders.

"I do hope they'll be back." Annie told herself it was the money they represented that worried her, but the truth was she rather liked the two spinsters.

Millie tugged her back toward the house. "I'm sure they will be. Neither one of them has any desire to leave Willow Shoals. They have too many ties here. It's killing both of them to miss this year's Christmas program. Why, the last few years, Kate made most of the costumes for the children, and Patience played the piano."

A little knot of tension eased in Annie's stomach. She could look forward to a few weeks with less work to do without having to worry about finding new boarders. The two sisters made very few demands on her and often offered to cook or help with the cleaning.

Millie steered Annie toward the parlor. "Why don't you have a seat? You've been up since way before dawn. I'll fix us some tea."

"That sounds lovely."

She sank down in the chair closest to the fireplace and let the warmth soak into her. Moments like this one, when the work was all done and she could afford a few minutes to relax, were few and far between. Not that she was complaining. She'd worked long and hard the past few years to establish a life she could depend on and be proud of.

And yet the memories of her past always hovered in the back of her mind, reminding her that she'd made choices that shamed her. She couldn't change what she'd done and wasn't sure she would if she had been offered the choice. After all, living with the guilt had made her the woman she was today, wiser and stronger, if sadder, than she had been.

But sometimes, when she closed her eyes at night, she wondered how her life would have been different if she had chosen differently. Millie came into the room and set down the tea service. After pouring each of them a cup, she sat down across from Annie. From the way she was worrying at her lower lip, Annie knew that something was up.

She sipped at her tea before speaking. "You might as well spit it out, Millie. That way you can drink your tea while it's still hot."

Her friend sighed deeply and set her cup aside. "Now, Annie, I know you aren't going to like this, but it sort of slipped out."

Annie fought down a brief flurry of panic. Millie

had no way of knowing anything about Annie's past that could cause her problems. It was only because it had been on her mind that she'd reacted so strongly. She took another long drink of tea.

"What exactly did you let slip?"

Millie squirmed a bit more and then grimaced. "You remember what I said on the way in about Patience playing the piano for the Christmas program."

Millie had been right. Annie didn't like where this line of talk was headed. Not one bit. She sat up straighter, not sure whether to hear Millie out or simply refuse before she had a chance to say another word. If it had been anyone else, she would have done the latter, but this was Millie, the woman who had come to be the sister that Annie had never had.

She'd listen politely and then refuse. "I remember."

"She was worried about who they would find to replace her." Millie was looking everywhere but right at Annie. "I reminded her how well you play."

Annie's stomach twisted in a guilty knot. "Lots of folks can play the piano."

"But not like you do." Millie's gaze finally met Annie's. Her chin came up, telling Annie more than words would that this was important to Millie.

"I've never played in a church." That much was true. She'd played in saloons, on steamboats, and once or twice in a brothel, but she wasn't going to mention that.

"No reason you couldn't."

None except she didn't want to. She might go to church most every Sunday, but even after several years of faithful attendance it wasn't always a comfortable experience. If the people in town really knew who she was or at least had been, they might not be so willing to welcome her as a member of the congregation. She could be misjudging them, but she didn't want to risk finding out that she was right. The result was she always felt a little out of place and was always on her guard.

What could she say?

"Surely they can find someone else, someone with more experience." She'd even help them look, if that's what it took.

Millie played her trump card. "If they don't find someone soon, Patience says they're going to ask Mrs. Dowell."

She picked up her tea and gave Annie a smug look. She looked for all the world like a cat with an extra big bowl of cream. And she had every right to feel that way. Mrs. Dowell was a lovely old dear who played the piano at church whenever Patience couldn't. Unfortunately, she had gotten rather deaf and the resulting effect on her playing was regrettable.

"I don't have a lot of free time." She waved her hand over her head to indicate the house that surrounded them. "I have a boardinghouse to run."

Millie gave an unladylike snort. "And right now, you have three empty rooms. That leaves you, me, and Miss Barker. Even if you didn't have me around to help, there isn't that much to do. At least look at the music. If you think it's too much or too hard or too anything, you just need to say so."

"When you get it, I'll look at it." Annie shook

her finger at Millie. "But that's all I'm promising—to look at it."

"Patience gave it to me after church yesterday morning. Wait right there. It won't take me a minute to get it." Millie scurried from the room.

Annie figured that if Millie had been really confident in her ability to convince her to play, she would have had the music with her. She'd look at it, but she already knew what her answer would be. She might be willing to disappoint Patience, and maybe even the children at church since she didn't know them all that well. It was Millie, and maybe herself, she wouldn't be able to face if she refused.

When Millie returned with the music, she was already sitting at the piano ready to play.

"Mrs. Dunbar, I can't tell you how grateful we all are that you are doing this for the children. You have a real gift, you know."

"Thank you, Pastor. It's really nothing."

He walked her to the door of the narthex. "Well, I can assure you that we consider ourselves blessed." He opened the door to a blast of frigid air and shivered. "I can't believe how bitterly cold it has remained. I haven't lived here all that long, but my understanding is that the winters usually aren't like this so early in the season. Please be careful on your way home." Rather belatedly, he asked, "Would you like me to see you home?"

"No, thank you, Pastor. I'll be fine. I only live a short distance away. It won't take me any time at all." She started down the steps.

"I shall look forward to the next rehearsal then, Mrs. Dunbar."

The temperature was dropping again to the point that the air stung her face and nose. She automatically sped up, wanting nothing more than to reach the sanctuary of her kitchen and something hot to drink. It wouldn't surprise her to find out that Millie was watching for her and would have the tea already made and a brick heating to warm Annie's frozen toes.

Despite everything, she wished Millie didn't feel so bad about getting her involved. Her friend had no way of knowing that playing piano publicly held such bad memories for Annie. Maybe if she talked about how lovely the music was and how cute the children were going to be, Millie would relax and not fret so. And maybe it was time for Annie to let go of her past and start looking forward again.

Sure enough, just as Annie turned the last corner, she caught sight of Millie's face in the window. She knew the instant she was seen because her friend waved before disappearing from sight. Then she was back, holding the door open, before Annie reached the top step.

"Come in and get warm." Millie helped her peel off several layers of clothing before settling her in the chair by the fire. A cup of hot tea and a plate of freshly baked cookies were already waiting for her.

"These smell heavenly. Did you use a new recipe?" She took a big bite and let the sweetness melt on her tongue.

Millie started to answer but then stopped and tilted her head to one side and looked puzzled. Annie didn't hear anything at first, but then she heard some shouting coming from behind the house toward the river.

"What on earth is that noise?"

"It sounds like someone is in the backyard."

Millie started toward the kitchen with Annie right behind her. Her heart was pounding so loudly she was surprised she could hear anything at all. Normally, Willow Shoals was a peaceful town, but occasionally some of the deckhands off the boats that tied up at the landing decided to get rowdy.

She considered running upstairs for the gun she kept loaded in her dresser, but there wasn't time. Whoever was raising a ruckus was already too close. Millie headed straight for the door, ready to look out, but Annie grabbed her arm.

"Don't. We don't know who is out there."

They stood frozen by indecision when the choice was made for them. A man's outline appeared through the narrow window. He raised his fist and pounded on the door.

"Mrs. Dunbar! Open up. It's Sheriff Stone."

"What could he be wanting?" Annie gave Millie a puzzled look as she walked past her to unbolt the door. She knew the sheriff well enough to say hello to, but the two of them had not spoken more than a few dozen words in the years she'd lived in Willow Shoals. She had nothing against the man, but her past experience with the law had left her reluctant to spend much time in his company.

Deciding caution was warranted, she opened the door only a few inches. "Sheriff, is something wrong?"

He immediately took off his hat. "Yes, ma'am. I hate to disturb you, but there's been an accident on the river. We have some injured men that we need beds for."

"How many?"

"Fewer than a dozen or so all told. Most are just wet and cold. They need a place to dry out and get warm, and your house is the closest. Once we get them sorted out, I'll see if the pastor can make room for some of them at the parsonage." He looked back over his shoulder. "Several have minor cuts and bruises. One man is more serious, though. He's the one we need to get settled somewhere right quick. They should be bringing him up soon. I came ahead to see if you had room for him."

One part of her wanted to refuse. But even if she could bring herself to turn them away, it would seriously damage her reputation in town. Millie was already filling pans with water to heat and reaching for the coffeepot. In truth, there was no choice in the matter. On a bitterly cold night like this, they would be lucky if the whole bunch didn't come down with pneumonia or worse.

She threw the door open wide. "Bring them in, Sheriff."

"Thank you, Mrs. Dunbar. I'll send one of my men down to the store to get dry clothes for all of them. Do you need anything else?"

"Did you already send for the doctor?"

"Yes, ma'am, I did, but he's not in town. He got called away to the Morris place to deliver a baby. He could be gone until morning. As soon as I can spare a man, I'll send word out there."

Her stomach plummeted. She had some experience in nursing wounded men, but it seemed like a lifetime ago. Before she could get mired in ugly memories, though, the first of the men came shuffling through her back door.

"Take them straight through to the parlor, Millie. I'll go get blankets." She knew she was being a bit cowardly by leaving the men in Millie's hands, but she desperately needed a minute or two alone to regain her composure.

She pounded up the stairs. Miss Barker peeked out of her door. "Mrs. Dunbar, I don't appreciate being disturbed at this hour."

Annie bit back her first reply. "I'm sorry, Miss Barker, but there's been an accident on the river. Sheriff Stone is bringing the wounded men here."

"Oh, dear. I'll get dressed and be right down."

Surprised at the offer, she shook her head. "That's not necessary."

"Nonsense, my dear. I may not be as young as I used to be, but I can make coffee, roll bandages, and cook soup if need be. It will take every willing hand to get those poor gentlemen settled."

She disappeared back inside her room, leaving Annie staring at the closed door in stunned silence.

CHAPTER TWO

"Sir, I see lights ahead!" A thread of excited relief colored Barton's voice as he stared out into the darkness and clung to the wheel.

Isaac squinted in the direction his pilot was pointing but didn't see anything at first. Finally, he saw a flicker of brightness when the trees thinned out along the shore.

"Keep her steady, Barton. We'll make it yet."

He hoped so. He hated like hell that the *Caprice* had already sustained considerable damage, but as much as he loved his boat, he cared more about the men who worked on her. He'd already come close to losing one to the river. Guilt ate at his gut, but he couldn't allow himself the luxury of regrets yet. Not until he had his crew on shore and safe.

Joe appeared at his side. "She's still taking on water, sir."

"I know, but every foot closer we get to that town up ahead, the better off we'll be."

"At least we don't have a load of cattle this time, sir." Joe grinned, the dim light from the pilothouse giving his face a ghostly look.

"I guess that we do have some things to be grateful for." He walked around the side of the deck and leaned down, trying to gauge for himself how bad the damage was. "If we can make it to the landing, we should be able to tie her up in the shallows where we can offload the cargo safely."

And it would be nice if they could let down the gangplank so they didn't have to swim for shore. The temperature was dropping so fast that ice was forming on the deck. His crew, all experienced men, had strung rope to hold onto wherever they could. It wouldn't take but a few minutes in the water to freeze a man through and through.

The lights were getting brighter. Hope struggled to life in his chest, counting each turn of the big paddle wheel as one more step toward sanctuary. He willed the river to stay deep and free of any more chunks of ice like the one they'd plowed into an hour ago. He'd had men watching the water ahead with lanterns, but the huge piece of rock-hard ice had appeared out of nowhere. It hit the *Caprice* with enough force to knock a hole in her side.

And if she took on much more water, they'd be sitting on the bottom of the river.

"I see the landing!" Barton's voice carried over the boat loud enough for the whole crew to hear. Several of the men paused what they were doing to check for themselves.

"Take her in easy, Mr. Barton." Isaac knew he didn't have to tell Barton how to do his job, but he wanted to keep things as normal as possible. Panic would be their worst enemy at this point.

"Yes, sir." Barton disappeared back into the pilot-house.

"Joe, tell the others to pack their stuff. Once we get ashore, it may be some time before we can safely come on board." His heart hurt at the thought of leaving his favorite lady to the fickle care of the river, but he had no choice.

He headed for the bow, wanting to oversee their final approach. Several of his men stood along the railing on the cargo deck below holding lanterns out. Finally, the landing eased out of the shadows, revealing enough detail to give Barton a clear target. The boat, sluggish to respond, gradually nosed toward the right.

Hope died, cut off by a terrified yell from Joe on the port side. "Ice! Lots of it!"

The words had hardly cleared his lips when they felt the first jolt. Quick reflexes saved him from being tossed overboard, but a loud splash from the port side told him that Joe had not been that lucky.

He screamed his friend's name, hoping against hope that he'd answer. When none was forthcoming, Isaac made his way across the deck. He wanted to run, but the footing was getting worse and if he slid out of control right into the water too, he'd be little help to his friend.

"Joe!" he called once, twice, and finally after the third time, he heard a faint response. His men had already come around to the deck below to light the river with their lanterns.

"There!"

One of them pointed at a spot about twenty feet

downstream. Isaac grabbed a handful of rope and charged down to the lower level. His fingers, stiff from the cold, fumbled to tie the rope around his waist. If Joe were badly hurt, he wouldn't be able to catch hold of the rope nor could he swim for shore. Someone was going to have to go in after him. And that someone was Isaac. His friend, his boat, his responsibility.

Tossing the end of the rope to the nearest man, he shrugged out of his coat, knowing it would only weigh him down. "Be ready to pull us out."

"But . . ."

Isaac didn't want to hear the man's protest. If there were a chance of saving Joe, he'd take it no matter what the cost to himself. He drew a deep breath and braced himself for the shock of hitting the water. Aiming for a shallow dive, he arced out over the water in the direction they'd last seen Joe.

No one had ever told him that cold could burn, but his skin was afire and freezing in the icy water. Movement became harder with each stroke, but he made some headway. His feet scraped bottom, allowing him to stand, bracing himself against the current.

He put his hands to his mouth and shouted, "Joe."

"Here!"

The answer was close by. After an eternity, he spotted his friend clinging to a log wedged along the far side of the river. He began wading, each step a fight against the current, the uncertain footing, and the chunks of ice slipping toward him through the darkness.

But he made it across to where Joe waited. His friend was still conscious, but his movements were sluggish. Whether it was because of the cold or his injuries, it was impossible to tell. There wasn't anything he could do about either one until they both got out of the water. He tied the rope around Joe, having to work by feel in the dark. But finally he managed to tie a knot that should hold against the worst the river could throw at them.

"PULL!" he yelled and was rewarded by an immediate tug on the line. He used what strength he could muster to lift Joe from the water and began to drag him back across. Joe managed to help some, pushing against the bottom of the river whenever he could, propelling them forward into the deeper water where Barton was holding the *Caprice* against the current.

Finally, hands reached out to pull Joe back up on the deck. Others tried to catch hold of Isaac, but his hands kept slipping away. His legs were hardly moving as he tried to tread water. He felt as if his feet had turned to stone, dragging him down and down.

Knowing death was swimming beside him, he gathered his last flicker of energy and tried to propel himself up high enough to reach the deck. But as a loud noise rocked the night, the *Caprice* settled on her side, raising the port side high out of the water. Belatedly, he realized the churning in the water was because he'd drifted too close to the paddle wheel.

"Damn, Cynthia is not going to forgive me," he whispered as he slipped into the cold embrace of the river.

* * *

It was a nightmare. Her back ached, her head throbbed, and her feet begged for relief. The worst part was that compared to the others in the room, she was in great shape. Men, all unknown to her, sat everywhere wrapped in her best quilts. For the most part, they'd warmed up enough to quit shivering, but their mood was as dark as the night sky outside.

"Does anyone else need more tea or coffee?" Agatha Barker came into the parlor, carrying what must have been the tenth pot of tea since that first fateful knock at the door.

One of the miserable-looking men bestirred himself enough to answer. "No, thank you, ma'am." He went back to staring into the fire, as if searching for answers that weren't to be found anywhere.

Miss Barker set the teapot down on a convenient table. "Mrs. Dunbar, you should sit a spell. You've been up and down those stairs too many times to count."

Annie let the older woman lead her back toward the kitchen where Millie kept a careful eye on the pot of soup she and Miss Barker had started. The air was redolent of bitter, black coffee and freshly baked biscuits. All three women sank wearily onto the chairs at the table.

"How is the injured man?"

Annie shrugged. "I cleaned him up as best I could. He has a sizeable lump on his forehead I'm worried about, but I don't think he has any broken bones. We'll need to keep an eye on him for the next few hours to make sure he can respond."

Millie shuddered. "He was sure enough blue when

they brought him in. I've never seen anyone look so cold."

"Those bricks you warmed have helped a lot, Miss Barker. His chills have all but stopped."

"I'm glad to hear that." She gave Annie a weary smile. "I do think after tonight you can call me Agatha, my dear. Nothing like a crisis to bring people together."

"And you must call us by our given names as well." Agatha was her newest boarder, one who had maintained a formal distance until tonight. "Thank you for everything you've done. I know all those men appreciate it as much as I do."

"It has been some time since I've had to nurse injured men." Her eyes took on a distant look. "The war, you know." Her fingers strayed to the brooch that she wore pinned at her neck.

Annie, who had done her own share of caring for the wounded, could guess all too well the images in Agatha's thoughts. She leaned forward to touch her arm. "At least with warm blankets and your soup, these men should all recover nicely."

"Except for the one they haven't found yet. The others are still looking for the . . ."—Millie glanced toward the parlor door before dropping her voice to a low whisper—"the body. The sheriff said there wasn't much hope."

"I must have been in with the one they call Joe. Do we know anything about the missing man?"

Millie shook her head. "No, except he was the captain, and a hero according to the others. Joe was knocked overboard, and this man dove in after him. But once he got him back to where the others could pull him out of the water, the boat shifted and the paddle wheel dragged their captain under."

No wonder all of the men in the other room looked so grim. Not only were their jobs in jeopardy because of damage to the boat, they had lost their employer as well. Her heart hurt for them, knowing all too well how it felt to have one's whole life change in the blink of an eye. For several minutes, the three of them sat in silence, each lost in her own thoughts.

Finally, Millie checked the soup again. "This is done."

Annie started setting out bowls. "I think we should make sure each of them eats a full serving. Afterward, we'll get them all settled for the night."

She'd already decided that she and Millie could double up in her room. Under the circumstances, she knew Kate and Patience would readily forgive her for allowing strange men to sleep in their beds.

They had put Joe in the one bedroom on the main floor of the house. It was located off the kitchen, and she normally rented it out only to someone who needed a place to stay for a short time. Otherwise she used it for her sewing room, a place she could escape to if she needed a few minutes to herself.

While Millie and Agatha badgered their weary guests into eating a hot meal, she checked on her patient. His color had continued to improve, and he seemed to be resting easy. She perched on the edge of the other narrow bed in the room and considered what to do next. If she slept in her own bed, she wouldn't be able to hear him if he needed something during the night.

She closed her eyes and offered up a prayer for his healing and for the others who had lost so much tonight and for their unnamed captain. She hoped Joe could live with the burden of knowing he lived because another man had traded his life for his.

She returned to the kitchen to dish up a cup of broth for Joe and set it aside to cool a bit. She could hear Agatha and Millie cajoling the men to eat up, telling them there was plenty more if they wanted extra. Figuring they had things under control, she started washing dishes. It was tempting to leave the mess until morning, but she'd hate herself later. Especially when she'd have these same men to cook for in the morning.

The pastor was supposed to see about collecting donations to help feed them, but he wouldn't be there by breakfast, that was for certain. She made quick work of the dishes already in the kitchen. It wouldn't take long to finish once the men were done with their bowls and spoons.

She was just wiping her hands dry when she thought she heard a noise from the next room. Picking up the mug of broth, she hurried back into the bedroom. Joe was doing his best to sit up.

"Please, you mustn't try to move yet."

He sank back onto the pillow and stared up at her in confusion. "Where am I?"

"My name is Annie Dunbar, and I own this boardinghouse. The sheriff brought you here after your boat hit ice." She straightened out the blankets, pulling them back up around his shoulders. "If I prop you up with another pillow, do you think you could sip some of this broth?"

He had more questions; she could see them starting to form in his eyes. She didn't want to be the one to tell him about the captain. Maybe if she kept spoon-feeding him broth, he wouldn't get the words out. He winced when she lifted his head to slip another pillow under him.

"I know that hurt. You've got an impressive bump on your head." She held out the first spoonful of broth with an encouraging smile.

Before he'd take a sip, though, he asked, "Where are the others?"

She stalled for time. "They are scattered all over my house trying to get some sleep. You can talk to them in the morning. Now, no more questions."

Joe's eyes began to drift shut before the broth was half gone. She set the cup aside and reached out to touch his forehead. So far, no sign of fever setting in. Considering everything he'd been through, if he managed to walk away from the experience with only a bad headache, he would be a lucky man indeed.

She turned the lamp down to a faint glow, enough so she could keep an eye on him, but not bright enough to keep either of them awake. She joined Millie out in the kitchen.

"How is he?"

Annie picked up a towel and began drying the bowls as Millie washed them. "He woke up long enough to eat some broth. He wanted to know where the others were. I didn't tell him about the captain. I figured he'd had enough of a shock tonight."

A tear slipped down Millie's face. "Those poor men."

Annie knew all about her friend's tender heart and had been expecting the tears to fall as soon as everything settled down. Millie had a will of iron as long as strength was needed, waiting until the crisis passed before falling apart. Annie wasn't much one for hugging, but she made an exception for her friend. She let Millie cry herself dry. When her sobs had eased into an occasional sniffle, she held her at arm's length.

"We did all we could for them, Millie. When they've had some time to think about it, they'll be grateful that only one man was lost." She dredged up a smile. "Now you go get some sleep. I'll need you more than ever in the morning."

"You've been up as long as I have. I should sit with him." She gestured toward the bedroom door.

"No, I will. I'll sleep tomorrow after Pastor Chesterfield gets them settled elsewhere." She gave Millie a gentle push. "Now go!"

Before her friend could argue any more, Annie went back into the bedroom and closed the door behind her. She checked Joe for fever again before stretching out on the other bed and let sleep come.

It seemed that no sooner had she managed to fall asleep, someone started pounding on her back door again. She fought clear of the quilt she'd covered up with and stumbled out into the kitchen. This time she didn't waste time asking who was there, knowing no one would come knocking at that hour without good reason.

"Sheriff Stone!" she stood back to let him inside. "What's happened now?"

His teeth were chattering from the cold. She

pulled out a chair at the table and poured a cup of coffee for him while she waited for him answer.

"We found the last man." He wrapped his hands around the cup to absorb the warmth. "He's more dead than alive, but we found him." His eyes were bleak. "He's in pretty bad shape, Mrs. Dunbar. I hope Doc gets back soon."

"Me, too." She brought out the quilt she'd been using and put it around the sheriff's shoulders.

"Thank you, ma'am. I think it might be days before I'm warm again."

"I wouldn't be surprised. I'll go get the bed ready for him." She hurried into the bedroom and pulled back the covers. She'd have the sheriff's men help remove the injured man's wet clothing before putting him to bed. The first step toward getting warm was getting dry.

The bricks would have to be heated again. She gathered up the ones she'd used in Joe's bed and brought them out to set on the stove. The sheriff seemed to have dozed off at the table. She tried to be quiet, but he gave a start when she added wood to the stove.

"Mrs. Dunbar, this town is going to owe you quite a debt for all you've done tonight." He cocked his head to the side. "And it's not over yet. They're coming."

He opened the door himself. "Bring him in here and lay him out on the table."

It took four of them to wrestle the final victim through her back door and up onto the table. She wasn't sure she wanted her kitchen table as a bed for a man who might have already breathed his last, but she didn't protest. If he were to live, they needed to act quickly. The men, all as cold as the sheriff, stood by, waiting for Annie to take charge. Reluctantly, she did so.

"One of you go to the steps and shout for Millie. I'll need her help."

The man closest to the parlor did as she asked. While she waited for her friend, she hurried to fetch her best scissors. This was no time to worry about saving the man's clothing. If he lost a shirt and trousers, it was a small price to pay to get warm that much faster. She began cutting away his shirt. His skin felt like ice, and he was covered with mud from the river.

She paused long enough to rest her fingers along the bottom of his jaw. They all seemed to hold their breath, waiting for her to feel a pulse. She closed her eyes, willing his heart to beat, his blood to flow. Nothing. She pressed harder and waited. This time she was rewarded with a soft flutter.

"His heart's still beating."

There was no mistaking the relief that swept through the room. After all, these men had risked their own lives to bring this one man back.

"I'll need a couple of you to help move him to the bed in the next room, but the rest of you should go on home. You're all exhausted, and your families will be worried."

"I'll stay."

It didn't surprise her that the sheriff was the first to volunteer. He'd had the most time to get warm. Another few minutes in her kitchen wouldn't hurt. Before anyone else could speak up, Millie came in followed by one of the men from the boat. They must have heard what she'd said because he spoke up as he pushed his way into the already crowded room.

"I'll help."

"Are you up to it?" Annie didn't want to refuse his assistance, but she needed someone she could depend on.

"He's my captain. I'll help."

She knew stubborn when she saw it. "Fine, then. The rest of you go on along home."

Another blast of cold air swept through the room as the men filed out. The sheriff added more wood to the stove without being asked while Millie filled yet another kettle with water to heat.

"How bad is he?"

Annie glanced up long enough to shake her head. "I haven't had a chance to check him over yet. I need to get these wet things off of him. Until he gets warm, we stand a greater risk of him coming down with a fever or worse."

"Do you have another pair of scissors?"

He clearly needed to be doing more than watching. She handed him hers. "I'll get my other pair."

"Thank you, ma'am."

"Call me Annie."

"I'm Barton." He set to cutting away the sodden fabric with fierce determination.

She brought her sewing basket with her. She'd made note of at least one cut that would need stitching. And from the angle it was bent, she suspected there was a broken leg to be set. But each thing in its own time. She spread a sheet over the injured man. He was beyond caring if he was naked in front of strangers, but she suspected it would bother the other two men in the room. Millie gave her a quick

wink, as if reading her mind, and helped to spread
the sheet.

When they had the last of the clothing gone,
Annie wrapped the warmed bricks in towels and
nestled them close to the captain's body. Then she
dug out the bottle of whiskey she kept for medici-
nal reasons. She caught the sheriff eyeing the bottle with interest and poured him and Barton each
a shot, figuring they could use it.

She cleaned the gash on her patient's arm and
then began the arduous process of stitching it closed.
Millie held a lamp over her head to give her the best
light. Slowly, she matched the edges as best she
could and brought the wound closed. She counted
it as a blessing that the cold had slowed the bleeding.

She turned her attention to the leg. Just as she
feared, it was broken. "Has anyone heard back from
the doctor? About how soon he'll be back?"

The sheriff shook his head. "I sent a rider out to
get him, but he may not be able to come until after
the baby is born. There's no telling when that'll be."

"Has anyone else ever set a leg before?"

Barton spoke up from right over her shoulder.
"I've seen it done once or twice, but that's all."

"Not me." Millie actually retreated several steps,
obviously not anxious to learn how.

"Sheriff?"

He looked queasy at the thought. "I'll try to help."

Annie weighed their options. Their patient had
worse problems than his leg being broken. If they
didn't get him warm, there might be no reason to
bother with the fracture.

"Let's get him cleaned up first, and then we'll

concentrate on getting him warm. If the doctor isn't here in a couple of hours, we'll worry about the leg then." She looked around at the others to see if they agreed with her decision. Mostly, they all looked relieved.

"Sheriff, why don't you go on home? Barton can lie down in the other room, so he can stay close by if I need anything. The three of us should be able to move the captain. If not, I'll get another one of the men down to help us."

Sheriff Stone's shoulders sagged with exhaustion combined with relief. "I'll do that, Mrs. Dunbar. I'll be back after I get some sleep to see what I can do to help. I'm sure that Pastor Chesterfield will be by later as well." He started for the door. "Don't hesitate to ask for help if you need it. I can always send another rider out to fetch the doctor."

"Thanks, Sheriff."

He let himself out while Millie got a basin full of hot water. She got a handful of rags and a bar of soap. Together, the two of them started washing away the filth that clung to their patient's skin. So tired she was almost numb, Annie wrung out her cloth and started on his shoulder and arm while Millie washed his face and hair.

As soon as they got him clean, they'd move him to the bed and reheat the bricks. Then maybe they'd have time to get a little sleep before the doctor arrived. When she turned his hand over to wash the back of it, she noticed a horseshoe-shaped scar. She'd known someone with a scar like this one. She wondered if the captain had gotten it from an ill-tempered horse, too. Curiosity made her take a closer look at the unconscious man now that Millie had washed the last of the mud from his face and had rinsed his hair clean.

When she saw the blond hair, her heart squeezed tight in her chest, leaving her short of breath. She had to be wrong. It couldn't be—but there was no mistaking that arrogant nose and stubborn chin. And without looking, she knew that his eyes would be a bright, vivid blue. She must be tired to have not recognized him sooner.

Hoping she sounded calmer than she felt, she said, "Millie, I don't believe I heard this man's name. Did you know it?"

Millie emptied the muddy water from her basin and refilled it with clean. "I believe they called him Captain Chase. No one mentioned his first name that I know of."

"I was thinking he might respond if we called his name." Annie forced herself to continue washing away the dirt. At least it gave her something to do besides panic.

Millie gave his shoulder a shake. "Captain Chase! Can you hear us?"

Nothing.

Annie felt a little stab of guilt for being relieved that he didn't answer, not that she wished him ill. No, not at all, but she needed enough time and enough rest to figure out how to deal with Isaac Chase reappearing in her life, in her home. Would he take one look at her and see a nightmare from his past? She could just imagine how he'd feel knowing she was the one who would nurse him back to health.

Of course, knowing Isaac, he would have crawled back to the river and jumped in before letting her touch him. He'd draw no comfort from knowing that it was taking every ounce of willpower she could muster to continue washing him clean. There was a time when she would have leapt at the chance to do this man's bidding, but that was in the past when both of them had been young and foolish.

Annie had left that girl behind and hadn't looked back. She'd changed everything about herself that she could—how she lived, where she lived, and even her name. She could only pray that it would be enough to keep this man from recognizing her.

"I think his color is improving." Millie set the water and soap aside and picked up a towel. "We should be able to move him into the other room as soon as you are done there."

Once again, their plans were interrupted by a knock at the door. Annie appreciated the excuse to put some distance between her and their patient, even if it was only the width of the kitchen. It was with some relief she found the town doctor waiting on the porch.

"Doc, come on in."

He wiped his feet before coming in. She appreciated the gesture, but after all the men trooping through the house all night, it was too late to care. Doc walked past her and headed right for his patient. He shrugged off his coat and set his bag on a handy chair.

"He the only one hurt this bad?"

Annie hung the doctor's coat on a peg by the door. "There's one more in the next room, but his injuries don't seem as serious. I need to check on him again, but I think his worst injury was a bump on the head. He seemed to understand everything I said to him when he woke up."

"Good. I'll take a look at him before I go." Without another word, he began a thorough exam of the man on the table.

"Which one of you stitched up his arm?"

"I did." Annie forced herself to move closer. "Is something wrong?"

"Not at all. You did a damn fine job. Next time I need some help, I'll know who to turn to." He made his way down to the broken leg. "We'll need to set this. I'd rather do it here than in a bed, if that's all right."

"That will be fine, Doc. One of his men is resting in the parlor in case you need help."

"I will. Do you have any boards we can use for a splint?" He rolled up his sleeves, ready to get to work.

Annie looked to Millie for an answer, unable to think of anything herself. Her friend didn't fail her. "We have a couple of crates we could break up. And an old sheet you can use for ties."

"Perfect. Why don't you get them while I check on the patient in the other room? Once we have everything together, we'll set the leg. Annie, will you stay with our man here until we're ready? I don't think he'll regain consciousness anytime soon, but you never know. The last thing he needs is to fall off the table."

"Sure thing, Doc. I'll keep an eye on him."

Not that she wanted to, not for an instant. But if she were to protest, she'd have to explain to Millie what was going on. As long as she acted as if everything were normal, she could pretend her life hadn't just undergone another major upheaval. At least until Isaac opened those beautiful blue eyes of his and saw the one woman in the whole world he'd professed to love—and then hated with equal passion.

She hadn't deserved the first emotion, but she'd earned the second all right. Even if he'd somehow found a way to forgive her for what she'd done, she hadn't.

She brushed a lock of hair back from his face and prayed for strength. They were both going to need it.

Pain. Lots of it. Voices, none of them making sense, just a constant murmur sounding worried and distant.

He fought against the current of darkness that wanted to drag him back down and down to where there was nothing but cold and fear. If only for a moment, he needed to listen, to learn where he was: heaven or hell or somewhere in between.

He shoved a single word through his lips. "Where?"

A gentle hand on his shoulder was his answer. At least it wasn't hell, drawing comfort from even that little bit of information.

"You're safe. Your friends are fine."

Relief came with understanding. He was safe. Joe was alive. For now that was enough. He wished like hell he could say how grateful he was for even that much, but why did the voice sound so familiar? It was too much to puzzle out with pain nipping at his every thought. The blackness swirled through his mind, easing the agony. He gave up fighting and slipped back down to where the pain couldn't find him.

CHAPTER THREE

The bones snapped back into place. Doc ordered everyone to hold their patient steady until he arranged the splints and tied them in place with the strips of sheets. Once he had everything to his liking, he had Barton ease off on the pressure. Annie and Millie had been responsible for holding the captain down while Doc and Barton worked on his leg.

Isaac hadn't even whimpered. Although it simplified setting his leg, she knew Doc was concerned. He kept lifting one of Isaac's eyelids and frowning. But they'd done all they could for the time being.

"Let's get him moved into the other room." Doc positioned himself at Isaac's head. "Barton, you take the feet. Millie, you help stabilize his broken leg while Annie guides us through the doorway."

Between the four of them, they managed to move the gravely injured man to his bed. Their maneuvering woke Joe up from a sound sleep. He immediately wanted to help, but Doc ordered him back to bed.

"We've done everything we can for now, son." Doc stood back and let Millie pull the covers up around Isaac's chest. Annie brought the warmed bricks wrapped in towels. "He's in God's hands now. The best thing we can all do is get some rest so we're ready to deal with whatever tomorrow brings. He'll need your strength then."

Joe reluctantly let himself be put back to bed. Millie brought him a glass of water to drink before they all filed back out into the kitchen.

"I'd better be going, Annie. I've been up since before dawn yesterday morning, and I suspect the same can be said for you and Millie here. I'll be back around noon or so to check on everybody, but don't hesitate to give me a holler if you need me sooner."

Annie busied herself washing down the table with lye soap. "Do you think he'll be all right?"

"Well, he's young and in good health. I'd say he's got a fighting chance, but he's got a long way to go before he comes out on the other side of this whole affair. I'd be surprised if he doesn't at least catch a nasty fever or worse. Then there's his leg. The break was clean and the cold kept the swelling down some. Keep him warm and feed him some broth and the like as much as you can." He took his coat down off its peg. "Don't sit up watching him. You need to protect your own health, for your sakes as well as his."

When he was gone, Millie shooed Barton back to his makeshift bed. "You've done enough for one night. We've got a few things to see to before we come up."

"Thank you, ladies, for all you've done for all of us, and especially the captain." He nodded in the direction of the bedroom. "I know he'll be grateful. Good night. Don't worry about us in the morning. In fact, if you don't mind, our cook is a fair hand in the kitchen, and he's used to preparing big meals."

Annie hesitated only briefly before accepting the offer. "Tell him to use whatever he needs. The town will make sure we're reimbursed for anything we run low on."

"Yes, ma'am. Until tomorrow, then." His smile was genuine, if a bit ragged around the edges.

Annie gave the table one last going over before drying it off. Millie turned down the last few lamps. Together they made their way up to the third floor where they were going to double up in Annie's room. Neither of them spoke a word. Annie had too much on her mind that she couldn't share, not even with her best friend. Millie was probably just too tired.

"I don't even have the energy to put on my nightgown." Millie pulled the pins from her hair and let it down. For a few seconds, she ran her fingers through it, working out the tangles.

Annie managed to unbutton her dress and let it slip to the floor. She left it there while she pulled her favorite, well-worn gown over her head. "Which side of the bed do you prefer?"

Millie stopped braiding her hair long enough to consider the matter. "I'm so tired that I could sleep under the bed and not know the difference. You pick."

Annie crawled in on the side closest to the window and stretched out. It felt strange to feel the other side dip when Millie joined her. How long had it been since she shared a bed with someone? Years. Longer than she wanted to remember.

"Good night." Millie already sounded half asleep.

"Good night." Annie rolled onto her back and stared up into the darkness. As weary as she was, sleep could be a long time coming. For tonight and perhaps for another day or so, her secret was safe. As long as Isaac remained unconscious, no one would find out that she'd not always been the prim and proper woman that the people of Willow Shoals knew.

But the minute Isaac recognized her, unless his temper had mellowed over the years, there would be hell to pay. The tears she'd been fighting slipped free in the darkness. Her chest ached with the effort it took to not sob in fear and frustration. But if Millie heard even one whimper, she'd be awake and demanding to know what was wrong.

Annie didn't want to tell her because her friendship meant too much. What would she do if Millie were to learn the truth and turn away from her with disgust?

The tears stung her face like acid. Blinking furiously, she fought for control. She turned on her side, facing the window. Morning was but a couple of hours away, and the new day would bring what it would. For now, she closed her eyes and tried to empty her mind of all the regrets that churned in her mind.

Gradually, exhaustion won out over worry and sleep came.

* * *

"Let her sleep. I'll come."

On some level, Annie was aware of Millie climbing out of bed and getting dressed. She knew she should do the same, but she couldn't muster the energy even to throw back the covers. She let Millie think she'd been successful in not waking her.

Was Isaac awake or had he taken a turn for the worse? Although, considering the shape he was in last night, he couldn't get much worse and still be breathing. She rejected that thought. If something were that wrong, whoever had knocked at the door wouldn't have been so quiet about it. No, it was more likely that the boat's cook needed help finding something.

Either way, the sun was up, and it was time for her to be stirring. The cold temperature in the room ensured that she didn't linger over her morning routine. After running a brush through her hair, she loosely braided it and exchanged her gown for a dress. A glance in the mirror made her wince. The dark circles under her eyes gave testimony to how little sleep she'd gotten.

But her unexpected guests wouldn't be overly concerned if their hostess wasn't at her best. Considering last night, she figured they'd understand. She walked slowly down the stairs, trying to make sense of the voices coming from the rooms below.

Bacon and hot coffee scented the air. Evidently the cook had been busy. And, unless she was mistaken, he'd made flapjacks. She couldn't remember the last time someone had cooked breakfast for her. Millie usually helped, but it was going to be a real pleasure to sit down and eat without having even cracked an egg. Her mood brightened immediately.

She glanced into the parlor on her way to the kitchen. Several of the men were perched on the chairs. They looked decidedly uncomfortable and out of place in the feminine décor she had chosen for the room. She hid a smile, not wanting to embarrass them.

Millie stood in the doorway to the kitchen and didn't notice Annie until she was right beside her. "Good morning, Annie," she said with a smile. "I was trying to get Jake to share his recipe for flapjacks with us. So far without success, I might add. They're simply incredible."

"Will he at least share the flapjacks?" Annie poked her head past Millie to get a peek at the cook.

Jake gave her a shy smile. "I saved some batter to make them fresh for you, ma'am." He looked to be about fifty or so, completely bald and portly. The tight fit of his shirt told her he was fond of his own cooking.

Millie moved aside so that Annie could take a seat at the table. Jake fussed about her stove, his motions efficient and capable. In short order, he set a plate loaded with flapjacks in front of her. He stood back and waited for her to take the first bite. She closed her eyes and savored the moment.

"Jake, these are heavenly."

He blushed. "Thank you, ma'am. It's little enough to do for you and Miss Millie here. All of us are grateful to you for taking us in last night."

"Anyone would have done the same."

"I'm not so sure about that." He took off the towel he'd tucked into his waistband as an apron.

"I'll let you eat in peace. Leave the dishes when you're done. I'll get a couple of the men to help me with cleanup."

When he left the room, Annie took another bite, hoping everyone would let her finish her breakfast before bringing up the topic of the two men in the next room. It wasn't to be. Millie poured them both a cup of coffee and sat down at the table.

"Joe ate a good breakfast this morning," Millie told her. "I think once Doc checks him over, he'll be able to get out of bed and move around some."

"That's good news. He's a lucky man."

"I'm concerned about Captain Chase. I've checked him a couple of times already. I think a fever is setting in." Millie gave a worried look at the door. "His skin felt clammy and too warm."

Just that quickly, Annie couldn't look at another bite. She shoved her plate away. "I'd better look in on him and see if we need to send for Doc."

Millie looked relieved. Annie took a steadying breath before opening the door to the bedroom. Joe was awake and sitting up.

"Good morning, Joe. I hope you got a good night's sleep." She allowed herself the small reprieve of ignoring Isaac's too still form.

"Yes, ma'am, I did." His attempt to smile was valiant, considering the size of the lump on his head.

"How do you feel?" She touched his forehead gently. "No fever, but I bet you have quite a headache still."

He closed his eyes and slowly nodded. "Feels like someone's hitting me with a hammer every few seconds. Could be a whole lot worse, considering everything."

"True enough."

Barton appeared in the doorway. "Excuse me, Miss Annie. I thought Joe might like to make a trip outside."

She should have thought of that herself. Joe was already struggling to get out of the blankets. She stepped back to let Barton help his friend to his feet. Together they shuffled out of the room. Millie followed along behind to open the door for them.

Alone with her other patient, Annie pulled a chair close to the bed, still managing to keep her eyes from settling on Isaac. Finally, she had no choice but to face him. Telling herself that she would offer the same care to any of the other men who had been brought to her house last night, she ignored the slight tremble in her hand as she reached out to touch his forehead.

Fever had clearly set in. His skin felt as hot as the bricks that she'd heated last night. She also pulled back the blankets to check his leg. His foot felt warm; the toes all had good color. For now it appeared his leg stood a good chance of healing. He might end up with a limp, but that was a small price to pay considering everything. She tucked the blanket back around his leg and foot.

She needed to do something to break the fever. Millie would help, she knew, as would any of the men. But this was her house and therefore her job. Besides, in some way, perhaps it was a way to make amends for the past. He might not see it that way, but it felt right to her.

Back out in the kitchen, she asked, "Millie, would you heat up some of the broth from last night?" Then she reached for a basin and filled it with cool water. "I'm going to try to bring his fever down some. When the broth is hot, bring it in. He's going to need nourishment to fight this off."

She set the basin down on the bedside table and closed the door before sitting down on her chair. As long as she thought about Isaac as a patient, she could see to his needs without embarrassment. However, he deserved some privacy from prying eyes. She had a feeling that all of his men would want to check on him at some point. As long as she had the warning of the doorknob turning, she could pull the covers back up in time.

She wrung out a cloth in the water and began by washing his face and slowly made her way down to his shoulders and chest. The rhythm soothed her. Stroke and stroke. Dip and wring. Stroke and stroke again. Once she reached his waist, she worked her way back up to his shoulders again. His skin still felt too warm, but she thought perhaps a little cooler.

Of its own accord her hand reached out to brush back his hair from his face. The color seemed darker than it used to be, but perhaps time had distorted her memories. Guilt had a way of doing that, she supposed. Had his face always been so chiseled? Did those lines around his eyes come from smiling or perhaps from squinting against the bright sun reflected off the water? She had no right to ask or even wonder. Her place in Isaac's life had ended a long time ago.

The sound of the door opening broke her out of her reverie. She quickly covered Isaac's chest and turned her attention to washing his face one last time. Barton stepped into the room, carrying a bowl of broth.

"I settled Joe in the parlor with the others for a while. He's awfully upset about the captain being hurt so bad on his account." He handed the bowl to Annie. "I keep telling him that it could have been any one of us in the river and that the captain would have done the same thing. We would have gone in after him, too, for that matter."

He frowned down at the still form on the bed. "Has he stirred at all?"

There was no use in lying. "Not yet." Recognizing Barton's need to feel useful, she asked him, "Can you prop him up for me? I'd like to see if we can get him to swallow some of the broth. Not enough to choke him, mind you. Just a little at a time."

With surprising gentleness, Barton eased Isaac up enough to slide in behind him. He braced his captain against his chest, trying to support him without jarring his leg.

"That's perfect." Annie held a small spoonful of broth to Isaac's mouth. "Open your mouth, Captain Chase." When he didn't respond, she pried his lips apart with the side of the spoon and let the broth dribble in his mouth. Some spilled down his chin, but most of it made it into his mouth. Their efforts were rewarded when he swallowed.

"That's it, Captain, take some more." Barton kept his voice low but insistent as they laboriously coaxed their patient into taking almost half the broth.

"I think that's enough for now." Annie set the bowl aside. "Too much may make him sick to his stomach."

She helped Barton ease Isaac back down on the pillow again. "I think his fever is down a bit, but I'll feel better when Doc checks in on him."

"How is his arm?"

"I was about to look at it when you brought the broth in." He watched over her shoulder as she unwrapped Isaac's arm. Blood had seeped through the bandage and dried. She had to soak the cloth with water to loosen it. Barton winced when she finally pulled the last little bit free from the wound. The stitches had held, but the injured area looked swollen and hot.

"Doc said he'd be by around noon. If he doesn't come by then, I'll send for him." She frowned. "Maybe I should put a poultice on it now."

"If you think it would help." Barton's eyebrows were drawn together in worry. "Do you have everything you need to make one?"

She closed her eyes and thought about it. "Yes, I think so. Do you want to sit with him while I make it up?" Until he regained consciousness, Isaac wouldn't know if anyone was nearby, but it was clear that Barton needed to be near him.

He took her place in the chair. "Do you want me to try to cool him off some more?"

"That would be fine. I'll be back in a few minutes."

She left the room, pausing outside the door to catch her breath. For the moment, the kitchen was empty, allowing her a few minutes of privacy. Maybe things would be easier once the rest of Isaac's crew either went back downriver or at least found other accommodations. There was little chance that she'd be shed of the entire group. Somehow she thought Barton and possibly Joe would insist on staying on longer to keep an eye on Isaac.

She couldn't blame them, but she hated having

her life in such an uproar. There went her plans for enjoying the quiet time while Kate and Patience were gone. Now she had even more mouths to feed. Sighing, she put water on to boil and looked for a piece of clean cloth to use for the poultice. She set the ingredients on to steep while she checked her supplies and tried to plan for the next couple of meals. Maybe Millie had some ideas.

Come to think of it, she hadn't seen her friend since she'd offered to hold the door for Joe and Barton. Where could she be?

"Millie?" No response.

She went exploring. There was no one in the parlor. Had they already moved on? Voices drifted down the staircase. Perhaps Millie was putting the bedrooms to rights. Before she could check out her theory, someone stepped on the creaky step.

Joe turned the corner on the landing with Millie hovering right behind him. He held onto the railing, but otherwise seemed to be getting around all right. When he saw Annie waiting at the bottom, his steps faltered a bit.

She forced a smile on her face. "You seem to be feeling stronger."

"Yes, ma'am." He glanced behind him toward Millie. "I was just helping Miss Millie straighten up the rooms the others used last night, although I suspect I only slowed her down."

Millie eased past him on the stairs and hurried down to the bottom. Unless Annie was mistaken, her friend was blushing. Now wasn't the time to find out what was going on, not with Joe standing only a few feet away.

"Were you looking for me?"

Annie nodded. "I'm making up a poultice for the captain's arm. I was wondering if you had any ideas about what to cook for all our guests? And how many we'd need to feed." She gestured toward the parlor. "Are some of the men gone?"

Joe answered. "The sheriff came by awhile ago and took them over to the parsonage. He said to tell you that he'd found rooms for everyone except me and Barton." He walked the rest of the way down the stairs as he spoke. "And the captain, of course. Miss Millie here said you had room enough for that many. If that's all right, of course. We'll pay whatever you normally charge for boarders."

It was no more than she expected—better actually, since she hadn't figured on being paid. "That'll be fine."

Millie seemed pleased by her response. "I'll tell you what. Since you're taking care of the captain, I'll start the cooking. Miss Barker said she would be gone most of the day. She and the church circle are over at the church working on the costumes."

Annie trailed after Millie to the kitchen, grateful that Joe had headed into the parlor instead. Once the two of them were alone, she whispered, "So was he a lot of help making the beds?"

She'd been right. Millie blushed again.

"He needed something to do."

Deciding that she'd teased her friend enough, Annie picked up the cloth she'd laid out for the poultice. "I'm sure he did. Barton is the same way. They're both worried about Captain Chase."

"How is he?"

"Feverish and his arm looks like infection may be setting in. I'll be glad when Doc comes back."

She crossed her arms over her chest, feeling a chill that had little to do with the cold weather outside. "Barton helped feed him some broth. I was thinking some weak tea with some honey might taste good to him."

She took the teapot down off the shelf. "I'd like a cup myself."

While she waited for it to brew, she finished assembling the poultice. "I'll go apply this to his arm and come back for the tea."

Picking up the hot compress, she braced herself and returned to her patient's side.

Her voice was back. The angel, the one whose fleeting touches drew him back to the edge of light. This time, perhaps he'd find some way to let her know that he heard her words even though he didn't understand them.

The struggle weakened him. He quit trying when another voice answered her, a deeper one, a man. This time the hands that touched his face and pulled down the covers were his, bigger and not as gentle. Something cold touched his chest briefly.

Pain screamed up his arm when the man moved it. What had happened? As the two voices whispered and conspired above him, he tried to take stock of his own condition. His arm was injured; that much was clear. And his leg felt heavy and stiff. It took some effort, but he managed to move his foot. Or at least he thought he did.

He'd heard horror stories about amputees who nearly went crazy from the sensation that their missing limb was still there. Is that what was wrong, why his wouldn't move? He tried to move the other leg. That one was easier. Until he was able to open his eyes, the best he could guess was that he'd managed to hurt one leg and one arm.

But how?

The soft voice would tell him, if only he could let her know he had so many questions that needed answering. Unless he was mistaken, the man had left the room, but she was still there. He could feel her warmth hovering close by. A cool cloth brushed across his forehead, easing the pain that burned behind his eyes.

He concentrated the little strength he could find on opening his eyes. Until he could do that much, he was a prisoner of the darkness and the pain. One try would be all he would get at the moment. Already he could feel his control slipping away again.

When she took his hand and caressed his arm with the cool cloth, he squeezed his hand around hers. He wanted to whimper when she let go and jumped back from the bed. Had he scared her? He hadn't meant to, but he had no words to tell her so.

"Captain Chase?"

He puzzled over the name and finally decided that it was his, another piece of information to tuck away and cherish. He was Captain Chase. That answered who he was, but where was he? And who was the angel with such gentle hands?

"You're safe, Captain Chase. All of your men are as well."

He could have listened to her talk for hours. Her hand grasped his again.

"Squeeze my hand again, Captain, if you can. Just so I know that you meant to the first time."

His heart raced with the effort, but he succeeded in closing his fingers around hers. She immediately squeezed his hand, letting him know without words that she knew he'd answered her.

"I'll be right back, Isaac. Stay with me."

Isaac? She'd called him Captain Chase before, but the names went together. Captain Isaac Chase. It sounded familiar, right somehow, especially when she said it. As if he'd heard her say his name a thousand times before.

Who was she? Before he could give the matter any serious thought, he heard more voices—men this time.

"Captain? Are you awake? It's me—Barton. Joe is here, too. Can you talk to us?"

A big rough hand took his and squeezed. "Captain, can you hear me?"

But it was too much for him. Wishing he could do as they asked, regretfully, he let sleep claim him. This time his dreams were restful. After all, she said he was safe.

Barton or Joe would be in to relieve her soon. She'd insisted on sitting with Isaac after dinner, hoping and fearing that he'd respond again. Doc had praised her care of their patient. The poultice had already reduced some of the redness around the gash on his arm. His face still felt feverish, but certainly no worse than it had been. He wasn't out of danger yet, but there was reason to think he might continue to improve.

She wished it had been Barton or Joe who had been holding Isaac's hand earlier, anyone but her. She hadn't wanted to feel a connection with him. As long as she could think of him as Captain Chase, and not Isaac, she was all right. He would not be pleased to find out that the voice he was responding to was hers. Not at all.

She closed her eyes and wished she knew how he was going to react when he had his wits about him again. Would he be grateful that she had nursed him, offered him the sanctuary of her home? Somehow, she doubted it. And once his friends found out about their shared past, they might not be too thrilled to be staying there either.

One of the first things she'd learned after leaving Isaac behind was how to ignore the stares and slights and disapproval of the so-called decent folks. Women especially were given to little shows of superiority when faced with someone they thought beneath them. She wouldn't claim that it hadn't hurt some, but for the most part, they'd been strangers.

The people of Willow Shoals had come to be friends and neighbors. If they were to shun her, it would hurt something fierce. She'd lost everything once. With hard work and some luck she'd patched her life back together. Now, in the blink of an eye, she felt as if she were out on the broken ice in the river and skidding toward disaster.

Voices from the next room carried through the thin walls. If she really concentrated, she could make out some of what they were saying. For the most part, it was nothing of consequence. But now Barton and Joe seemed to be talking about Isaac, telling Millie about the man they worked for and also considered a friend.

She closed her mind to their words. Even now, she could wash his brow and change his bandage without really thinking about who he was. She didn't want them to make him seem more real to her.

Dipping a fresh cloth in the water basin, she twisted it tight to remove the excess water. Once again, she began the long process of washing Isaac's face, neck, and so on. When the cloth felt warm to the touch, she refreshed it, hoping the cool water would ease his fever.

If her life was headed for disaster, she wanted it to come fast because the suspense would tear her apart. Or so she told herself.

Focusing her attention solely on the moment and keeping her hands busy, she hoped the monotonous activity would distract her. Slowly, however, she realized that someone was watching her. Blue eyes stared up at her, struggling to focus, trying to make sense of his surroundings.

She wanted—needed—to run before he succeeded. Of all things she'd once hoped to see in his gaze, loathing wasn't it. Right now, he was still too dazed to do more than look at her with questions in his eyes.

She backed away from the bed, out of the dim circle of light cast by the single lamp on the table. She fought down the panic, holding onto her control by the thinnest of threads. With a calm she certainly didn't feel, she opened the door to the kitchen and called for reinforcements.

"Barton, Joe, it appears that your captain is finally awake."

Just as she'd hoped, the two men pushed their way into the room. She inched past them, planning on allowing them some privacy.

But a single word stopped her. Barely a whisper, his voice was rough and painful to hear.

"Belle?"

She froze, for the space of a heartbeat, wishing she could either run or disappear completely. But that wasn't going to happen. She made herself look at him, made herself respond in a calm voice.

"My name is Annie, Captain Chase. You are a guest in my house. These men are your friends Barton and Joe. They'll stay with you now."

Turning her attention to them, she admonished, "Be careful not to wear him out. He may not even stay conscious for long. But while he is, you might help him drink some more broth. I'll be back to check on him before I retire for the night."

If they thought her behavior odd, neither of them commented. She walked out, pulling the door closed behind her before Isaac could whisper her name again. And break her heart.

CHAPTER FOUR

She found herself in the parlor staring at the piano. Her fingers trailed down the keys softly, the notes drawing her closer. Music was a luxury that she rarely had time for. But tonight, she needed the distraction. Telling herself that she should practice the music for the Christmas program, she pulled out the bench and sat down.

The piano had been left behind by the previous owner of the house. In truth, it had been the real reason she'd been drawn to this particular house in town. There had been one or two others that would have served her just as well to take in boarders, but none of the others offered the added feature of a piano in the parlor.

The poor thing had been badly abused, no doubt the reason it was left behind. She'd seen past the scars and scratches to the possibilities. Step by step, she'd brought it back to respectability. In some ways, she had done the same with her own life. She'd slowly made herself into someone she could respect again.

Until Isaac Chase reappeared and called her Belle. But she'd worried and fretted enough about him for one day. She shoved all thought of him aside as she reached for the music for the Christmas program.

After the first few notes, she lost herself in the melody. The song was new to her, but already her fingers were learning the rhythm and flow of the piece. Despite her initial reluctance, she couldn't wait to hear the voices of the congregation singing along, all drawn together in a night of celebration. Perhaps this was the chance she'd been waiting for, the one that would make her feel a legitimate member of the community.

Concentrating so hard on the music and the possibilities it offered, she didn't realize that she had attracted an audience. When she finished playing with a flourish, her efforts were rewarded with a round of applause. The noise startled her into leaping to her feet. Barton and Joe had somehow entered the room without her noticing.

"Sorry, ma'am, we didn't meant to disturb you. That's some of the nicest playing I've heard in a long time." Joe's smile was apologetic.

When he started to stand up, she motioned for him to stay seated. "No need to apologize. It wasn't your fault that I wasn't paying the proper attention to my guests."

"You were doing a fine job of entertaining us, even if you didn't know you were doing so." Barton stood leaning against the door frame. "I assure you we don't feel neglected, especially since we weren't invited guests to begin with." He pushed away from the wall. "Miss Millie offered to sit with the captain for a spell. I'm going to take her place. Joe has the right of it, though. You've got a real talent for the piano, that's for certain."

"You're too kind, gentlemen." She pushed the bench back up to the piano, done practicing for the night.

"Your captain—did he say anything else?" She straightened the sheets of music in a neat pile to keep from looking at the two men.

"No, just that one word. I guess his thoughts are still scrambled a bit. I didn't hear any bells." Joe sounded puzzled.

She could tell him that Isaac hadn't heard a bell; he'd seen one. Not that anyone had called her by that name in years. Feeling a bit guilty for leaving his friends confused and worried, she decided to look in on Isaac one last time and then retire for the night.

Millie had turned up the lamp in order to read. She looked up from her novel and smiled. "All is quiet in here. He hasn't moved much at all since I came in, but he seems to be resting easy."

She marked her place in the book and stood up. "I'll give you a minute or two with your patient and then send Barton in. You should get some rest soon. All of this excitement has worn me out, so I know you must be tired out."

"I'll be up as soon as I check his arm. I may need to make a new poultice, but otherwise I shouldn't be far behind you."

She began uncovering the wound as Millie left. Since Isaac seemed to respond to her voice more than anyone else's, she spoke softly and explained what she was doing. "I know this might hurt some, Isaac, but Doc wants me to keep a close watch on your arm. It was a pretty nasty cut to begin with, but all that river mud didn't help matters."

He stirred slightly when she tugged the last bit of bandage free. The redness had faded, which pleased her. As she reapplied the bandage, she kept talking. "I think you're arm is healing up fine. Now if your fever would break, we'd all be a lot happier."

She meant to keep her touch brief and impersonal as she felt his forehead. When she realized that she was brushing his hair back, she tried unsuccessfully to convince herself that it was to make it easier to check his temperature. The truth was that she'd always envied his thick blond hair and bright blue eyes. It seemed so unfair that she was the one who was stuck with plain old brown hair and brown eyes.

But none of that mattered, not anymore.

"Good night, Isaac." The temptation to press a small kiss to his cheek surprised her. She had no business thinking such a thing. Knowing she needed to keep her distance, she quickly left the room. He'd be in good hands with Barton stretched out on the other bed.

Millie waited until her friend was about to get into bed to ask the question that was keeping her awake. "Do you want to talk about him?"

Annie's response was too casual to be believed. "Which him? Barton, Joe, or Captain Chase? Although, there isn't much to talk about that you don't already know. The captain's arm is better and his fever is certainly no worse than it was."

Millie watched as Annie climbed into the other side of the bed, being so very careful to avoid looking in her direction. Considering those dark circles under Annie's eyes, she knew she should let her friend go to sleep without another word. But something wasn't right and hadn't been since shortly after Sheriff Stone and his men had carried the injured man into the house.

None of the others had put that worried look in Annie's dark eyes. Of course, it could be just concern for an injured man, but Millie didn't think so. There was more to it. Something that looked all too much like fear.

Rather than press the issue, she settled for a simple offer. "I'm here whenever you need to talk, Annie. I'm your friend. Nothing can change that."

For a few seconds she thought perhaps Annie had already fallen asleep and hadn't heard her. But as her own eyes were drifting closed, she thought she heard Annie whisper, "I can only hope that is true."

"Annie?"

This time there was no response at all.

He was biding his time, ready to act when the circumstances were right.

Sometime during the night his mind had cleared, and he remembered it all. The sickening crunch when the first ice hit the *Caprice*. The long hell of praying they could make it as far as the next landing without her settling to the bottom of the river.

Then the brief flare of hope when the lights of Willow Shoals loomed up out of the darkness along the shore.

Then Joe's scream swallowed by the river. Even now, his chest hurt with the need to get to his friend before the ice or the freezing water claimed his life. He remembered feeling Joe being pulled back up onto the boat and then the roiling water sucking him under before he could reach safety himself.

Darkness and bitter, numbing cold were his only other clear memories.

Where was he?

Once she came back, he would demand answers. There had been others in and out of the room. He was pretty certain that he'd heard Barton and Joe talking over him several times. And there was at least one other woman in the house.

But there was only one who mattered. The one whose voice and face had made him cry out a name he hadn't uttered in years. He knew that the resemblance was probably only superficial; no doubt his feverish dreams had supplied a name to go with a strange face.

Belle.

He would be lying to himself to say that all thoughts of Belle had faded away, enough so that he no longer hurt whenever something triggered his memories of the time they'd spent together. But now wasn't the time to stir up all that hurt and bitterness again. He had other, more pressing problems to figure out.

The snoring from the next bed reached a new volume. If he had enough energy to complain, he would have even knowing that nothing ever stopped Barton from making such a racket. Whenever possible, he assigned the pilot private quarters to keep the peace on the boat. No one else could sleep much whenever Barton got started.

In between the bursts of noise, Isaac thought he heard someone stirring in the next room. It was difficult to tell for sure, but it seemed likely that the mysterious woman was up and about. His pulse sped up, waiting for a knock at the door. His good leg stirred restlessly.

Evidently, that was enough noise to awaken his companion. He could hear Barton struggle to sit up on the edge of his bed. A match flared, creating a small island of light in the darkness.

"Captain? Are you awake?"

He blinked up at Barton's worried face and managed to nod. A big grin split Barton's face.

"Welcome back, sir. You've had us all worried." He reached for his trousers. "I'll be right back."

Isaac turned his head enough to watch the doorway. He could hear the rumble of Barton's excited voice in the next room and then two sets of footsteps coming his way. The owner of the gentle touch and the cool cloths would walk through the door in only seconds. He braced himself, wondering if she was half as sweet as he imagined her.

"He hasn't said anything yet, but his eyes look clear." Barton came through first but then stood back out of the way, holding a second lamp up to give her a brighter light.

Isaac blinked again, trying to adjust to the sudden light. He'd been living in darkness for what seemed like an eternity.

"Good morning, Captain Chase. I'm glad to see you're finally awake." She managed to hover just outside the light. Her voice sent the first tendrils of suspicion tearing through his gut.

He managed to string some words together. "I'm sorry, I didn't catch your name."

Her first reaction was to take a step backwards. "My name is Annie, Captain Chase."

Years of dealing with people of all sorts, not all of them strictly honest, had honed his skills at detecting when someone had something to hide. All the alarms were sounding. She didn't want him to know who she was. If she were a total stranger, she'd have no reason to fear him. Which meant he did know her or had at some point in the past.

"I suspect I owe you a great deal, uh, *Annie.*" She took a sharp breath at his slight emphasis on her name. "Please come closer so that I can thank you properly."

"I'm sorry, but I have something on the stove I need to check on." She disappeared without a backward look, leaving both men staring after her.

Barton picked up on the undercurrents in the conversation and gave Isaac a puzzled look. "Miss Annie and her friend have opened up their home to us, Captain. Annie stitched your arm up herself when the doctor couldn't get here in time. I don't know how many hours the two of them have sat beside you, trying to get your fever down."

"And the rest of the crew? How are they?"

"Joe took a good knock to the head, but he's doing fine. The rest of the men were moved out to other places once they got warm and dry. The whole town has done their best to help us."

For the moment, Isaac was just as happy not to confront a living memory from the past. "And the *Caprice*?" He braced himself for the worst.

"I haven't been out to check on her myself, but I was planning on going today. The sheriff and a couple of his men told me that she's still listing to one side, but most of her is still well above water. The river is almost solid with ice now. I'd guess as long as it stays that way, she won't be going anywhere."

Isaac let out a breath. The news was bad, but not as bad as he'd feared. There was a good chance that they'd be able to salvage the rest of the cargo, and with luck the *Caprice* herself. He hoped so because he wasn't sure he had it in him to start over— again. Which brought him back to the woman in the next room.

For the moment, he'd accept Barton's opinion that this Annie and her friend were damn near angels. He was warm, dry, and on the mend. He owed them both for that. But there were older debts that may come into play, ones he'd waited what seemed like a lifetime to collect. Before he could pursue that thought, Joe came into the room.

It felt so good to see his friend up and about and looking a hell of a lot better than he had the last time Isaac had seen him. When he'd gone into the river after Joe, he'd half expected to be retrieving his dead body. Instead, he was the one who was almost back to normal while Isaac was abed and in pain.

"Is my leg broken?" He felt stupid for having to ask, but so far no one had told him any details about his own condition.

Barton smacked his forehead with the flat of his hand. "I'm sorry, Captain. I should have told you straight off. Your leg is busted, but the doctor and Annie managed to set it straight. I don't know much about broken bones, but I think you'll heal up fine as long as you don't do anything else to it. You've got a sizeable gash on your arm that Annie stitched up. She's been using some kind of poultice to keep the infection down. And you've been running a fever almost from the first night." He reached down with his rough hand and touched Isaac's forehead. "It seems to be breaking up finally."

"I suppose I have Annie to thank for that as well." He allowed some of his bitter suspicion to seep into his words and regretted it. "I'm sorry. I don't handle being sick very well."

"I've never met a man who did." Another woman entered the room. "I'm Millie, Captain Chase. I'm glad to finally make your acquaintance." She gave him a brief smile. "Barton, Joe—Annie will have breakfast on the table for the two of you in a few minutes. Go on in and wash up while I check on our patient."

"We'll be back shortly, Captain." The two of the disappeared from sight.

Millie drew up a chair and reached for Isaac's arm. As she unwrapped the bandage, he studied her face. She looked to be slightly older than he was, maybe by a couple of years. Life had left a few marks on her face, but he suspected that when she smiled, men would sit up and take notice.

"Your arm is improving steadily."

"Doesn't feel that way." He winced when she lifted it to wind a clean bandage around it.

Her eyes crinkled at the corners. "Just be glad you still have an arm, even if it hurts some. If it weren't for Annie and her poultices, I suspect you might have lost it."

He shuddered. He'd witnessed a few amputations during the war and still had nightmares from the memories. "I'll be sure to thank her."

"You do that, Captain Chase. We all helped care for you, but she's the one who knew what to do." Millie picked up the old bandage. "I'll be right back with something for you to eat. Annie was getting a tray ready."

"I appreciate everything you've done for me." This time it wasn't hard to sound sincere.

Figuring she'd be back almost immediately, he tried his best to prop himself up on the pillows so that he could feed himself. After the third try, he gave up and waited for Millie or Barton to help him. He really hated feeling so damned helpless. He didn't know which was worse—having women wait on him or his own men.

Joe came into the room, carrying a tray. "We sure hit it lucky when the sheriff brought us here. Miss Annie and her friend are both terrific cooks." He set the tray down and pulled the chair closer to the bed. He gently eased Isaac up higher on the pillows and even tugged the covers back up around him.

"I'm not totally helpless, Joe," he grumbled and slapped his friend's hands away.

"No, you're not, but you'll get better faster if you don't overdo." Joe grinned. "I know, because that's what everyone's been telling me since I got here."

"Are you all right?"

"Yes, thanks to you. I ended up with a big knot on my head and a hell of a headache." He pointed to the black circle under his eye. "As the lump goes down, the worse my eyes look, but it doesn't hurt."

"Could have been worse."

Joe's eyes turned bleak. "A lot worse. Hell, I thought I was a dead man the second I hit the water. Never felt such cold before."

"I know the feeling." He doubted if he'd ever forget the terror he felt when the wheel came so close to killing him. "But we're both on the mend. That's the important part to remember."

"True enough." Joe reached for the plate on the tray. "Miss Annie said for you to take it easy and eat slowly. This is the first solid food you've had in days."

Isaac wanted to say that if she were so worried about how he ate, why wasn't she the one in there supervising the whole process? But he held his tongue. If Miss Annie was who he thought she might be, he didn't want her holding a knife in her hand when he found out.

He'd managed to eat about half the food on the plate when chewing became too much of an effort for him to continue. Joe nagged him into drinking more water before he'd let him rest.

"Barton is getting ready to go check on the *Caprice*. If the ice is solid enough, he may even go on board. I hope he can because most of us need to get some of our stuff off the boat. He said to tell you he'd give you a full report when we get back."

Isaac managed to nod before sleep claimed him.

*   *   *

The house was empty again, except for her and
the one person in the world she didn't want to talk
to. Maybe she was being cowardly by not confronting
Isaac with the truth of who she was, or at least who
she had become. Would he even care?

The ticking of the clock on the mantel seemed
to echo too loudly, each second stretching her
nerves to the breaking point. Finally, she gathered
the ragged edges of her courage around her and
prepared to face the inevitable. He would either
accept her or not. His decision, not hers. But if he
were going to explode, she'd rather have it happen when the rest of the household wasn't there to
stand witness to it. Once she knew how he was going
to react, she could better prepare for explaining the
situation to the others.

She closed her eyes, wanting to pray for deliver-
ance, but she didn't expect that to happen. Maybe
she couldn't get on with her life until she managed to make peace with her past, especially the
one person she'd wounded the deepest.

If she didn't walk into that room in the next few
minutes, she'd lose the best opportunity she'd had
to talk to Isaac without interruption. After checking her appearance in the mirror and shaking her
head over the folly of that, she started toward the
back of the house. She stood outside the bedroom
door, willing her hand to knock on the door. Now
that he was conscious, she felt he deserved that
much courtesy.

He answered before she had a chance to knock
twice. Her stomach churned as she reached for
the doorknob and turned it.

She crossed the threshold, feeling as if she were leaving her whole life behind. Isaac had managed to prop himself up on his pillows. It had taken some effort, considering how hard he was breathing. For several seconds, they stared at each other without saying a word. For her part, she didn't know what to say. He, on the other hand, looked as if he couldn't decide what to say first.

"Isaac." She stood at the foot of the bed, near the door and waited.

His eyes looked like blue ice. "Well, I'll be damned. I was hoping I was having nightmares when I saw you, Belle."

"I'm sorry I didn't come in earlier." That much was true. If she had, this whole mess would be behind her.

"I wondered if I'd have to wait until I could walk to find you." His lip curled. "Still taking the coward's way, Belle?"

"I go by Annie these days."

"Did you think changing your name would change who you are or what you did?"

"No, nothing can change the past." One could have regrets but that wouldn't fix anything.

"Well, if you've come in to ask my forgiveness, you can forget it. You stopped meaning anything at all to me a long time ago." Despite what he said, fury dripped from every word. "Barton and Joe mentioned a couple of women living here, but no man. Did you run out on Nick the same way you did me?"

His words lashed out at her like a whip. She stumbled back a step before she managed to stand her ground. "No, I didn't."

"Then where the hell is he? Is he waiting to see how I reacted to seeing you again before he puts in an appearance? It's just like the son of a bitch to hide behind your skirts." He looked around as if he expected Nick to pop out from under the other bed or from behind the dresser.

"Nick's dead, Isaac." She took mean pleasure from seeing the shock on Isaac's face. "He's been gone for almost five years."

"What happened?" Then he shook his head. "No, don't tell me. Just leave."

"But . . ."

"I said leave, Belle or Annie or whatever you decide to go by tomorrow." He laid his good arm across his face, as if to ensure he couldn't see her anymore.

Her own temper was running high. "This is my house, Isaac. Mine. I come and go as I like, and I won't be ordered around by any man, especially you."

He ignored her. Finally, she walked out, but only because she wanted to.

Nick was dead. He tried to get his mind around that idea. He'd thought a lot of things about Nick over the years, but that hadn't been one of them. Hell, Nick was—or would have been—twenty-eight, a year younger than Isaac was himself. Despite everything he'd done, he'd died too damn young.

How had it happened?

Eventually, he might ask Belle to tell him, but he wasn't ready for that. Not when he was still reeling from the shock of seeing her again. He wasn't about to ask her to sit down and reminisce about old times.

He shifted a little, wishing he could get out of bed and walk off some of his agitation. Even sitting up was beyond him at the moment. Until he regained some of his strength, all he could do was lie there and fume. Maybe when Barton and Joe came back, they'd read to him or play cards or do something to keep his mind occupied.

The sound of footsteps and a soft knock at the door caught his attention. Since he hadn't heard anyone else's voice for a while, he had to assume that Belle was wanting in.

"What do you want now?"

She opened the door a crack and peeked in. "I've made soup. Do you want to eat or would you rather starve?"

He considered the choices. If he refused to eat just because of her, it would only slow down how quickly he healed and therefore how quickly he could get the hell out of her house. Which meant he had no choice at all.

"I'll eat."

"Fine."

She waited for him to struggle to sit up, obviously no more eager to touch him than he was for her help. When he was ready, she set the tray on his lap and handed him a spoon. Evidently she would cook for him but feeding him was beyond what she was willing to do for him now.

After she arranged everything to her satisfaction, she stepped back and waited to see how he managed on his own. When he proved himself able to get a spoonful of soup to his mouth without dribbling too much, she sat down on the other bed and waited for him to finish. She kept herself occupied reading a book.

The silence dragged on; the only noise was the occasional turning of a page or the clink of the spoon against the bowl. When he couldn't stand it any more, he managed to pick up the tray one-handed and set it on the chair she'd left by the bed. He eased back down the pillow and closed his eyes, even though he didn't feel at all sleepy.

A few seconds later, he heard her pick up the tray and silently walk out of the room. He listened to the door close and wished like hell that he were the one leaving.

As soon as she heard Millie return from shopping, Annie reached for her coat. The brisk walk to the church for another rehearsal would go a long way toward improving her mood. She'd worked hard all afternoon around the house. But no matter how busy she was, she remained painfully aware of Isaac's presence. It was like a bleak fog following her every footstep.

"I'm going to the church for a couple of hours." She didn't want to explain that she could just as well practice on her own piano. "I'll be back in time to help with dinner."

"Don't hurry. I can take care of things here." Millie reached for her apron. "How is our patient?"

"I haven't checked on him recently. He was able to feed himself some soup, so he's getting stronger."

Millie gave her a puzzled look, but before she could ask any questions, Annie hurried out the door. Once she was out of sight of the house, she paused to take some cleansing breaths. The air had a cold bite to it, but it felt good.

She set off at a brisk pace, anxious to reach the church. The chance to lose herself in the music beckoned to her. For as long as she could remember, it had been her one escape. Once her fingers rested on the keys, everything else in her life faded into the background. She'd played everything from classical to saloon music, but it all brought her a sense of joy and peace.

The pastor must have seen her coming because he opened the door for her as soon as she reached the steps.

"Mrs. Dunbar, this is an unexpected pleasure! Come in, come in." He helped her with her coat, hanging it on a peg just inside the door. "I was taking a short break from writing Sunday's sermon for some tea and some of Mrs. Chesterfield's best cookies. Would you care to join me?"

It was on the tip of her tongue to pass because the music was calling her, but he looked so glad to have company, she couldn't refuse.

"I'd love some tea and cookies. I hear that Mrs. Chesterfield has quite a talent for baking."

He beamed with pride. "That she does, and for all kinds of cooking." He patted his potbelly with a wry smile. "I sometimes think maybe she's too good."

Annie followed him through the church to the small office where he worked. Papers were scattered all over his desk, evidence that perhaps the sermon wasn't going smoothly. He gathered them up and set them in a disorderly pile out of the way.

A tray with a teapot, several cups, and a huge

plate of cookies sat on a nearby table. "Have a seat while I pour."

Annie pulled a straight-backed chair closer to the desk. "Were you expecting company?" she asked, gesturing toward the cups.

"No, but I never know who is going to stop by during the course of the day. My wife always sends along extra, just in case. Now, do you take sugar in your tea?"

"No, that's fine, Pastor." She accepted the cup and the two cookies he insisted she take.

When he was settled in his own chair, he peered at her over his glasses. "I have to say that you have the gratitude of the entire town for opening your home to those unfortunate men the other night."

She felt uncomfortable accepting praise for something she'd done only reluctantly. "Anyone would have done the same."

"I'd like to think so, Miss Annie, but we both know that it isn't true. But even more, Doc tells me that you did as much for that Captain Chase as he could have."

Now she was blushing. "But Doc set his leg."

"That may be true. But according to Doc, if you hadn't acted so quickly with his other injuries and getting the poor man warm and dry, Captain Chase might not have lasted the night until Doc got there." He looked a little sheepish as he reached for his third cookie. "Where did you learn so much about nursing?"

"During the war." That much was true, but she had treated more knife wounds and gunshots in the backroom of saloons. She figured he didn't really need to know that.

"How is Captain Chase doing?"

"He's improving. Today he was up to feeding himself."

"That's wonderful news. I'll include him in my prayers today. It was truly one of God's miracles that no one died out there on the river." He smiled. "We should all be grateful that He watched over those men. And I'm sure that they know that they were blessed when the sheriff led them to you."

Somehow she doubted that was true for Isaac, but she didn't want to disappoint the kind man sitting across from her. She changed the direction of the conversation. "What happened to the rest of his men? Are they all right?"

"I think the sheriff was going out to the river with them today to see what could be salvaged. If they can retrieve their personal belongings, several of them plan to head back downriver by the next stagecoach. However, I believe two of the men plan to stay on as long as Captain Chase may need them."

She nodded while inwardly she winced. It would be weeks before Isaac's leg was completely healed. Did that mean Joe and Barton planned on staying at her boardinghouse for the duration? For that matter, what about Isaac himself? She couldn't imagine living with the tension that she'd been feeling since the minute she recognized him. It couldn't be good for him either, considering how riled up he got every time she walked into his room.

On the other hand, where else could he go? If she suddenly insisted that she had no room for him, people would ask questions she had no interest in answering. Millie, especially, would have something to say on the matter.

Some of her thoughts must have shown on her face because Pastor Chesterfield set down his cup and leaned forward. "Now don't you worry, Miss Annie. I'll make sure that you get all the help you need to deal with the extra burden of unexpected boarders. I know it's more work, what with Captain Chase being injured and all, but at least his friends are willing to help with his care. I think that speaks well of the kind of man he is."

"Barton and Joe have both been wonderful." If he read anything into her leaving Isaac off the list, so be it. She wasn't going to lie to a pastor, even if she didn't tell the complete truth.

She finished the last of her tea. "Thank you so much for the refreshments. The cookies were every bit as good as you said they'd be."

He stood when she did. "I just realized. I never asked what brought you by. Did you need me?"

"I came here to practice the music, unless that will bother you." In case he wondered why she wasn't using her own piano, she added, "Each instrument is different, so I wanted to practice some on the piano that I'll actually be using on the big night."

"Another thing we have to be grateful to you for, Miss Annie. I don't know what we would have done with Miss Patience being called away. I know the children and their families appreciate you accepting this calling for Christmas. It will add so much to the celebration."

"I love music. It will be a pleasure." That much was true. "Thank you again for the refreshments."

"You are most welcome. Perhaps your playing will inspire me." He gave the stack of papers a mournful look. "So far, I have to admit that my sermon lacks a little something."

"I'll do my best, Pastor."

"I know you will, Mrs. Dunbar. Remember, God never gives us more of a burden than we can bear. And when we find the going hard, all we have to do is reach out to Him and our friends."

"Yes, sir, I'll keep that in mind."

Once she was safely out of sight, she shook her head. Pastor Chesterfield had no idea how much of a burden she was carrying. Her past seemed to loom over her, threatening to overwhelm her. Would he really be so willing to reach out that hand he talked about if he knew the truth of who Annabelle Dunbar really was?

Rather than find out, she sat down at the piano and sought solace in the music. After only a few notes, she found peace, at least for the moment.

CHAPTER FIVE

"Damn it, Isaac! Use some common sense."

Barton stood across the room glaring at him. He had his arms crossed over his chest, a sure sign that he was digging in for a fight. Isaac had won more than his fair share of arguments with his pilot, but the man was definitely his equal when it came to being hardheaded.

"Get me up. If you won't help, then I'll do it on my own." His threat would have been more convincing if he'd been able to at least sit up without assistance. At least his arm had improved to the point he could use it. Some. At least when he had to and no one was around to see how much it hurt when he did. He'd damn near bit through his lip to keep from yelling earlier when he had tried to do too much. He was getting good at stringing together a line of whispered curses.

"Let me ask Annie if you should be moving around."

That did it. The last thing he wanted was to have his every move reported to her. "What I do is none of her damned business. Now get me up."

"No. Not until either Annie or the doctor say you can be moved. If they say it's all right, Joe and I will carry you out to the parlor for a spell." He shot Isaac a triumphant look, knowing full well that without his cooperation, Isaac wasn't going anywhere.

"Fine. Ask the doctor then."

"He's out of town until later this afternoon. I've already asked him to stop by when he can." Convinced of his victory, Barton dragged a chair over by the bed. "How about a few hands of cards?"

Isaac wanted to tell him what he could do with the cards, but that would only leave him with nothing to do at all. "Fine. Deal."

"What shall we play for?"

"Buttons, toothpicks, rocks. Hell, I don't care as long as I have something to do."

"Fine. I'll be right back."

He returned with a plate full of cookies. He divided them into two stacks. Before Isaac could take his portion, Barton snatched one off his stack and ate it.

"Hey! Those are my chips." Isaac's outrage was only partly in jest.

Barton grinned unrepentantly as he picked up the cards. "The house gets a part of the take." Like most men who made their living on the rivers, Barton had a great deal of experience at card games. He shuffled the deck with a skill to rival the most experienced gambler.

Isaac arranged his hand, careful not to jar his

bad arm. If he showed any weakness at all, Barton would snitch to the doctor. At least the cards he'd been dealt liked him: two queens and a pair of tens. "I'll take one." He tossed down the deuce of clubs and picked up its replacement. Another queen.

The sight of the three ladies and their matched escorts raised his spirits considerably. He tossed a cookie down on the chair and then added another one for good measure. Barton gave him a narrow-eyed look before matching his bet and called.

Isaac tossed down his full house and reached for the pot.

"Not so fast there, sir." Barton laid down his hand, a set of four kings that seemed to be smirking.

"How the hell . . ."

Before he could finish, Barton raked in the cards and started laughing. "Did I ever tell you what I did for a living before I got my license to pilot the rivers?" His eyes twinkled, daring Isaac to guess.

"No, you didn't, but I assume you have more than a nodding acquaintance with dealing a deck of cards."

Barton did a few fancy maneuvers as he shuffled again that would have amazed even the most jaded cardsharp. "From the time I was old enough to see over the top of a poker table, I earned enough to keep myself fed and clothes on my back. I wasn't always so concerned with how honest the game was if it meant the difference between eating and starving."

He dealt the cards again, this time slowing down enough so that Isaac could actually see a card or two slip off the bottom of the deck into Barton's hand. It was done so slickly that Isaac was impressed, even though he knew he was being cheated. Of course, losing a cookie or two wasn't the same as real money. He still didn't like it, not one damn bit.

"Remind me never to sit down across from you in a real game again." He picked up his cards. Nothing. He eyed Barton's hand with justifiable suspicion.

"How many do you want?"

"You tell me."

"Smart man."

Grinning, Barton dealt him four cards. Isaac picked up three jacks and a ten. Normally, he'd place a good-sized bet. Considering his friend's talent with cards, though, he hesitated. Even though he was playing with someone else's cookies, he hated to lose.

"I fold."

"I never took you for a coward, Isaac."

Barton tossed his own hand down for Isaac to see even though he didn't have to. A pair of twos. When Isaac saw them, he made a lunge for Barton's cookies. He managed to grab two before Barton jerked the plate out of reach.

"Now, if I promise to deal straight, do you still want to play?"

Isaac considered the matter. He trusted his boat and his life to Barton's competent hands. He supposed he could trust him in this. They played a few hands laced with some good-natured insults and daring bets. He realized that he was enjoying himself for the first time in days.

Without looking up from his cards, Barton quietly asked, "So who is Belle?"

Isaac almost dropped his cards. "What did you just say?"

Barton rearranged the cards in his hand before glancing up to meet Isaac's gaze. "I asked who Belle was. Joe thought you were talking out of your head the other night, like your ears were ringing. But you've been like a bear with a thorn in its paw ever since you first laid eyes on Miss Annie. I figure she must remind you of someone from the past."

He spread his cards out for Isaac to see. "Or maybe she *is* from your past? Either way, I thought you might want to talk about it."

"You thought wrong." Isaac shuffled the cards, ignoring the pain in his arm. The one in his chest hurt worse anyway. "Ante up."

"I'll take three." Barton tossed the same number down on the chair. "That Annie sure is a nice woman, and so is Millie." He picked up two cookies and set them in the pile. "In fact, I suspect Joe might be a bit taken with Millie, not that I blame him."

Isaac knew his friend was fishing for information, but he wasn't going to bite. Belle was a painful part of his past, one that he wasn't in any mood to discuss with anyone. Maybe with Matthew because he was there when it all happened, but Barton and Joe didn't need to know that their boss had been such a damn fool.

"Millie does seem nice." And damned protective of her friend, although somehow he doubted that Annie had told Millie much about her past. Maybe it wouldn't matter, but he suspected that no one knew the truth about Annie. If they did, the townspeople might not be so welcoming of her.

A knock at the door caught his attention. "Come in."

The town doctor poked his head through the

door and smiled. "You must be improving if you're up to playing poker. I'm going to wash up and then I'll be in to look at your arm and leg."

Barton gathered up the cards and what was left of the cookies. "It's hard to keep track of who is winning when we keep eating the chips. I'll stop in the store later and see if I can find some real ones."

"Thanks for keeping me company. I do appreciate it even if I am acting like a bear." Weariness that didn't come from playing cards made him glad to be alone for a few minutes. He lay back down on the pillows to wait for the doctor.

After she had already mastered most of the songs that she needed to play for Christmas, Annie found several music books that belonged to Patience. She'd thumbed through them and found several other pieces to try.

When she'd been playing for an hour or so, Pastor Chesterfield came out of his office. He sat down in the front pew and closed his eyes with a peaceful smile on his face. Since he didn't seem to want to talk, she continued playing, going from one song right into the next. Finally, she stopped when her fingers begged for a rest. When she stood up to put the music away, the pastor stirred in his seat.

"Mrs. Dunbar, I cannot remember the last time that I heard such a lovely performance. The good Lord surely blessed this town when you took up residence here." He smiled as he stood up. "I would love to hear you play an entire concert for us sometime."

She blushed, not accustomed to such flattery, especially when it was so sincerely offered. "Thank you, Pastor. It's been a long time since I've played in front of people."

"Well, let me know when you are interested in doing so. I, for one, would take great pleasure in an evening of music." He stretched his arms and sighed. "I should return to my sermon. I can only hope that your music has inspired me."

Annie felt compelled to say, "I always enjoy your sermons, Pastor. You have a true gift for explaining things so that I can understand them."

"That's nice of you to say so." He trailed after her while she gathered her things. "Please feel free to practice here anytime, not just for the Christmas program."

Since he seemed to really mean it, she thought she might just take him up on the offer. She didn't have a lot of free time, but maybe she had been ignoring her music too long. Her piano at home was nowhere near as good as the one at the church.

Walking home, Annie felt better than she had in days. Her good mood lasted until she walked into her parlor, only to find it had been invaded by the one man she didn't want to see. At least when he was confined to the back bedroom, she could pretend he didn't exist. Now, she had no way to avoid him, not without raising questions among the others that neither of them wanted to answer.

Millie looked up from her sewing. "How did your practice go?"

"Fine. They have a nice instrument." She took off her coat and hung it up. She sniffed the air. "Did you already start cooking, Millie? I would have done that." And been grateful for the excuse to leave the room.

"It's just stew. I thought it sounded good, and it's easy enough to make." She snipped off a thread and then held up a man's shirt. "There, that's the last one."

Considering the pile of clothes sitting on the floor beside her chair, Millie had been busy indeed. Annie hoped the men were properly grateful.

"That was nice of you to mend those for us, ma'am. I wish you'd let me pay you for your time." Isaac's smile was genuine, containing none of the bitterness that he always turned on Annie.

"I'd do the same for any boarder, Captain. Besides, sewing gives me a perfect excuse to sit by the fire for a spell." That was when she realized that Annie was still hovering near the door. "Come and sit with us, Annie. You have to be cold after sitting in the church all afternoon and then walking home."

She felt Isaac's eyes on her, watching to see if she'd come in or if she'd turn coward and run. Steeling her resolve, she took a seat on the far side of the room, angling it toward Millie—and away from him.

"Where are the others?"

"Agatha went upstairs to take a nap. Barton and Joe left with the sheriff to look at the boat." Millie glanced up toward the clock on the mantle. "I would have expected them back by now. Do you think something is wrong, Captain Chase?"

He looked a little worried himself, but he shook his head. "I'd guess they may have found a way to reach the boat. If so, they'll be unloading everyone's personal gear first. I'll be sending most of the crew back downriver by coach to be with their families. I can send for them again once the *Caprice* is free from the ice and the repairs are done. Then we'll sail back south until spring."

Perhaps because she knew him so well, at least in the past, she realized that Isaac was nowhere near as confident about what would happen to his boat as his words sounded. His wouldn't be the first steamboat to sink in the river. They'd been lucky that no one had died, but he could stand to lose everything if the damage to the *Caprice* was bad enough.

"I'd better go check on dinner." Millie set her sewing aside. When Annie immediately jumped up to go with her, she waved her back. "No, you rest awhile. This won't take me long."

An uncomfortable silence filled the room. Annie watched the flames in the fireplace flicker and dance, trying without much success to imagine that she was alone in the room. Even though he hadn't said a single word to her since she came in, she couldn't completely ignore Isaac either. Especially when he shifted on the sofa and winced in pain.

"Is it your leg or your arm?" No matter how much she didn't want him there, she wouldn't let him suffer unnecessarily.

"Both, if you must know." He grimaced as he tried to shift his position.

"I'll be right back."

"Don't hurry on my account."

He sounded more like a crabby little boy than a daring steamboat captain, making her smile despite herself. "I won't."

As soon as she stepped foot in the kitchen, Millie looked up from tasting her stew and frowned. "I thought I told you to stay in the parlor. Don't you trust me to prepare a simple meal?"

Now, what was making her so testy? "Of course I trust you. I'm just getting the brandy for Captain Chase. His arm and leg are bothering him, and I thought it might help."

After wiping her hands on her apron, Millie began laying out the ingredients for biscuits. "I'm afraid he's been up too long. Doc said he could sit up for short periods of time, but he's been on the sofa for at least two hours. I didn't expect his friends to stay away so long." She stood at the window, staring in the direction of the river.

"It's already getting dark. I'm sure they'll be along soon." Suspecting her friend was more concerned about Joe than Isaac's comfort, she added, "They know what they are doing, Millie. I'll bet they were able to get on the boat and wanted to unload everything they could."

"Maybe. Tell Captain Chase that if he needs to get back to bed, maybe we can help him."

"He's heavier than he looks. I'd think he'd rather wait for them to support him. The brandy should help him wait that long."

She poured him a good-sized glass of the brandy. She started to put the bottle away, but then thought better of it. Deciding he shouldn't drink on an empty stomach, though, she put together a sandwich for him and carried everything back to the parlor on a tray.

Isaac didn't look up when she walked in, giving her a chance to study his face briefly. Lines of pain bracketed his mouth, and he held himself as if every move hurt. No wonder he was feeling out of sorts. She set the tray down on a small table and moved it within easy reach for him.

"What's that?"

"I thought Joe was the one who got knocked on the head. If you can't recognize brandy when you see it, maybe I should send for Doc again." She stepped back and waited to see if he could manage on his own.

When he reached out with his bad arm, he winced and muttered a curse under his breath.

"Here, let me get it for you." She picked up the plate and set it in his lap and then held out the glass, so that he wouldn't have to move to reach it.

"I'm not helpless, Belle."

She immediately pulled the glass back out of reach. "My name is Annie."

He sneered. "Changing your name doesn't change a damn thing."

"It's still my name. Now do you want this brandy or not?"

"Hell, yes, I want it. Now hand it over, Annie, or get out of here and let me suffer alone."

As soon as she handed him the glass, he drank down about half of it in one gulp. When he started to finish it off, she snatched his hand back away from his mouth.

"What the hell is wrong with you? Why did you pour it for me if you didn't want me to drink it?"

"The last thing I need is a drunk sitting in my parlor. You can have the rest of it after you eat that sandwich."

"Since when are you that particular about the company you keep?"

His words lashed out and wounded her. She expected better of him, but it was obvious that he didn't intend to make any effort to remain civil when they were alone. She supposed she should be grateful that so far he'd behaved in front of Millie and his friends.

"Shut up, Isaac. I don't need or want your abuse, especially when you're a guest in my home. Now either eat the sandwich or the brandy disappears." And so would she. She wasn't about to put up with his foul mood a minute longer than she had to.

Finally, he grabbed the sandwich and took a healthy bite out of it. Once she was sure that he'd continue to eat, she refilled the glass and handed it to him. Before she could decide whether or not to sit back down by the fire, she heard a commotion at the back door.

Obviously, his friends were back. That made her decision for her. Let them take the brunt of his temper. Without a word to him, she returned to the kitchen. Barton and Joe and several of the others were filing through the door, each of them loaded down with stuff they must have retrieved from the boat.

She smiled at Barton. "Looks like you've been busy this afternoon."

"Yes, ma'am. A successful one, too. We were able to get on board long enough to get our personal gear off. If the weather stays this cold, we hope to unload most of the cargo tomorrow." He pulled his coat off and accepted the cup of coffee that Millie had poured for him.

"And what about the boat?" She wanted to ask how soon they could fix it and get out of her way, but she managed to hold her tongue.

Joe answered. "Most of the boat is above water and dry. The ice knocked a sizeable hole in the starboard side right about the water line. Once we can get it patched, she should make it downriver. Isaac would be a better judge of when that can happen."

That didn't sound too promising. She'd been hoping that the damage had been such that they could move the boat as soon as a warm spell broke up the ice. They'd all be happier when Isaac was back on his boat, even if they had to carry him on a litter to get him there.

The thought of weeks of him living under her roof soured her stomach. She sipped at her coffee, wishing she knew what to do to make things better. Pastor Chesterfield might be willing to advise her, but she didn't want to do anything that might make him think less of her. She eliminated Millie from the list of people she could talk to for the same reason.

Which left no one. She stared into her cup, listening to the chatter going on around her, and had never felt so alone in her whole life.

"Easy, damn it!"

Isaac gritted his teeth and waited for the pain to ease. He knew his friends were doing their best. But every time they bumped a doorway or banged him into a wall as they maneuvered him down the narrow hallway, it hurt like hell. He'd been out of bed longer than he should have been, but it had been such a relief to look at something besides the four walls of the small room they'd given him.

"Now, hold on tight. We're going to back you through the door and then you're home free."

"I'm not home at all." Damn, he wished he was, but his home was the *Caprice* and she wasn't livable right now.

Joe and Barton finally helped him to stretch back out on the bed and pulled his covers up. Both of them immediately sat down to catch their breath. He hadn't forgotten that they'd both put in a full day's work unloading the boat.

"How is she?"

Neither of them made the mistake of thinking he meant a real woman. It was Barton who answered. "I think she'll be fine with a little work, but we need to offload the cargo as soon as possible. I'd guess we've already lost some to the water and ice, but a fair portion is still above water for now. We can't wait too long, though. If the weather were to warm up enough to melt the ice, she could sink further."

"Son of a bitch." He closed his eyes, wishing he could get out to her to see the damage for himself. "Do the best you can. Ask the sheriff if there's some place dry that we can store the cargo. If anyone would know, it would be him. See if a couple of the crew would be willing to stay in town to stand guard over it. If not, that's something else you can ask the sheriff about."

"Joe and I can take turns."

"I appreciate the offer, but you can't be there twenty-four hours a day. We'll need at least another man or two to help." His eyelids were getting too heavy to keep open. As they closed, he heard his friends stand up to leave. "One more thing, ask Doc about getting some crutches for me."

"I will. Get some sleep. I'll wake you for dinner."

* * *

"Isaac, wake up."

He smiled, glad that Belle had managed to find her way into his room. His ma would pitch a fit if they were discovered, but he didn't care. All that mattered was that she was there. He held his arms out in welcome, anxious to hold her close.

"About time you got here, Belle."

"I told you earlier to call me Annie."

She didn't sound all that happy to be there, but he'd coax her into a better mood with a few kisses. "I'll call you anything you want, sweetheart. Just crawl in here with me, and we'll both be happy."

"Wake up, Isaac! I'm not your sweetheart." She punctuated her statement with a hard punch to his shoulder. "Open your eyes now."

He struggled to do what Belle wanted, wondering what he'd done to make her so mad. Had it only been last night that the two of them had snuck off to the woods to do a little kissing?

His eyes finally fluttered open to see one very annoyed woman glaring down at him. No, it hadn't been yesterday that he'd kissed her. It had been years ago, and kissing her again was the last thing he wanted to do.

"What the hell do you want?" He rubbed his eyes, trying to clear out the cobwebs of his mind, as well as the memories of how sweet Belle's kisses used to be. Now she was Annie, and she hated him. That was fine with him. He felt the same way about her.

"It's dinnertime. Do you want to eat in bed or do you want me to have your friends help you into the dining room?"

"Get Barton."

"Fine, I will." She gave him a nasty smile. "Right after I change the bandage on your arm."

He braced himself, figuring her care would be thorough but not particularly pleasant. To his surprise, her hands cradled his arm gently as she slowly unwound his bandage. When the last layer stuck to his wound a little, she winced as she tried to work it free without hurting him.

"Go ahead and yank. It won't get any easier by going slow."

She did as he suggested, but she didn't look too happy about it. When the wound was completely exposed, she studied it carefully for any signs that it was getting worse.

"It's finally on the mend. I think we'll leave it uncovered for a while and let the air get to it. Either Millie or I will cover it again before you go to sleep for the night." She gathered up the soiled bandages and started for the door. "I'll send Barton in for you in a few minutes."

"Fine." Then, before she made it out the door, he called her name. "Annie?"

She visibly braced herself before answering. "Yes, Isaac?"

"Thanks."

Her dark eyes looked down at him in confusion. "For what?"

Maybe he should have kept his mouth shut, but she had taken good care of him and his friends. He owed her for that. "For everything. Thank you."

She obviously didn't know what to make of his sudden desire to be polite. Rather than just accept his words at face value, her eyes narrowed. "I'm just trying to make sure you get well as fast as possible. Then I can have my life back."

She was gone before he could say another word.

Dinner was a relaxed affair. The stew was thick and savory, the biscuits light and tasty. Isaac wasn't particularly hungry, but he forced himself to keep eating. The others managed to keep a conversation going in between passing the butter and the biscuits. The only two who contributed little to the discussion were he and Annie. He was tired and he hurt. He wondered what her excuse was.

"So, Captain Chase, tell us how you came to own a steamboat. Did you always want to spend your life wandering up and down the river?" The question came from his left. Agatha Barker gave him an encouraging smile, as if trying to coax some civilized behavior out of him.

He kept his eyes from straying in Annie's direction. "No, ma'am. At one time I hoped to settle down with a wife and maybe raise a family. When that didn't work out, I felt restless. I served on a couple of different boats during the war and developed a taste for living on the river."

"I've made a few trips on steamboats, and I've always enjoyed it. I can see how it would hold some appeal." She turned her attention to Barton and Joe. "And you, gentlemen. Do you also have wandering souls?"

Isaac wondered if he was the only one who noticed Millie sit up a bit straighter, as if Joe's response had special interest to her. Maybe Barton was right about the two of them.

Barton answered first. "My pappy was a wandering sort, so we were always moving on. I guess I never learned how to put down roots."

Joe took over. "I served under Isaac here during the war. When the fighting ended, I didn't have any home to go back to, so I've sort of followed wherever he wanted to go. I don't mind the work, but the river's not in my blood the way it is in his and Barton's."

Now that was news to Isaac. Joe had never said a word about wanting to do anything else with his life. But then maybe he hadn't had a reason to say anything until now. Well, he'd miss Joe's easygoing nature, but he wouldn't begrudge him leaving if he found a reason to stay in one spot.

He decided to turn the tables on Miss Barker. "And you, Miss Barker, how did you come to live here in Willow Shoals?"

"I came to visit an old friend. It seemed like a nice town, so I stayed." She nodded in Annie's direction. "I can tell you that it is not easy for a single woman to find a comfortable place to live. I've seen my fair share of boardinghouses, and Mrs. Dunbar runs one of the best I've ever stayed in. I doubt I could find a place I like better."

From the stunned look on Annie's face, her boarder clearly had never said anything of the kind previously. "Why, thank you, Agatha. That is kind of you to say that."

"Kindness has little to do with it, Annie. It's nothing but the simple truth. Life is not easy for women alone, as you well know. We often have to make difficult decisions and hard choices. But you have made a fine home here for yourself and are good enough to share it with others." She set down her napkin. "Now if you all will excuse me, I would like to retire to my room."

Barton and Joe immediately rose to their feet as she swept from the room. For several long seconds they all stared after the older woman. Finally Millie spoke up.

"Well, I'll be. I wonder what brought that on. She's never said anything of the like before, has she?" She looked to Annie for confirmation.

"No. She always pays her money on time and rarely makes any special demands." She grinned. "Other than insisting that we avoid the squeaky step on our way past her room. I suppose that isn't much to ask."

The mood at the table felt lighter after that. When the last piece of pie was gone, the women started clearing the table. Isaac watched as his friends hastened to help them, leaving him alone. He couldn't put his finger on the reason, but somehow he suspected that Agatha's comments on Annie's boardinghouse were directed more at him than they were at Annie.

Well, if she knew the truth about Annie, she might just feel differently about her. But maybe not. There was no understanding women or the way their minds worked.

A few minutes later, his friends returned from the kitchen. Joe complained, "They ran us out."

Isaac arched an eyebrow when he looked at his friend. "I didn't know you had such a fondness for washing dishes. I'll have to keep that in mind the next time the cook needs a hand in the galley."

Joe actually blushed, which set Barton to laughing. "I think we should get him one of those fancy aprons like Miss Annie wears. What do you think?"

"I think so. Something with lace and lots of embroidery."

"Go to hell, both of you." Joe flopped down in a convenient chair. "I was trying to be polite. We've been a lot of extra work for both of them."

"Don't get all sulky, Joe. And you are right about us being a burden. I was going to ask if either of you know if there's a hotel in town we could move to?" He shifted slightly, trying to ease the ache in his leg.

"I did ask when we were trying to find rooms for the rest of the crew. No hotel and this is the only boardinghouse that had room. The only reason Annie could take us in was that two of her boarders went east for the holidays." Barton pulled out his pipe and lit it. "The pastor worked hard to find room for everyone."

"Were you able to get everyone's belongings off the boat today?"

Joe answered. "Sure did. They were all mighty glad to get their things. The stage should come through day after tomorrow. I bought tickets for everybody that wanted one."

Another expense he hadn't counted on when he decided to make one last run up the river. "Was there enough money in the safe to cover everything? If not, I'll send word to Matthew with one of the men."

"There was plenty. I put some in the drawer in your room when you were asleep. There's a bank in town, so I opened an account in your name for the rest."

"Thanks, Joe. I'm almost embarrassed to say I hadn't even thought of it. I'll send word to Matthew anyway and ask him to pay the men the wages they're due." And let him know that the payment on the boat might be late, if he could scrape it together at all. It would depend on how much of the cargo he'd lost to the river and what it would cost to repair the *Caprice*.

Millie came in, wiping her hands on a towel. "Annie and I are going to sit in the parlor. You are all welcome to join us for coffee or brandy."

Joe brightened considerably at the offer. "I'd like coffee."

"Brandy would be nice, if my pipe doesn't bother you."

She smiled and shook her head. "I've always been rather fond of the smell of good tobacco. And how about you, Captain, what can I get you?"

"Nothing, thanks. I think I'd better turn in for the night." He was tired and besides, he'd spent enough time in Annie's company for one day.

Barton and Joe immediately came to help him back to bed. They'd done it enough now to make the entire process go more smoothly. They managed to whack his injured leg only once between the dining room and his bed. A definite improvement over the previous attempt.

As they made the final turn into the bedroom, Annie looked up from the tray she was preparing. "Once they have you tucked in, give me a holler so I can wrap your arm again."

"All right."

His friends helped him out of his pants and shirt and then waited while he washed up some.

He rubbed his hand over his jaw. "I must look pretty damn scruffy. Remind me to shave tomorrow."

"I don't know, I think you'd look pretty dashing with a beard. We'll have to ask the ladies for their opinion."

"Don't bother. I can already tell you that Annie has always hated them." He could have bitten his tongue for letting that little fact slip out. After all, how could he have known that? "We, uh, discussed it earlier when she looked at my arm."

He wasn't sure that either of them believed his explanation, but he was going to stick by it. When Annie came in, he'd have to tell her what he'd said, assuming she was no more anxious than he was to discuss their past.

"Enjoy your coffee and brandy."

"We will. And I'll send Annie in, if you're ready for her."

"Might as well."

"See you in the morning. If Doc doesn't show up with the crutches he promised, I'll go looking for him." Barton pulled the door closed, leaving Isaac alone to wait for Annie.

When she came in, she had a shot of brandy for him. "Thought this might help you sleep better."

"Thanks." It seemed as if every other word out of his mouth was to thank somebody for something. The whole situation was starting to chaff.

"Your arm is healing nicely. Next time Doc comes in, he'll probably want to take those stitches out." She quickly wrapped his arm and tied the bandage in place.

He almost let her leave without telling her what

he'd said. Finally, he blurted it out. "I told Joe and Barton that you'd always hated beards."

She frowned. "How did that particular fact happen to come up in conversation?"

He explained the circumstances. "I told them we'd discussed it when you checked my arm. I didn't know what else to tell them."

"You might have considered the truth. Eventually, one of them is going to figure out that we've met before."

"Maybe we should have told them as soon as we recognized each other, but I think it's too late now."

"Fine. If they ask, we talked about beards because it's such an interesting subject. Do you need anything else?"

There were a hundred questions he'd like to ask her, about where she'd been, and why she'd done what she did. But now wasn't the time. "No, nothing."

She took the lamp and left, leaving him in the dark.

CHAPTER SIX

A loud thump was followed by what had to be a string of curse words. Annie and Millie looked at each other and grinned. The thumping started up again, this time coming in their direction. Immediately, they both wiped the smiles off their faces. If Isaac hated his crutches, he hated being laughed at even more.

He made it to the parlor door with only a few more curses. Annie calmly looked in his direction when he came into the room. His dark blond hair was mussed, as if he'd been running his fingers through it, or else had been trying to pull it out in frustration. Then there was the spark of anger that seemed to make his blue eyes even bluer. It wouldn't take much to set off a full-blown temper tantrum if they weren't careful. Annie found the idea tempting, but Millie didn't deserve to suffer the brunt of his anger just because Annie was itching for a fight.

"Come in and sit down, Captain Chase."

Millie moved from the sofa so that he could sit down and prop his injured leg up on the seat. He started to come in but stopped when he saw Annie was in the room. Abruptly, he turned away, teetering on his crutches before regaining his balance.

"No, thank you. I've been sitting too much."

He started walking back toward the kitchen. Annie watched him disappear from sight, wondering if she had left anything breakable in his path. He was having some trouble maneuvering around the house on the pair of crutches that Doc had brought him. If he would take his time, he'd be all right, but he wasn't used to being inactive. Not to mention that he was angry—with the situation and with her.

She supposed that a big part of the problem was that he couldn't be out on the river with his men supervising the work on his boat. A tendril of sympathy wound its way through her. Everything he'd built his life around was in jeopardy out there, trapped in the ice and vulnerable. He knew as well as she did that every day men pitted themselves against the river, and sometimes the river won. It wouldn't do any good to remind him how lucky he'd been to survive at all.

He wouldn't appreciate the sentiment, especially coming from her.

She realized she'd been staring at the same page in her book for fifteen minutes and couldn't recall a single word she'd read. Rather than try again, she gave up and closed it. Maybe she should get out of the house for a while. She could get in some practice at the church, Millie could enjoy some peace and quiet, and maybe Isaac would quit wearing out her hallway.

"I think I'll go over to the church for a while, unless you need me for something."

Millie looked up from her embroidery. "No, I think that would be a good idea." She glanced toward the door as if to gauge how close Isaac was to their end of his route. "But sometime, I want to know why the two of you work so hard at avoiding each other."

Annie closed her eyes and sighed. "It's not a very interesting story."

"That may be, Annie, but I'm not the only one who's noticed. Barton and Agatha both watch the two of you whenever they think you're not looking, and Joe has made a comment or two."

Maybe she could deflect Millie's curiosity by turning the tables on her. "And how about the way Joe watches you all the time? I think he's quite taken with you."

"He is not. Besides, I think he's too young."

Annie figured if Millie was worried about his age, she must be interested in the man. "If I'm any judge of men, I'd have to say that any difference in your ages is the last thing on his mind." Annie stopped to rest a comforting hand on her friend's shoulder.

"Really?" Millie's gray eyes looked more hopeful.

"Really." That much was true.

Millie went back to sewing. "Well, it doesn't really matter. Once they get the boat fixed, he'll be gone."

"From what Barton has been telling Isaac, that won't be anytime soon." Which brought her back to the reason she needed to leave her own home for a while. "I'll get my coat."

She ran into Isaac in the hallway. He managed to back out of her way long enough for her to get her coat off its peg in the kitchen.

As soon as he saw it, he asked, "Where are you going?"

"I'm going to the church to practice."

"Can I come?" Somehow he managed to sound belligerent and hopeful at the same time.

He was the whole reason she was going. Why would he want to tag along with her?

"No."

"Why not?"

What could she say? Because he wasn't welcome. Because she hated him. Because he hated her. Because her skin ached with the need to touch him whenever they got too close. Because the memories he stirred up still hurt despite how many years had passed them by.

"You're on crutches."

"How far is the church?"

She could have lied about the distance, but eventually he'd find out. There were already too many lies between them; she wouldn't add to the list. "It's about two blocks."

"I can make it that far if you go slow enough for me to keep up." He frowned at her, as if expecting her to either argue or even refuse him altogether.

"Do you have a coat?"

He relaxed some. "Barton hung it in my room."

When he didn't move, she realized that he expected her to fetch it for him. Rather than argue, she got it for him and even helped him put it on. However, she drew the line at buttoning it for him.

She'd seen a dark blue cap, the same color as the coat, and brought it as well. "I figured this was yours, too."

"Thanks." He didn't sound particularly grateful, but at least he wasn't taking his bad mood out on her either.

"Let's go."

If Millie thought it odd that Annie would let Isaac tag along on her escape, she didn't say anything. Once they were outside, Isaac held onto the railing as he hopped down the steps on his good foot. When he made it to the bottom without mishap, he grinned. The smile quickly disappeared, as if he'd had to remind himself who he was with.

She led the way down the street, shortening her steps to match his more halting ones. It didn't take long for the effort to take its toll on him. "Do you need to stop and rest for a minute?"

"Is that the church up ahead?"

"Yes."

'Then I'd rather keep going. I can rest once we get inside."

He would only ignore any suggestion from her that he was asking too much of himself, so she continued on her way, letting him follow as he would. Once they reached the front of the church, she stopped and studied the steps.

"How are you going to manage going up the steps? I don't think you can hop like you did coming down."

"Sure I can."

He put both crutches in one hand while he held

the railing with the other. Then he drew a deep breath and managed to hop up on the first step. After another few seconds, he managed to take two steps in a row. By the time he reached the top one, her heart was pounding as if she'd been jumping right along with him.

He even managed to open the door on his own and then stood back to let her walk in first.

"You didn't have to play the gentleman, Isaac."

"I wasn't. I wanted to see if the roof fell in when you crossed the threshold. If it held up for you, I figured I was safe."

She shushed him, looking around for Pastor Chesterfield. "I'll have you know that I attend this church regularly."

"I never thought I'd see the day that Belle Dunbar took religion." He shook his head with wonderment at the idea.

She wanted to kick his bad leg. "You don't know anything about me, Isaac. I'm not the woman you knew."

"Considering everything, I don't guess I ever knew you at all, Annabelle. If I had, I wouldn't have been so surprised when you ran out on me."

"Call me Annie or we're right back out of here."

He considered calling her Annabelle again, but the need to fight with her wasn't all that strong. He wasn't even sure why he'd given in to the urge to tag along with her to the church. It was hard enough for him to see the Belle he used to know in the woman who called herself Annie. The looks were the same, allowing for a few extra years, and the temper certainly hadn't changed much, but there were more differences than similarities.

So he conceded the point. "Annie, can we sit down now?"

He hadn't meant the question to be a plea for sympathy, but that's what he got, along with a lecture on overdoing things. She not only led the way to a pew, she offered her support as he hobbled his way to the front of the church near the piano.

"Now stay there. I can't believe I let you talk me into letting you walk this far." She helped him with his coat and tossed it and hers on the seat beside him. "If you get too tired, stretch out there and use those as blankets."

"Yes, ma'am," he said, doing his best to sound meek. Inside, though, he realized he was amused by her attempts to bully him into taking better care of himself, that and a little touched. It had been a long time since a woman fussed over him.

She gave him a narrow-eyed look, filled with suspicion and a little worry. That last little bit shouldn't please him, but it did. He'd all but died when she walked—no, make that ran—out of his life. It was only right that she suffer some, even if it was too late to make any real difference to him.

But since she didn't look as if she were going to go sit at the piano until he was settled, he did as she ordered. Gingerly, he eased his leg up onto the pew and then leaned back and waited for her to turn her back before giving in to the urge to grit his teeth in pain.

He distracted himself from the throbbing by watching Annie set out her sheet music. When she had everything arranged to her satisfaction, she began playing the simple tunes she'd always used to warm up her fingers before starting in on the complicated stuff.

Somehow, he'd forgotten what pure joy it was to hear her play, regardless of the kind of music she was indulging in. When she launched into a hymn, though, it made him uncomfortable on some level. She kept telling him that her life had changed, that she was no longer the woman he'd known. He hadn't really believed her at all, but here she was playing piano in a church, of all places. The image was more than his beleaguered mind could decipher. Rather than try to puzzle it all out, he closed his eyes and let the music carry him away.

Just that quickly, the years rolled back, taking him back to the one time in his life when he thought a woman loved him and that the future held nothing but good things for the two of them. His fist closed on nothing, as if he could clasp the hand of that laughing girl in the past and hold onto her. But that wasn't going to happen now, not when it hadn't happened then.

It hurt to know that.

A voice spoke from right behind him, jarring him back into the present. He glanced over his shoulder to find a man sitting in the next pew back. He wore a cross on a chain around his neck. Even with his mind all jumbled up, Isaac could recognize a pastor when he saw one.

"You must be Pastor Chesterfield." He turned as much as he could and held out his hand. "My men and I appreciate all that you have done for us."

"And you must be Captain Chase. It's a great thing to see you up and about. Although from what I've been told, if it weren't for Mrs. Dunbar acting so quickly, I might not have ever had the chance to meet you." He nodded toward where Annie sat lost in her music, oblivious to her audience. "I have to say she's been the answer to more than one prayer this week."

Isaac knew the man meant well, but he had to wonder what the pastor would think if he knew the truth about Belle and the kind of woman she was, at least when Isaac first met her. Yes, she had a real talent for music, but this was the first time he'd heard her play a hymn. Hell, when the two of them met, she'd been playing piano for a local saloon.

Here she was in a church, wearing somber colors and a simple hat. She was still pretty—honesty made him admit that. But the Belle he had known sparkled, always dressed in bright colors and a spray of feathers in her hair. Her laughter had made men stop in their tracks just to hear it. And when she'd looked at him with her dark eyes flashing, he'd dropped his heart at her feet and never looked back.

Until it was too late, and she'd walked all over it.

"How is your leg feeling?" Pastor Chesterfield had leaned forward to cross his arms on the back of Isaac's pew.

"It hurts like . . ." Isaac managed to catch himself in time. "It hurts a lot, but not as bad as it did."

The deep lines at the corner of the pastor's eyes crinkled, telling Isaac without words that he'd heard his unspoken oath anyway. "Well, I'm glad that it is improving. And your men, are they all well? I know you rescued one of them from the river yourself."

"That's Joe. He's doing fine, except for the prettiest shiners I've seen in a long time. They're already starting to fade into shades of purple and green." He shuddered at the memory of his friend's scream when the river tried to claim him. He closed his eyes to shut out the echoes in his mind.

The pastor's hand felt warm on his shoulder. "Fear, whether remembered or real, has a nasty way of sneaking up on you. I find when that happens, I feel better if I pray."

"I haven't had much practice at that, sir." Hell, his ma had done her best to raise him right. On the other hand, his pa would have laughed himself sick over seeing Isaac sitting in a church, much less talking about praying.

"Maybe you haven't gotten down on your knees, Captain Chase, but don't you think God was listening when he helped you fetch your friend back out of the river and almost certain death? Someone was watching out over the both of you that night."

Isaac preferred to think of it as luck, blind stupid luck.

"What kind of fear sneaks up on you?" Maybe it was rude to ask, but something about the man made Isaac think he wouldn't mind.

"I fought in the war." Suddenly, those lines that Isaac had assumed came from smiling, took on a whole different appearance. His fingers strayed to the cross around his neck. "This came afterward. The only way I could live with myself and what I'd done was to find something better than I was. My wife, blessed woman that she is, supported my decision and helped me. I didn't find my own peace for quite some time after the fighting stopped."

Then he was smiling again. "But now, when the past and its fears come creeping out, I have all the help I need shoving them back where they belong. You have friends, Captain Chase, and people who care about you. And the people of Willow Shoals, who'd never seen you before, all stepped up to help you through hard times. It's enough to remind us why we celebrate Christmas with such joy."

Annie launched into another song, the various strands of the melody ringing out in the room. Both men watched and listened. Once the hymn ended, she immediately moved on to another song, this one a dance tune. A grin tugged at his mouth. He bet it was the first time that particular song had been played on that piano and in this church.

He risked a quick peek at Pastor Chesterfield, half expecting to see a look of disapproval on his face. Instead, he was grinning and, if Isaac wasn't mistaken, he was actually tapping his toe in time to the music. Before Isaac could come to terms with that, the music ended.

The pastor surprised him again by applauding. "Well done, Mrs. Dunbar, well done."

She blushed as she turned to acknowledge her audience. "Thank you, Pastor. I hope you didn't mind that last piece. Sometimes my hands seem to have a mind of their own."

"Not at all, my dear. I truly believe that music is one of God's greatest gifts to his people. But now that the concert is over, I had better get back to work. Captain, can you make it back to Mrs. Dunbar's home without assistance?"

He would or die in the attempt. "Yes, sir, I will."

"Please come visit again, Captain." The older man clapped him on the shoulder. "I'd love to tour your boat sometime. Perhaps when you're ready to begin repairs, I can be of help. I know most of the people in town and what skills they have."

"I would appreciate that, sir." Isaac found himself liking the man and feeling more at ease than he would have expected, considering how little experience he had with men of the cloth. "I'll keep that in mind."

He hobbled toward the door with Annie walking beside him. The pastor trailed along behind them to close up after them. Isaac made his way down the steps without mishap and began the slow walk back to Annie's house.

"You're still a hell of a piano player."

"Thank you."

"Does the good pastor know where you learned to play so well?"

"No, he doesn't." Her tone made it clear this was a topic she didn't want to discuss.

They walked on in silence for a while. He needed most of his energy to maintain his balance and to keep going. That didn't keep him from mulling over everything he'd learned about Belle. From what he could tell, the whole damn town, from the sheriff to the pastor to her boarders, thought she was a fine, upstanding citizen in their town.

Of all the possible fates he'd envisioned for her, he would never have guessed she'd end up respectable. Not just that, she was apparently well liked. And if that didn't beat everything all to hell and back, she was playing piano for a church. He knew her well enough to know that she'd never have given up her music because she took such joy in it. But the Belle he had known had been much better suited to playing in a saloon or a whorehouse.

And for some reason, the whole situation made him furious. She had managed to make quite a life for herself, all built on the ashes of his. No doubt the preacher would tell him to let bygones be bygones, but to hell with that. Despite everything she had done for him, she still owed him the money she and Nick had stolen from him. Money he was going to need to repair his beloved *Caprice* and his own life.

Frustration and regrets and pain mixed together in a volatile brew. He lashed out at the nearest target. "So tell me, Annie Belle, when are you going to tell all your *respectable* friends the truth about yourself? I'd think it would bother you something fierce, what with your new life and all, to live with so many lies. Doesn't it worry you that it could all come tumbling down around you?"

He hated that she looked at him with wounded eyes, silent and full of past memories that haunted them both. Even more, he hated that it made him want to reach out to comfort her. Even if she would have accepted such a gesture from him, he knew he couldn't risk touching her, not that way.

Instead, he pushed past her and bulled his way up the steps, ignoring the shards of pain that flashed up his leg, ignoring the girl from his past, and the woman of his present. Most of all, he ignored the guilt that tore through his gut and made him want to take it all back.

Annie had no choice but to follow Isaac into the house. If she turned around and left, there would be questions. If Millie caught sight of the tears that threatened to spill down her cheeks, there would be questions. And if she walked into the house and broke the nearest vase over Isaac's thick skull, there'd be questions.

None of which did she want to answer.

So she straightened her shoulders, made a quick swipe across her eyes with her sleeve and marched in as if nothing was wrong. Inside, the house was quiet except for the sound of Isaac thumping his way back to his room. The parlor was empty, so Millie must be upstairs or in the kitchen. Rather than risk running into her immediately, Annie hung up her things and then sat down on the sofa. Safe for the moment from prying eyes and angry men, she leaned back and tried to make some sense out of everything that had happened over the past few days.

She knew Isaac was having a hard time reconciling himself to his memories of her as Belle and his new acquaintance with the woman she'd become as Annie. And maybe he'd never accept the changes she'd made in her life and forgive her for the mistakes of the past. She even understood that; much of the time she had trouble forgiving herself. But despite what he thought, in some ways it was best that she had left him when she did. He wouldn't have believed that then, and he obviously didn't believe it now.

Maybe he never would.

Her mind spun in circles inside of circles, not making sense of anything at all. Finally, she let her eyes drift closed and took refuge in sleep.

Had Captain Chase and Annie come home? She had thought so but couldn't hear them when she came down the stairs. Millie paused on the bottom step and listened. Perhaps they had left again. But as soon as she looked in the parlor, she realized Annie had fallen asleep. She picked up a small quilt they kept thrown over the back of a chair and spread it over her friend. Annie stirred slightly and snuggled into the warmth.

Millie backed away, not wanting to wake her. Those dark circles under Annie's eyes were worrisome. She knew for a fact her friend wasn't sleeping well at night and that she was fretting about something. There wasn't much Millie could do, not when Annie didn't trust her enough to share the problem with her. That hurt, but she tried to be patient. Eventually, one way or the other, the problem would come out and then she'd help Annie deal with it.

She did have her suspicions, though. All of this started the night they carried Isaac Chase into the house and not a minute before. No matter how careful Annie thought she was being, she would have to be plain stupid not to notice the tension hovering in the air every time Isaac and Annie were in the same room. When they were together, it felt as if a storm of anger and hot desire was about to erupt.

It was all the more puzzling since Annie hadn't shown a lick of interest in a single man as long as she'd known her. Although Annie rarely referred to her late husband at all, Millie suspected it had not been a happy marriage. Could Captain Isaac be part of the reason for that?

Well, if Annie wouldn't give her any answers, there was one other person who might. She backed out of the parlor and braced herself to confront Captain Chase. He might not like it, but she wasn't going to let him make her friend miserable without trying to do something about it.

She rapped on his door with her knuckles to give him fair warning but didn't wait for him to acknowledge her before barging in. Unfortunately, the trip down the church had evidently worn him out, too. He was stretched out on his bed, snoring softly. He had the same dark circles under his eyes, so at least Annie wasn't the only one affected by whatever was bothering the two of them.

Good.

The muffled sound of voices caught her attention. Evidently, Barton and Joe Cutter were on their way in. She quickly returned to the kitchen, not wanting to be caught hovering over their beloved captain. She also checked her appearance in the reflection of a window, blushing as she did so. It was of no concern to either of the returning men what she looked like.

That didn't keep her from wishing that she had worn a nicer dress today. However, she didn't have all that many, and she couldn't afford to wear her Sunday best to clean house in. If he—no, they—didn't realize that, too bad. At least her apron was clean and her hair neatly arranged.

She opened the door for them and held her finger up to her lips. "Your captain just dozed off and Annie is sleeping in the parlor."

Barton nodded as he came in. Joe was right behind him. He smiled at her, sending her pulse racing along at an embarrassing pace. She really needed to get control of herself. The man was younger than she was, after all. But that didn't keep her from thinking about things that she had no business thinking about. She'd had a good marriage and still missed her late husband. Daniel had been a wonderful man, and she wasn't at all sure that she was ready to remarry. If she did decide to do so, she wouldn't settle for less than she'd had.

But for whatever reason, Joe Cutter made her think about all that she was missing, especially when she turned out the light for the night and crawled into an empty bed. Truly, as much as it shamed her to admit it to herself, she'd even wished she wasn't a lady. Would a few nights of shared passion ease the longing she felt whenever she thought about Joe? Would he even be interested?

The scrape of a chair snapped her out of her reverie. Both men were staring at her with big grins on their faces. She blushed, knowing she'd been caught daydreaming. Her one comfort was that neither one of them, and especially Joe, could possibly know what she'd been thinking about.

"I don't know where you were, Millie, but it sure wasn't here with us." Barton was lighting his pipe.

"I'm sorry. I guess I was woolgathering something fierce. Can I fix either of you something to eat? It wouldn't take long to heat up some of last night's stew."

"If it's not too much trouble, that sounds good to me." Joe gave her one of his sweet smiles.

Barton shook his head. "I just stopped in to get warm. I need to go check out a place the sheriff found for us to store the cargo."

Joe jumped to his feet. "I forgot we promised we'd meet with him this afternoon. I guess I'll have to pass on the stew, Millie." There was real regret in his voice.

"It won't take both of us to look at an empty space, Joe. You stay here in case the captain needs you for something. I won't be gone long." He went back out the way he came, leaving Millie and Joe alone.

Looking a little unsure of what to do next, Joe sat back down at the table. Rather than stare at him, Millie got busy heating up the stew. While she waited for it to get hot, she cut a couple of thick slices of bread and spread butter on them. In short order, she set the meal down on the table.

"Thank you, Millie. You know you don't have to wait on me. I could have heated it up myself." That didn't keep him from eating with a satisfying enjoyment.

"I don't mind. I'll leave the rest on the stove in case Captain Chase would like some when he wakes up." The kitchen, normally one of her favorite rooms in the house, felt uncomfortably crowded with just the two of them in the room.

"Won't you sit down with me?"

Millie wished she had something pressing to do, something that would force her to turn down his invitation. But she'd made the beds, dusted the upstairs, and the dishes were washed except for the bowl Joe was using. She took the chair opposite him, putting the safety of the table between them.

The twinkle in his gray eyes hinted that he was fully aware of her fidgets. Well, that was fine, content to let him think what he would. A woman had a right to be a little nervous around a man she hardly knew. The silence, though, was becoming unbearable. Perhaps if she asked the right questions, she could find out more about Captain Chase.

"I believe you mentioned meeting Captain Chase during the war." She clasped her hands in her lap, determined to hide her nervousness.

"Yes, we were both assigned to guard boats on the river." Some of the smile in his eyes died.

"Because you knew about steamboats?" Somehow she didn't think so.

"No, because I was a sharpshooter."

The grim set to his mouth hurt her to see. Normally, his smile was so easy and warm. She regretted bringing up the subject at all. Few people had good memories from the war, but some had a worse time letting go of the ugliness. Maybe Joe was one of them.

"I'm sorry, would you rather talk about something else?"

"No, that's all right. You've a right to know more about the men who've invaded your home." A small grin eased the tension in his jaw. He leaned back in his chair and stared past her at a spot on the wall. "When I enlisted, I wasn't good for much, but I could pick a June bug off a rock at a distance. They needed men with that particular talent to keep the Johnny Rebs from killing off the troops being shipped up and down the river."

"I'm sure the men with you appreciated what you did for them. There are times being a good shot is a real gift."

"That's true enough I guess, but it's a gift I have no more use for."

Something bad had occurred. She could see it in the furrow of his brow and the way his hands clenched and unclenched. Would it hurt him more to talk about it or to keep it shoved back in his memory?

"What happened, Joe?"

"A sweet woman like you shouldn't hear about such things. Besides, it all happened a long time ago."

"Not so long, Joe." She reached across the table to lay her hands on his. "I'm willing to listen if you need me to."

With some effort, he refocused his eyes on her for a few seconds as if to wonder if she really meant it.

"As the war dragged on and on, the Reb soldiers seemed to get older and older or worse yet, younger and younger." His gaze flickered back to the wall again. "One day, I was the one standing duty. I thought I saw something flash in the bushes along the east bank of the river and started firing into the brush. You see, a bunch of Rebs had been following us on the shore for days. We'd learned to shoot first because those boys in gray were some damn fine shots."

"Boys." He paused and shook his head. "That's all they were, too. A bunch of kids dressed up in ragtag uniforms and carrying guns. I killed two of them before I realized it."

"Oh, Joe, how awful for you." Her heart hadn't felt such pain since the night her husband had died in her arms. It was tragic for the boys, too, but he was the one who had to live with what he'd done. It was all part of the horror of war, but that brought little comfort to Joe or anyone else.

The door behind her opened and Isaac hobbled into the kitchen. "What he's not telling you, Miss

Millie, is that those same boys, as he calls them, had managed to pick off about half a dozen of our men and wounded at least that many again. If he hadn't managed to stop them when he did, we might have lost even more. Considering I was one of the wounded, I figure he saved a lot of lives that day."

But at what cost to Joe? she wanted to ask. Perhaps he was younger than she was, but he'd lived through experiences that could make a man old before his time.

Figuring she had asked all the questions she could for the moment, she stood up and offered her chair to Isaac. He put both crutches in one hand and braced himself on the back of the chair with the other as he lowered himself down onto the seat.

"How did Annie's rehearsal go?" She dished up the rest of the stew and set it before Isaac on the table.

"She played well, and I met Pastor Chesterfield," he said between bites. "He seems like a nice enough sort."

"The whole town likes him. He's brought a lot of folks back to the church since he took over as pastor a couple of years ago. I like the way he preaches acceptance and forgiveness rather than hellfire all the time." Should she sit down or leave the two men alone? She decided to stay for a while at least to keep Joe from thinking that she was leaving because of what he'd told her.

She was horrified, but that didn't mean that she thought any less of him. If he had been unaffected by the incident, she would have been more upset. Somehow she'd have to find a time to tell him that.

"He seemed right pleased with Annie playing

music for the church." He frowned, as if that idea somehow surprised him.

Why would it, unless he knew something about Annie that she didn't know? Again, it was one more indication that there was something between the pair that none of the rest of them knew about.

"Would either of you like to play cribbage? Or perhaps chess? I have my husband's set upstairs in my room."

"Have you played much?" It was the first time Joe had spoken since Isaac had interrupted their conversation.

"A little." Actually, a lot, but he didn't need to know that. She had meant for the two men to play.

"Then I'd like a game. Isaac here doesn't have the patience for the finer points of chess. He's better with a deck of cards. The pretty people on the face cards fascinate him."

His friend took good-natured offense at his comments. "Listen here. Just because I don't take twenty minutes to make my move doesn't mean that I don't understand chess."

It was good to hear Joe laugh. "As I recall, you haven't won a single game since we've been playing. Even Barton is better than you are."

"He cheats at cards."

"So do I, but you've never managed to catch me at it."

Now both men were laughing. While they continued bickering, she took the opportunity to leave. She supposed she had no choice but to get the chess set and play Joe a game. After all, she was the one who had brought up the subject in the first place.

Annie was still asleep on the sofa, and Agatha was quietly knitting in the corner. Millie stopped in the parlor long enough to add another log to the fire before making her way upstairs.

"Do you need my help with anything in the kitchen?" Agatha whispered.

"Not right now. I'm going to my room to get a chess set. I thought the captain and Mr. Cutter would like to play."

And perhaps they would. She hoped so, because she really didn't think she was up to sitting across the small board from Joe, touching the same pieces he touched, learning how his mind worked from the way he attacked the game. It sounded like something a schoolgirl would get all worked up over, but her courting days were that long ago.

She opened her dresser drawer and lifted out the worn box that had belonged to Daniel for so long. The cover had a thin layer of dust on it that she wiped off with her sleeve. On some level, it felt like a betrayal of his memory to hand the game over to another man. Perhaps it was because of the guilt she felt in how she was looking at that same man. In her heart, she knew Daniel would have wanted her to find happiness again.

Telling herself it only a game after all, she clutched the box and the memories it held and hurried back down to the kitchen.

CHAPTER SEVEN

Annie shifted in the half-world between slumber and awareness. Her neck protested the position it had been in too long, vanquishing the last cobwebs of sleep from her mind. Slowly, having a care for her neck, she sat up and stretched out the kinks.

"I wondered when you'd awaken, my dear. You must have been quite tired. People have been coming and going for some time now, and none of it disturbed you in the least." Agatha smiled at her from across the room.

"What people?"

"Oh, that nice Mr. Cutter and his friend came back from the boat, and then Barton left again. The doctor stopped by for a few minutes, as did the sheriff. I think he and Barton were making arrangements where to store the boat's cargo and needed to talk to Captain Chase." She stopped to count her stitches before continuing.

"For now, all is quiet. Millie and Mr. Cutter are in the midst of a hard-fought game of chess. I do believe they are fairly evenly matched." Her smile looked particularly satisfied. "I do believe they might have more than a passing interest in each other."

Annie feared the same thing. She wouldn't begrudge Millie finding a little happiness, but she hated the thought of losing her friend. She had come to depend on Millie's companionship and good common sense.

"Mr. Cutter won't be here all that long." She hoped she didn't sound too anxious for that to be true. But if he was still around, it likely meant that Isaac would be, too. "I mean, once they get the boat fixed, they'll all be anxious to get back home."

If Agatha thought anything was amiss, she gave no indication of it. She seemed content to concentrate on her knitting. Annie checked the clock to see how long she'd been asleep. The last thing she remembered was hurting from Isaac's latest attack on their way back from church. She wasn't sure how much longer she could stand living with the tension of wondering when he'd finally announce to one and all what he knew about her.

"I'd better get dinner started." If Millie hadn't beaten her to it again.

Agatha nodded. "Let me know if you need my help with anything."

The offer warmed Annie's heart. "If I haven't thanked you for being so understanding about this unexpected invasion of our home, I will now. You expected a quiet home when you moved in, and now we have all these men clomping in and out."

The older woman surprised her again. "I don't know if I should admit this or not, my dear, but I have rather enjoyed all the commotion. It's rather too easy to settle into a rut. I think a little excitement now and then is good for the soul. Especially when the excitement has such striking blue eyes."

He did have beautiful eyes, at least when they weren't full of disgust and something that looked all too much like hate. There wasn't much she could say to Agatha's comment that wouldn't raise questions, so she just smiled and left the room.

She could hear the rumbling of male voices before she reached the kitchen. It sounded as if both Joe and Barton were there, so even if Isaac were as well, she wouldn't have to deal with him directly. And if she kept herself busy cooking, she might not have to talk to him at all.

The scene in front of her surprised her on several fronts. First, Millie and Joe sat with their heads bent over a chessboard, totally oblivious to anything but each other and the game. Annie had never much cared for the game, but she understood it enough to know that so far they were pretty much tied.

Barton and Isaac were playing cards. Isaac was busy counting his move along the cribbage board while Barton shuffled the deck. He was the first one to notice her.

"Did we wake you up? I tend to get noisy and obnoxious when I'm getting beat." He winked at her, taking the heat out of his complaint.

"No, I didn't hear much of anything until my neck started complaining about being in one position too long." She reached for her apron. "I hope you like fried chicken." She already knew that Isaac did. It was, or at least used to be, one of his favorites.

"Sounds good to me. Are we in your way? We can always move to the captain's room or the dining room."

As tempting as that idea was, she shook her head. "No, I can work around you." She let them play on while she peeled a pile of potatoes and set them on to boil. Next, she put her favorite cast-iron skillet on the stove to heat. After she put the lard in to melt, she went to work on a pair of chickens with a cleaver. When she turned around, Isaac was watching her.

"What's wrong?"

"I was just sitting here thinking how glad I am not to be a chicken right now." He picked up his cards and waited for Barton to take his turn.

"Miss Annie, if he keeps dealing me hands like this one, I might like to borrow that cleaver for a few minutes." The pilot muttered in disgust as he watched Isaac move his peg a fair distance along the board. "I'm convinced he's doing some shady dealing, but I can't catch him at it."

She could have told Barton that she knew first-hand that Isaac was lousy at cheating. Those striking blue eyes, as Agatha called them, revealed too much of what he was thinking for him to be any good at it. Nick, on the other hand, had a real talent for it until he ran into someone who was better.

"Checkmate!" Joe announced as he knocked Millie's king over with a flourish.

"How did you do that?" Millie demanded as she studied the board. "I never saw that one coming.

You're quite a player, Mr. Cutter." She stood up. "Well, it was time to stop anyway. I need to help Annie."

He was already putting the pieces back in the box. "That was a great game. It's been a long time since I've seen anyone better."

Annie watched her friend blush with pleasure. "I used to play with my husband. Daniel taught me to play after we were married."

"He must have been a good teacher because you sure enough made me work hard for that victory."

"He was. Patient, too."

Joe handed the chess set back to Millie, who hugged it close as if it brought her some kind of comfort. "I'll put this away and be right back, Annie."

"No hurry, Millie. I've got everything under control."

For the most part, she was able to ignore the trio of men clustered around her kitchen table. Every so often, she'd catch something one of them said, but for the most part, keeping an eye on the chicken held her attention. When Millie returned, she ran the men off, telling them that she needed the table to roll out the biscuits.

It didn't take long for her to have the pan of fresh dough ready for the oven.

"I'll mash the potatoes and then put the biscuits in to bake." Millie stood beside her wiping her hands on a towel. "That chicken looks delicious."

"Thanks. I just hope I made enough for all of us." She turned a few pieces to brown them evenly. "I've never cooked for three men before. Even if I make twice as much as usual, it all disappears."

Millie laughed. "They probably appreciate home

cooking more than your regular boarders because they don't get it all that often. I'm sure their cook does a fine job, but there's a limit to how much he can cook in quantities to feed their entire crew."

"I never thought about it that way. You're probably right."

As Millie worked on the potatoes, she cleared her throat a couple of times. Annie braced herself for another round of questions she didn't want to answer. When her friend finally managed to speak, her question wasn't at all what Annie expected it to be.

"Do you think Daniel would have minded me letting Mr. Cutter use his chessboard?" She looked up from her task long enough for Annie to see the real worry in her eyes.

"His chessboard isn't what you're really concerned about, Millie." She set down the fork she'd been using to turn the chicken and slipped her arm around Millie's shoulders. "You want to know how Daniel would feel about you looking at another man the way you're looking at Joe. I can't answer that for you because I never knew Daniel. However, I can say this much—from everything you've ever said about him, he was not a selfish man. You're a young woman. He wouldn't want you to dedicate the rest of your life to missing him. You loved him as much as any woman ever loved her husband when he was alive; that should be enough for anyone."

Millie sniffed a couple of times before nodding. "You're right, of course. I think I just needed to hear someone else say it." She set the potatoes aside as she gave Annie a shaky smile. "I'm not saying that there's anything between me and Mr. Cutter. It's just such a shock to find myself interested in a man again."

"Then it's time. Before now, you weren't ready to let go of Daniel. He'll always be in your heart, of course, but he's left plenty of room for someone else to be there, too."

Millie cocked her head to one side as she looked at Annie. "That's pretty fancy talk coming from a woman who hasn't looked at another man in that way in an even longer time. Until now, anyway."

Annie recoiled from the smug knowledge in Millie's eyes. She wouldn't be able to keep her secret for much longer. And maybe it was time to confess her past life to her friend. If Millie wasn't too disgusted, perhaps she could help her figure out how to deal with it all.

"If you'll step aside for a minute, I'll put the biscuits in and then set the table."

Annie did as Millie asked, glad that for the moment her friend wasn't going to press the matter. Later that night, though, Annie would try to find the right words to explain everything. That would give her the most time to cry her heart out without anyone but Millie being the wiser.

Until then, however, she needed to find the strength to get through the rest of the evening without falling apart. She'd done some harder things in her life, but not many.

Isaac let her check his arm one last time. The doctor had told them both that the stitches could come out in another few days, so there wasn't much left for her to do except change the bandage as needed. His leg still hurt, but he was learning to get around on the crutches without much trouble.

He remained silent during the entire process of her wrapping his arm. She was all too aware of him watching her as she tied off the last knot. After trimming the ends of the bandage with her scissors, she straightened up and gathered her things, preparing to leave.

"Dinner was extra good tonight."

The compliment startled her. "Thanks. You always did like fried chicken."

"Not exactly. I always liked your fried chicken." He flexed his arm, wincing only slightly as he did so. "You seem to have a knack for getting it crisp, but not greasy."

Why was he being nice to her? It was bad enough if he lashed out at her, but at least she'd learned to expect it. But when he turned around and talked politely to her, sharing the occasional good memory, it left her feeling raw and skittish.

"It only takes practice."

"Maybe." He pushed himself back up to his feet. "I think I'll turn in for the night. See you in the morning."

"Good night, Isaac." She followed his progress across the room. Even with a broken leg and crutches, he moved with a strength and grace that drew her eyes every time. She had no business thinking about him that way, but she couldn't seem to help herself.

"Good night, Annie."

At least he got her name right this time. She hated the way he called her Belle, taunting her with the power he had over her. Maybe she deserved it, but he sure wasn't her judge or jury. She'd done things she wasn't proud of, but not all it of was her fault. Not that she was making excuses for herself. Not at all.

The click of his door shutting reminded her that it was time to be seeking out her own bed. Millie wanted to finish up a few things before coming upstairs, but Annie wanted to ask her to join her in her room for a while. She didn't want to go another day trying to keep up appearances. As unpredictable as Isaac was, she didn't want her friend to hear his version of their shared past instead of hers.

She stopped in the parlor. Barton and Joe were both there reading the newspaper. Millie was hemming a dress she'd started a few days before but hadn't had a chance to finish with all that had been going on. Evidently, Agatha had already retired to her room.

"Good night, gentlemen. By the way, Captain Chase has turned in for the night."

"Think he needs any help getting ready for bed?" Barton looked at her through a haze of pipe smoke.

"He didn't say so. He seemed to be getting around all right, though."

Barton set the paper aside. "I'll go check on him. As stubborn as he is, he wouldn't ask for help if he fell flat on his face."

Joe chuckled. "That sounds about right. Give me a yell if you need me to help pick him up off the floor."

"I will. Good night, ladies."

"Good night."

Annie realized that once she left the room, Millie

would be alone with Joe. She didn't have the heart to drag her away from the man who'd put a spark back in her eyes. She could carry her burden alone for another day. Perhaps tomorrow would present a better opportunity for them to talk alone. She hoped so.

"I'll see you both in the morning." She wasn't sure either one of them was aware of her leaving.

Joe tried to concentrate on the article he was reading, but the words were starting to blur. He couldn't have repeated a single sentence he'd just read. Finally, he gave up trying altogether to quietly watch Millie chew on her lower lip while she deftly wove her needle in and out of the fabric of her dress. He bet her stitches were neat and regular. From what he'd been able to see in the past few days, there was very little that she didn't do well.

She'd even come damn close to beating him at chess. He wasn't given to bragging, but that was one game that he rarely lost. He would have never imagined how much fun it would be to match wits with a woman over a chessboard. She'd chewed her lip then, too.

He wanted to taste it for himself and wondered if she'd slap him for trying. He knew she was a widow, but he had no idea how long ago she'd lost her husband. That she'd loved the man was painfully obvious. It felt odd to be jealous of a dead man he'd never even met, but he was. And he suspected that Millie would be shocked to hear how he felt.

He knew the instant that he'd been caught staring. Her needle stilled as she froze. Slowly she looked up from her handwork, her expression wary. He hoped his smile was reassuring rather than predatory. It must have worked because she gave him a tentative smile in return.

"You must think I'm poor company." She set her sewing aside. "I'm afraid when I get a needle in my hand, I forget everything else around me."

"Not at all, Millie." He liked the sound of her name. "It's been a long time since I've had a chance to spend a quiet evening in the company of a beautiful woman."

He might have gone too far with that remark. Her smile dimmed slightly, as if she were unsure how to take his comment. Or perhaps it had been a long time since someone had told her just how lovely she was. What would she say if he told her that her smile was enough to warm him through and through? He held back the words, though, for fear she would bolt from the room.

She always seemed a little skittish around him, more so than she was with either Barton or Isaac. He drew some comfort from the fact that she'd agreed to play chess with him earlier, especially with her late husband's set. He hadn't been lying—she did play a hard-fought game. But for him, the real pleasure in the playing was sitting so close to her for the better part of an hour. He figured if she spent more time in his company, some of her nervousness would fade.

"Were you married for a long time?" The question surprised him as much as it did her.

Her eyes focused on some point in her past. "Almost twelve years, but I'd known Daniel most of my life. We grew up near the same town and went to school together." She smiled at something only she could see. "I think I knew he loved me the day he put a frog down my back at a church picnic. We were ten at the time."

Joe laughed at the picture that made. "Maybe that's why I've never married. I didn't know that was how to get a girl to notice me."

The sparkle was back in her clear gray eyes. "Well, I have to admit that frogs might not hold quite the same appeal for me now."

"That's just as well," he told her. "It's the wrong time of year for them. I can testify firsthand that it's too cold to be wading around out there in the river hunting for the slippery little critters."

She started to laugh again. But then her laughter trailed off as she realized what he was really saying—that he was interested in her as a woman and wanted to let her know. Her brow furrowed as she considered his comment and how she wanted to respond. He held his breath, surprised at how important her reaction was to him.

"I'm a widow, Mr. Cutter."

"Joe. My name is Joe."

She nodded reluctantly. "Joe. I've been a widow for some time now, but that doesn't mean that I'm in the habit of looking at other men. I loved Daniel with my whole heart. I haven't forgotten that—or him."

"You wouldn't be the woman I've come to know in the past few days if you had, Millie. I'll go as slow as you need me to, but I thought you should know that I'm interested. Real interested."

She stared down at her hands clasped in her lap

for a long time. Finally, she looked him straight in the eye. "I won't be hurried, Joe. I won't be pushed, and I won't be making any promises I can't keep."

But she wasn't telling him no, either. That was the important part. "Then we understand each other, don't we, Millie?"

"I suppose we do." She picked up her sewing, preparing to leave. "I had better be getting up to bed."

"Good night. I'll see you in the morning." And he was damn glad to know that.

Isaac sat up slowly, doing his best not to wake Joe. His friend had turned in about an hour before and had fallen sound asleep almost immediately. On the other hand, Isaac hadn't been able to do more than doze for a few minutes. Then his mind would latch on to something and refuse to let go. Right then, he was remembering how happy Annie had looked playing that piano at the church. That was one thing he'd always loved about her— the sheer joy she brought to playing her music. Not that he loved her anymore. That much was true, but his feelings about her were so tangled up and twisted that he had no idea how he really did feel.

Maybe he never would until he had some answers, and there was only one person who could give them to him. He had wanted to confront her earlier, but until he had his strength back, he wasn't sure he was up to dealing with the situation.

He eased his leg down off the bed and reached for his crutches. Joe stirred in his sleep. Isaac froze for a few seconds until he was sure that he still slept soundly. The last thing he wanted to do was explain himself. Finally, he pushed himself to his feet and managed to limp out of the room in the dark without bumping into anything or knocking something over.

The kitchen was cold, making him wish he'd thought to drag his quilt along with him. He didn't dare risk going back for it. Joe was normally a light sleeper. He might have gotten past him once, but he couldn't count on doing so again.

If he remembered correctly, there was a quilt in the parlor that he could use. He felt his way along the wall, trying to remember where everything was. It was one thing to wake up his friend, and quite another to bring the whole household running because he broke some silly gimcrack or other worthless thing women liked to leave sitting around.

The going got easier once he reached the parlor because the moonlight filtered through the curtains to light up the room enough for him to pick out the outline of the furniture. He found the quilt draped over the back of a chair. He considered returning to the kitchen but thought better of it. The sofa would be more comfortable for his leg.

It felt good to sit down again. He was getting stronger, but walking any distance on the crutches surely did wear him out. Maybe he was lucky to be alive, but he wished like hell he hadn't managed to break his leg. It not only slowed down his recovery, but it was going to be damned inconvenient when it came to repairing the *Caprice*.

He stared out the window, trying to make some sense of the mess his life had become the last few days. A few minutes later a whisper of air warned him that he was no longer alone in the room. A feminine form hesitated in the doorway. He swore he could have recognized Annie in total darkness, but he didn't have to this time. The moonlight gave her enough substance.

"You're not alone." He gave her that much warning in case she wanted to make a quick retreat.

She took that final step into the room. "I know. I was on my way down when I heard you in the hall. Are you in pain?" There was a brief flare of light as she struck a match and held it to the lamp. The yellow glow reached out far enough to encircle the two of them but left the rest of the room in shadow.

"I don't hurt worse than usual, but for some reason, I couldn't settle down to sleep." He didn't say why, figuring she wouldn't be particularly happy knowing how much she was in his thoughts.

"Me either. As tired as I was, I thought sure I'd drop off right away." She perched on the arm of a nearby chair, maybe afraid to really sit down for fear she couldn't escape if she decided to run from his company.

"Some nights are like that." Especially when the past kept stirring around in his mind.

"I was thinking about making some warm milk to help me get back to sleep. Would you like some?"

He shuddered at the thought. "No thanks."

His reaction made her smile. "How about some brandy instead?"

"That might help." He didn't much like depending on alcohol to get to sleep. Under the circumstances, though, he thought he would make an exception.

However, as she walked away, he wondered why

she was being so accommodating. Maybe it was the way the darkness shrouded the rest of the world, allowing both of them to forget everything else for a short time. This could be his chance to force their shared past to the forefront, to find out what really happened to make her leave him without any warning. It was hard to find time when the two of them were alone in a household full of people.

And no doubt she preferred it that way.

From the chill in the room, the temperature outside had to be dropping again. He was never much one for winter weather, but as long as the river stayed frozen, maybe the *Caprice* wouldn't shift or sink. He figured the worst danger would be when the ice started breaking up, although that was just a guess. But the thought of losing her was more than he could stand, so he'd cling to whatever hope he could.

He tucked the quilt closer around him, more to ward off the chill of a grim future if he lost the *Caprice* than the winter weather outside the door. He was almost relieved when he heard Annie coming back down the hall. She came in quietly and handed him a glass half-filled with brandy. He took a big swig, glad to feel the burn all the way to his stomach. He could feel its heat spread through him, offering its false comfort.

Annie sat in a nearby chair, huddled under a quilt and with both hands wrapped around her mug of hot milk. He didn't know how she could stand to drink the stuff, but absorbing the heat of it made good sense.

"How did he die?"

She didn't pretend not to understand, but neither did she look in his direction. Maybe it was easier for her to speak of such things that way. "Does it matter?"

"Maybe not, but I still want to know."

"Why should you care?" There was an edge to her voice that hadn't been there seconds before.

"Because . . ." He paused, searching for words and reasons. "Because he was my friend, I suppose. Or maybe just curiosity."

She lifted her drink to her mouth and drank it down. "He died. That's enough for you to know."

Then she disappeared into the darkness, leaving him alone in the dim circle of light. He bit back the desire to call her back, wishing he hadn't driven her away, if only because he didn't want to be alone and so cold.

He finished off his brandy as quickly as she had the milk and set his glass aside. Sitting alone no longer held any appeal for him. He reached for his crutches and pushed himself to his feet. He left the quilt laying on the floor next to the one Annie had dropped in her haste to get away from him. As far as he was concerned, she could pick them both up in the morning.

Despite his effort to move quietly, Joe woke up as soon as he opened the door to their room.

"What's the matter?"

"Go back to sleep, Joe. I'm fine."

He hurried as best he could to get back under the blankets and settle in. Joe waited until he was satisfied that Isaac could manage on his own and then turned over.

"Good night, Captain."

"Good night." This time the silence gently settled around him and let him sleep.

"I'd like to cut some greens for the house."

Millie looked up from her needlework. "What brought that on?"

Annie shrugged. "I've been thinking we should decorate a bit for Christmas. I know we don't usually do a lot, but I thought it might brighten the place up a bit." And it would get her out of the house and away from Isaac for the time it took to ride out to the countryside to collect the greens.

"I'd love to go, but how will we get there?"

"The pastor mentioned that he and Mrs. Chesterfield were going to make a trip out past town to gather some and invited us along." She glanced at the clock. "He said that if we wanted to come, we needed to be at the church around one o'clock."

"All right. I'll be ready."

Annie dug out a couple of baskets to put their cuttings in and some shears to use. She was about to change into some warmer clothing when she heard a knock at the front door. Joe got there ahead of her.

"Is Mrs. Dunbar available?"

She recognized the voice immediately and her heart sank. If Pastor Chesterfield had come to her house, it had to mean a change in plans. He was just coming through the door when she got there.

"Pastor, is there something wrong?"

"Well, I regret to say that I won't be able to drive you and my wife today. She's come down with a bit of a cold and doesn't want to risk making it worse with a chill. I know how disappointed you would be, so I stopped by to see if perhaps one of Captain Chase's men has experience handling a sleigh. If so, he might want to drive for you."

Joe immediately joined the conversation. "It's been awhile, but I've driven one several times. I'd be delighted to take the ladies if they'll accept me as a substitute."

Annie thought Millie might have something to say on the matter, but she wasn't about to miss a chance for an outing. "If you're sure you both don't mind, I'd love to go."

The pastor looked pleased. "Well, then I'm glad that's settled. Just stop at the stable and tell them that I've given you the loan of my horse and the sleigh. It's cold out, but the day is clear and sunny. I'm sure you'll have a wonderful time."

"Would you like us to bring some greenery back for you and your wife?" Annie was already figuring which other baskets she could bring.

"That's mighty nice of you, Mrs. Dunbar. I know Mrs. Chesterfield would feel better if she had a little Christmas cheer about the house." He stepped toward the door. "Take your time this afternoon. There's no rush getting my rig back. I have work enough at the church to keep me busy, and I don't want to stray far from home with my wife not feeling her best."

"Give her my regards."

"I will and thank you for it." She watched from the window as he headed off down the street.

Joe spoke from over her shoulder. "So do you want to tell Millie that I'm your new escort or shall I?"

"Do you think it will upset her for some reason?" She still wasn't sure how she felt about Joe's interest in her friend.

"Not upset her exactly, but she might have enjoyed an afternoon away from all of us."

That was more true for Annie than it was for Millie, but she didn't say so. "I'm sure she'll appreciate your volunteering. I know I do."

"I figure you have some misgivings about me, Annie, but I don't intend to hurt her." He glanced around to make sure they were alone for the moment. "Some men on the river have a woman at every stop, but I don't and never did. I don't know how things will turn out between me and Millie, but I'm not a frivolous man."

Since she had figured him for the steady type from the first, she didn't argue. Instead, she offered him the truth. "I'd miss her."

He placed a hand on her shoulder that was meant to comfort. "I'm not in a hurry to go anywhere. And I think Willow Shoals seems like a fine town."

Maybe they were getting ahead of themselves, but still his words helped to ease the little knot of worry she'd had in her chest since she first noticed the way he looked at Millie. And that she was looking back.

CHAPTER EIGHT

Annie sat tucked as far in the corner of the sleigh as she could and fumed. This outing was supposed to be her chance to get away from Isaac and his men and the problems they represented. She had already made one concession by letting Joe drive when Pastor Chesterfield had to cancel, thereby having to share Millie's attention with him.

Now she was huddled up under covers with the last man in creation that she wanted to spend time with. She'd have been better off staying home and scrubbing floors than go along on this disaster. She kept her eyes firmly fixed on the countryside ahead of them, but that didn't mean she wasn't almost painfully aware of Isaac's presence only a few inches away.

She would have much preferred to ride up front with Joe or else have Millie in the back with her, but that's not the way it worked out. She would have accused Joe of arranging the seating arrangements to his own benefit, but she knew that wasn't exactly true. Having Millie sitting next to him no doubt made Joe happy, but the real reason Isaac ended up in back with her was his leg. The back seat was a little roomier, giving him enough space to sit comfortably.

It was that simple and that complicated. She couldn't protest without answering a lot of questions she would just as soon not have to address. So instead, she was sulking like a two-year-old who'd been denied a piece of candy. The sudden realization how childish she was acting had her shaking her head.

Even if she didn't want to be with Isaac, that was no reason she couldn't enjoy the brisk air, the bright sunshine, and the company of at least two of the other people along for the ride. She sat up straighter to better see the countryside as the sleigh slid over the glistening snow. The bells on the harness jingled as the horse moved along at a sharp pace.

Isaac drew a deep breath and then another. She quickly looked to see if he was in distress. Instead, he was grinning broadly, clearly enjoying himself. The impact of his smile made her heart skip and skitter, and her mouth curve up in response. It was a beautiful day and bad moods had no place in it.

"Have you done this before?" She leaned closer to make herself heard.

"Not in a long time. I'd forgotten how peaceful it was." He pointed toward the woods. "Can you see the deer?"

A pair of does had frozen in mid-step, watching as the strange contraption sped past them. Then in a flurry of hooves and flying snow, they went bounding off and out of sight. It was just the sort of thing that Annie had been needing in her life: something wild and free and beautiful. Her new life suited her in most respects, but sometimes it was too calm and too predictable. She'd never go back to her old ways, but there were days when she felt the need to dance and laugh and play wild music.

And damn Isaac, every minute he was in her sight, he reminded her of those days. But for the next few hours, she wasn't going to let that bother her. The sleigh began to slow down. Millie was talking to Joe and pointing toward a stand of trees off to the right. He guided the sleigh in that direction and gradually brought the horse to a halt.

"How does this look?" Millie's cheeks were bright with color and her eyes sparkled. "There's plenty of pine boughs within easy reach, and it looks like there might be some holly mixed in as well."

"I'm not picky. As long as there's enough to cut some for us and for Mrs. Chesterfield, I'll be happy."

Joe climbed down first and tethered the horse to a nearby tree. He used his long legs to break a path to the closest trees before returning to help Millie and Annie out of the sleigh.

When Isaac started to climb down right behind them, Annie protested. "Do you think you should risk it with your leg?"

"I'm not an invalid, Annie!" he snapped. "I can handle a little snow. Pretend I'm not here if you don't want me around."

His words stung, partly because there was some truth to them, but mainly because she'd spoken only out of real concern for his safety. "Fine, be bullheaded if you want to. I was only worried that you might further injure your leg."

Then she walked away with a huff, but not so far that she couldn't get back to him if he ran into trouble.

Damn, he'd done it again. She'd put aside their differences so that they both could enjoy the day out of the house. And his damnable pride had spoiled it for both of them. He leaned back against the sleigh and wished he had more control of his temper and his mouth. Instead of being across the way with his friend and two attractive women, here he stood with an aching leg and a horse for company.

He'd give Annie a few minutes alone with Millie and Joe before he tried to join them. Once she'd had a chance to relax in their company, perhaps she wouldn't hit him over the head with a tree branch for coming near her again. He shifted slightly, letting his good leg take most of his weight while he waited.

As he watched, Annie pulled some needles off a handy branch and crushed them with her fingers. She held them to her nose and took a deep breath. Her eyes closed and a soft smile erased the last signs of tension from her face. His fingers itched to touch the soft curve of her cheek and to brush that stray lock of hair back from her face.

The idea shocked him as much as the intensity of the desire. He had no business thinking such thoughts about the one woman who had all but destroyed him once. He'd have to be some kind of fool to allow himself to get entangled with her, no matter how much she claimed to have changed since leaving him behind.

He gathered his courage and began the slow walk to where the others were busy cutting holly and some kind of greenery. Their easy laughter only served to make him more resentful. Maybe he should have stayed back at the house, but he wasn't used to being shut in. If he couldn't be out on the river, then he'd settle for this.

He was almost upon them before Joe managed to tear his eyes away from Millie long enough to notice. He immediately handed his basket to Millie and started toward Isaac.

"Sorry, Captain, I didn't see you coming." He stopped short of Isaac's position, obviously at a loss how to help. "Do you want me to find you a place to sit down?" Each word he said hung in the air in cold puffs of white.

"No, I'm fine. It feels good to be out moving around."

Even if the cold makes my leg ache, but he kept that comment to himself. If Joe knew the weather was making him feel worse, he'd probably insist on bundling them all back into the sleigh immediately. It wouldn't take all that much longer for the women to fill their baskets. He could hang on that long if they could.

A flash of red flitted through the tree overhead. A male cardinal finally landed a short distance away on a bare branch. Isaac looked around, trying to spot its mate. It appeared the bird was alone. The two of them apparently had that much in common. He wondered if the handsome fellow had trouble attracting a mate or if he'd had one and lost her. Or maybe some other handsome devil had offered her a warmer nest.

"Poor bastard."

"I beg your pardon. Were you talking to me?" Annie was on her way past him, her basket overflowing with her cuttings.

"Uh, no, actually I wasn't."

She made a point of looking around, as if checking to see who else was within hearing distance. Millie and Joe had moved farther away, leaving Annie the only one he could have been talking to.

He nodded in the direction of the tree behind her. "I was thinking about that cardinal and wondering how he stood the cold. I didn't realize that I spoke out loud. Sorry if I offended you." At least the bird was still there. If it had flown off, she would never have believed him. Or else, she would have thought he'd lost his mind.

"I always leave food out for the birds whenever I can. I don't know how they stand it when the weather gets so cold." She shifted her basket to her other arm.

"I'm sorry I can't carry that for you." He followed after her, finding it easier to walk where someone else had broken a path. "It looks heavy."

"It's nothing I can't handle. I've been carrying things for myself for a long time now." At least she didn't sound angry any longer.

Not that he cared, he reminded himself.

"Joe and Millie will be along shortly. She wanted to cut a few more holly branches." She set the basket up on the seat and climbed up on her own, another show of her independence.

He braced himself on one crutch and managed to pull himself up into the sleigh on his second try. His leg protested a bit, but he felt pretty proud of himself for making it on his own. Joe would probably grumble about it, but Isaac was tired of being coddled. He had bigger things to worry about than his leg right now.

"Here they come now." Annie shifted slightly farther away from him, setting the basket between them and then tucked her blanket around her, leaving him to fend for himself.

He managed to get the blanket situated before Joe got there, saving himself the embarrassment of being treated like a child. His friend handed Millie up into the front seat and then put her basket at their feet.

"Thank you, Joe."

"You're welcome."

Joe looked absolutely besotted with the woman. Isaac had an uncomfortable suspicion he was going to be looking for a new first mate when he was ready to sail back downriver. The thought bothered him because he and Joe had been together for so long. He supposed it shouldn't come as a surprise that his friend might like to marry and settle down, but he hadn't thought it would come so unexpectedly.

"Everybody ready?" Joe turned around to check on the two of them.

Annie smiled at him. "I'm fine, Joe. And again, it was sure nice of you to offer to drive us out here. I'm sure you had better things to do with your time."

"Not that I can think of, Miss Annie. I'd be hard pressed to come up with something I'd rather do than squire two beautiful women around."

"I'm fine, too." *As if anybody gave a damn,* Isaac added to himself. Hell, Joe was too busy flirting with Millie and Annie to notice how his boss was doing. He shivered and pulled his own blanket up higher on his chest and prayed the trip back to town would go quickly.

"Do you need another quilt, Captain Chase?" Annie had produced another one from somewhere.

"Don't you need it?" The temperature was dropping quickly. He was cold, but there was enough of a gentleman left in him to defer to a woman, even Annie.

She pursed her lips. "We could share." She sounded about as excited about the prospect of sharing as he was.

"It might be a good idea." He could stand it if she could.

He reached for the basket at the same time she did. When their hands touched, she jerked back as if burned. He gritted his teeth and refrained from commenting. He managed to scoot toward the middle of the seat and put the basket on his other side. She quickly flipped the extra quilt over them both. He noticed she was careful to keep her first one to herself.

The sun was going down by the time they reached the outskirts of town. Joe pulled up in front of the house and dismounted. He helped Millie down and then offered his hand to Annie. Both ladies had their arms full of quilts to carry inside. Joe set Millie's basket on the steps and then held out his hands to take Annie's from Isaac.

Finally, he came around to help Isaac down. This time he accepted his friend's offer of assistance.

Barton came down the steps and between the two of them, they helped Isaac into the house and into the parlor. The heat from the fireplace felt damn good.

"I'll take the sleigh back to the stable and drop the last basket of greens off at the parsonage. I shouldn't be gone long."

Millie trailed after him. "We'll have coffee and hot soup ready when you get back."

Joe flashed her another big smile. "I could get used to having this kind of service all the time."

Barton raised his eyebrows in an unspoken question to Isaac. All he could do was nod. When both Annie and Millie left them for the kitchen, Isaac relaxed, content for the moment to be warm and alone with his friend.

"So any suggestions who would make a good first mate?"

Barton puffed his pipe as he considered the matter. "I'd guess by rights that the second mate would expect the promotion, but I'm not convinced Jones has had quite enough experience yet. Can't complain about his work, though. He seems to have a good feel for how things should be done."

"That's my thinking, too," Isaac stared into the fire. "It may turn out that we won't need to worry about it, but I'd rather be ready. If Joe ends up staying here in Willow Shoals, I think I'll offer Jones the job on a trial basis. If he does a good job, say after six months I'll make it permanent. Otherwise, he can go back to being second mate."

"Sounds fair." Barton poked and prodded at the tobacco in his pipe and then went back to sending clouds of smoke into the air. "How was your outing?"

"Fine. It felt good to get out of the house for a while, even if it was on a fool mission to cut branches off innocent trees and bushes." The scent of pine was already scenting the air, reminding him of the look on Annie's face as she'd held those first few needles close and breathed deeply. "I guess the next step will be helping the women spread the stuff all over the house."

Barton nodded. "I suppose so. You know, I can't remember the last time I spent Christmas in someone's home. It's been years. Wonder when the baking frenzy will start." He grinned around the stem of his pipe. "I can't wait."

The idea held some appeal for Isaac as well, but once again he had a hard time imagining the woman he'd known years ago with flour on her hands as she created a world of spicy cookies and fragrant pies. He closed his eyes and tried to picture it.

A blast of cold air was the first indication he had that he'd drifted off to sleep in front of the fire. Barton was no longer in the room, giving him to believe that he'd been dozing for some period of time. The sound of stomping feet cleared the last cobwebs from his mind. It appeared that Joe had then returned from disposing of the sleigh and delivering the greens, so perhaps he hadn't been sleeping for too long.

"Damn, but it is cold out there." Joe crossed the room to stand directly in front of the fire. Holding his hands out to the blaze, he shivered. "It took me some longer than I thought because I had to unharness the sleigh myself. The stable owner was busy, and I didn't want to leave the poor horse standing in its traces and hungry."

"I'm sure both the horse and the stable owner appreciated it."

His friend's willingness to offer a helping hand wherever needed had always impressed Isaac. Friends like Joe were all too rare. He'd miss him like hell.

"I talked to the pastor for a few minutes about you." Joe kept his back to Isaac. He suspected it was more to keep from seeing Isaac's reaction to what Joe was about to say than to get warm.

"What about?"

"Well, I know you're worried about the *Caprice,* so I asked if I could borrow the sleigh again tomorrow for a couple of hours. I thought you might like to ride down to the river and see her for yourself."

Joe knew that Isaac hated feeling beholden to anyone, but in this case he was willing to make an exception. Besides, he could always offer to pay the man for the use of the sleigh. If he wouldn't take money for himself—and Isaac suspected that would be the case—he'd find a way to put the money in the church offering plate. Not that he'd attend services himself, but Millie would probably take care of that little chore for him.

"Thanks, Joe. It's been killing me to not check on her." He would have walked to the river, but he knew by the time he managed to go that far, he'd be too tired to get back on his own.

"You're welcome. I told him we'd use it in the morning and have the sleigh back for him by noon or so. That suited him fine."

Barton came back in. "Annie sent me to fetch

both of you for dinner. The meal is ready to be served."

His friends automatically offered Isaac assistance to his feet. Once he was secure with his footing, they stepped back and let him lead the way back to the dining room. He was glad to sit down again so quickly because the day's adventures were beginning to take their toll on him. Once the meal was over, he thought he'd turn in for the night. He wanted to be well-rested before tackling the inspection of his boat in the morning.

Caprice held his future in her beams and boilers. Without her, he would be as lost and alone as he'd been when Belle and Nick had disappeared from his life. He wouldn't let that happen again.

Everyone seemed to be in a quiet mood tonight, he thought, as he looked around the table. Barton ate with his usual gusto, content with both the quality and the quantity. Miss Barker was her usual dignified self, dining with the manners that would befit a lot fancier company than three boatmen in a remote Missouri boardinghouse.

Joe, of course, was too busy sneaking peeks at Millie to pay much attention to anyone else at the table. She was just as busy avoiding meeting his gaze. Annie, on the other hand, kept a wary eye on everyone, ensuring the butter got passed or another bowl of soup was served up quickly. He was impressed with her dedication to her chosen profession, but then she'd always had a way with people. She didn't smile as often as he remembered, but she lit up the room when she did.

And there he was, wishing like the fool he was,

that she'd smile once more for him. Maybe he was more tired than he thought. He set down his spoon and reached for his crutches. It was definitely time for him to seek out his bed.

Annie watched him go, feeling unsettled and wishing she didn't. Most of the time, Isaac looked so grim and cold. But every so often, she caught a glimpse of the man she used to know. The truth be told, she wasn't sure which was worse. She didn't want to remember anything about the past. Too much time and too much pain had passed.

Would Isaac have been happier if it had been Nick who had survived instead of her? The two had been as close as brothers at one time, but she and Nick had managed to betray Isaac. With Isaac's strong sense of honor and pride, perhaps he wouldn't have forgiven his friend any more than he would forgive her.

As one by one, her guests finished their meal, she began to carry the dishes back to the kitchen. Millie followed after her with another load. Joe was right behind her.

"Now, Mr. Cutter, you're a paying guest in my home. There's no need for you to do a lick of work while you're here." Annie took the dishes from his hands.

"I'm used to keeping busy and carrying a few dishes isn't going to kill me. Now, drying them just might." He winked at her and turned tail and ran for the safety of the parlor, leaving the two women laughing.

"Your Mr. Cutter is a nice man." Annie shaved

some soap into the sink and added hot water from the reservoir on the stove. "I like him."

"He is nice, but he's not mine." The wistful look in Millie's eyes betrayed her true feelings on the matter. "I truly don't know if I'm ready for this, Annie."

Annie wagged her finger in her friend's face. "Wasn't it you telling me how nice it would be to have a man to share my bed on these cold winter nights? Seems to me that you're pretty good at handing out advice and not so good at taking it for yourself."

She kept her voice low, all too aware that Isaac was still moving around in the next room. It was one thing to tease her friend, and quite another to embarrass her in front of Joe's good friend and employer. The last thing she wanted was for Isaac to overhear something he shouldn't.

"I'll finish these dishes myself, Millie. I'm sure you have sewing to do."

Millie sometimes took in sewing to earn a little extra money. This time of year, she was kept pretty busy helping others get their finery ready for Christmas. She had also volunteered to sew candy bags for the tree at church to be handed out to the children Christmas Eve.

"If you're sure . . ." Millie hesitated, even though she was already taking off her apron.

"I'm sure. Go on. I'll be along presently."

Although she could hear the murmur of voices from the parlor, she relished the few minutes alone. It sometimes seemed that she never had a minute to herself, especially since the men had moved in. For some reason, the women who boarded with her usually spent more time in their rooms. Perhaps

Take A Trip Into A Timeless World of Passion and Adventure with Kensington Choice Historical Romances!
—Absolutely FREE!

Enjoy the passion and adventure of another time with Kensington Choice Historical Romances. They are the finest novels of their kind, written by today's best-selling romance authors. Each Kensington Choice Historical Romance transports you to distant lands in a bygone age. Experience the adventure and share the delight as proud men and spirited women discover the wonder and passion of true love.

4 BOOKS WORTH UP TO $24.96— Absolutely FREE!

Get 4 FREE Books!

We created our convenient Home Subscription Service so you'll be sure to have the hottest new romances delivered each month right to your doorstep—usually before they are available in book stores. Just to show you how convenient the Zebra Home Subscription Service is, we would like to send you 4 FREE Kensington Choice Historical Romances. The books are worth up to $24.96, but you only pay $1.99 for shipping and handling. There's no obligation to buy additional books—ever!

Save Up To 30% With Home Delivery!

Accept your FREE books and each month we'll deliver 4 brand new titles as soon as they are published. They'll be yours to examine FREE for 10 days. Then if you decide to keep the books, you'll pay the preferred subscriber's price (up to 30% off the cover price!), plus shipping and handling. Remember, you are under no obligation to buy any of these books at any time! If you are not delighted with them, simply return them and owe nothing. But if you enjoy Kensington Choice Historical Romances as much as we think you will, pay the special preferred subscriber rate and save over $8.00 off the cover price!

We have 4 FREE BOOKS for you as your introduction to
KENSINGTON CHOICE!

To get your FREE BOOKS, worth up to $24.96, mail the card below or call TOLL-FREE 1-800-770-1963.
Visit our website at www.kensingtonbooks.com.

Get 4 FREE Kensington Choice Historical Romances!

♡ YES! Please send me my 4 FREE KENSINGTON CHOICE HISTORICAL ROMANCES (without obligation to purchase other books). I only pay $1.99 for shipping and handling. Unless you hear from me after I receive my 4 FREE BOOKS, you may send me 4 new novels—as soon as they are published—to preview each month FREE for 10 days. If I am not satisfied, I may return them and owe nothing. Otherwise, I will pay the money-saving preferred subscriber's price (over $8.00 off the cover price), plus shipping and handling. I may return any shipment within 10 days and owe nothing, and I may cancel any time I wish. In any case the 4 FREE books will be mine to keep.

Name_____

Address_____ Apt._____

City_____ State_____ Zip_____

Telephone (___)_____

Signature_____

(If under 18, parent or guardian must sign)

Offer limited to one per household and not to current subscribers. Terms, offer and prices subject to change. Orders subject to acceptance by Kensington Choice Book Club.
Offer Valid in the U.S. only.

KN094A

‖‖.ıı..‖‖....ıl‖.ı.ıl.ıı.lı..ıl.‖.ıll.ıl.ı.ıll.ıl..l

KENSINGTON CHOICE

Zebra Home Subscription Service, Inc.

P.O. Box 5214

Clifton NJ 07015-5214

PLACE
STAMP
HERE

they felt the need for solitude more than the men-folk did.

Once the last dish was dried and put away, she wiped her hands on her apron and then hung it on its peg on the wall. She looked around the kitchen to make sure that she hadn't missed something. Satisfied that she was done for the day, she started to join the others. At the last second, she stopped and knocked on Isaac's door.

She heard a muffled answer and opened the door. He was sitting on his bed, still in his clothes and playing a game of solitaire using the seat of the chair as a makeshift table. Did he so despise her company that he'd rather hide in his room than spend the evening in the parlor with his friends?

She wasn't about to ask him. Instead, she asked, "Do you need anything?"

He arched a suggestive eyebrow in reply. "What are you offering?"

So he was back to hating her again. She was getting awfully tired of the game he was playing.

"I thought you might appreciate a brandy to help you sleep."

He didn't look particularly disappointed. "I don't want to get in the habit of drinking every night. My leg aches, but it's not unbearable."

"I'm glad today wasn't too much of a strain on it." She started to leave when she realized he wasn't done talking.

"Me, too, because I'll be going out again tomorrow. Your Pastor Chesterfield agreed to let Joe borrow the sleigh again. We're going to go take a look at the *Caprice.*"

His frown didn't seem to have anything to do with

her, but more likely his concern over the damage to his precious boat. Had it come to mean more to him than people? No, that was too extreme. It was obvious that he had friends who cared about him, ones that she had come to respect.

"Well, I had better let you get some rest. Do you need Joe or Barton to help you?"

He tossed the cards down and muttered something under his breath. "Yeah, send one of them."

She nodded, not envying his friends' having to deal with him when he was in such a mood. "I'll tell them. Good night, Isaac."

"Good night, Annabelle."

She winced at the use of her full name but decided that some battles were better not fought. Closing the door behind her, she left him muttering as he gathered up the cards.

The day dawned cold and clear. The snow still lay crisp and clean as far as he could see except where a few hardy folks had walked or ridden, leaving their tracks behind. His feet were already chilled and his nose stung with each breath he drew of the frigid air.

He should have waited inside for Joe to bring the sleigh, but he'd needed to get out. No matter how miserable he might be standing outside, it was far worse to be trapped in the house. As each day passed, hated memories of Belle faded into the new images of Annie and the life she'd built, all without him.

They still hadn't spoken of Nick. Eventually he would pin her down and make her tell him. Once he knew everything, he could finally lay the past down to rest and get on with his life without looking back or thinking about dark eyes and dark hair and smiles that warmed the heart. And if he kept telling himself that often enough, he might actually get around to believing it.

The sound of bells caught his attention. Joe was just turning the corner down the street. When he saw Isaac was already waiting outside for him, he slapped the reins, asking the horse to speed up. He pulled up right in front of where Isaac stood with a spray of snow and ice.

"And was there some particular reason you couldn't wait inside like any sane person would?" Joe clambered down out of the sleigh to help Isaac up into the back seat.

"I don't suppose you believe that I couldn't wait a minute longer to see your smiling face." He grunted with the effort to pull himself up into the seat. He yanked the covers over his legs and settled back to enjoy the ride.

"Is Barton coming?" Joe asked as he settled back in the driver's seat.

"He walked down awhile ago. He said he wanted to do a little exploring before he'd let me risk walking on board." It rankled something fierce that his employees continued to fuss over him. They were as bad as the women were.

The bells chimed on the harness, making the few other people who were out turn and wave. He returned the greeting, doing his best to smile pleasantly. But the closer they got to the river, the more worried he became. In the safety of Annie's house, he could tell himself that the damage to his boat wasn't too bad, that they'd be able to repair her in no time and be ready to sail as soon as it was safe to do so.

But Barton and Joe had both been too vague about what they'd found, their eyes shifting away whenever he brought up the subject. It was bad, maybe beyond bad. He needed to know, to see it for himself so that he could start making plans one way or the other.

Barton was walking up and down the shore, stomping his feet and waving his arms trying to stir up some heat. He stopped when he saw them coming. The welcoming smile he pasted on his face looked forced, sending a chill straight through to Isaac's stomach.

He looked past his friend to where his poor lady sat in the river, listing to one side and looking worse for the wear. For once he didn't protest when his friends manhandled him down out of the sleigh and half-carried him to the gangplank.

Barton stood blocking his way. "Are you sure you're up to this, Captain? She's not going anywhere."

Except possibly to the bottom of the river, but no one had the nerve to say so aloud. He was grateful for that much.

"I have to see it sometime. Putting it off won't change a thing." He stood his ground and waited for Barton to move out of his way. Instead, the pilot spun on his heels and led the way up to the deck.

"There's ice almost everywhere, so watch your step." He put a steadying hand on Isaac's shoulder. "You can pretty much walk anywhere on the texas deck, and the pilothouse is dry and intact. The boiler deck is above water as well."

He could see that much for himself. That meant that three out of four levels were unaffected by the damage, at least so far. He hoped that boded well for the chance of salvaging the boat. Barton continued with his description of the damage.

"The wheel itself seems fine. We were afraid that it might have hit your hard head and sustained considerable damage."

Isaac laughed a little, mostly because it was expected, but also because each bit of good news was appreciated. "And the cargo deck?" It was the one part of the *Caprice* that Barton had yet to mention. "How bad is it?"

"There's water in the cargo hold. It doesn't look like the engines or boilers are under water, but it's impossible to tell until someone can get a good look in there."

And that someone wasn't going to be Isaac. He wouldn't have hesitated if he had two good legs, but he couldn't risk it. Not yet. And it was obvious that the *Caprice* wasn't going anywhere as long as the ice held her captive. Once the temperature started to rise, though, the picture would change.

"Were we able to offload all of the cargo?"

Joe entered the conversation. "Almost all of it. A few things got wet, but we're working on drying them out. I'd guess we lost maybe ten percent, certainly no more than that."

That didn't sound like much until he added that onto the cost of repairing the boat. He had some insurance, but not enough. He'd have to talk to Matthew soon about his financial situation.

He peeked in a few windows, wishing he could see a hell of a lot more. The rooms looked pretty much as he expected. His crew had gone through them, hauling out everything that wasn't nailed down. It was all stowed with the cargo. He kept telling himself all was not lost. Eventually the cargo would reach its rightful owners, absolving him of those debts at least.

His gut ached. He was enough of a gambler to know that sometimes the cards were with you and sometimes they weren't. It would be some time before he knew which way this hand would ultimately play out. For now, though, he had to figure out how much money he could lay his hands on in the near future.

He'd have to wire Matthew soon. Before he'd set off on this run up the river, his friend had made it clear that the bank would allow him to delay his final payment if necessary. But that was when he had a boat he could depend on. What would their attitude be now that the *Caprice* had taken on water and her future was unclear?

Hell, he wasn't sure he wanted to know. But he owed it to his friend to let him know how things stood. His own code of ethics required that much of him. He made one more halting lap around the boiler deck, before hobbling up the stairs to the texas deck. He found more of the same—empty rooms, stripped and bare. He didn't bother checking on the pilothouse, figuring Barton would have already done so.

"I'm ready to go." He knew he sounded abrupt, but his friends wouldn't take it personally.

He made it down the gangplank, only losing his

balance once along the way. Barton managed to catch him before he went down. He hated how much of a relief it was to reach land, even though the footing wasn't much better there. The three of them rode in silence back to the boardinghouse, each lost in his own thoughts.

As the sleigh slowed to a stop, Isaac leaned forward. "Do I need to see the storage for myself?"

Joe shrugged. "That's up to you. There's nothing much to see. It's dry, and we've got someone checking on it regularly. It should be fine."

"All right. I'm going to need to send a telegram to Matthew. I'll figure out what I want to say and then maybe one of you can see to it that it gets sent. Tomorrow should be soon enough."

Barton helped him down and into the house. After he hung up his coat and hat, he stood there for several seconds, trying to decide what to do next. Maybe he'd feel better if he tried to work out his finances on paper. No matter how bad it was, it was worse not knowing.

He went in search of Millie, or failing that, Annie. He found her in the dining room, setting the table for the midday meal. She put the last plate in place before looking up.

"Did you need something?"

"I was wondering if you had a pad of paper and a pencil I could use. It can wait until after we eat, if you're too busy right now."

"Not at all. There should be something you can use in the desk in the parlor. Help yourself." She disappeared back into the kitchen.

Before he'd gone two steps, Millie joined him.

"You might as well sit down now. We'll be bringing in the food in just a second."

He wasn't really hungry, but neither was he in a hurry to start working on his budget. Either way, he needed to get off his feet soon. Maybe he'd do better to get a good meal under his belt and perhaps take a nap before tackling the numbers that would foretell his future.

Satisfied with the decision he'd made, he pulled out his chair and settled in to wait.

CHAPTER NINE

Isaac didn't bother to look up when the front door opened. He'd already added the column of numbers twice and ended up with two different answers. He wasn't about to stop halfway down and have to start over again. If someone needed him, they could damn well wait until he was done.

He crowed with success when he came up with the same answer he'd gotten the first time. Even if he'd made the identical mistake twice, he didn't care. He had an answer he could live with. Setting down the pencil, he turned around to see which one of his friends was waiting patiently for his attention. It took him a second to realize who it was.

"Matthew?"

His friend grinned at him. "I told you it was a bad idea."

"And leave it to you to so nicely point that out to me. It may surprise you to know that I managed to figure it out for myself."

"Was it the ice or the broken leg that convinced you?"

"Go to hell, Matthew." He said it without any real rancor. At least he'd had enough practice with his crutches to stand up without falling down or yelling for help. A few hopping steps and he was within handshaking distance of his friend. "How did you get here so fast? I was going to send you a telegram this afternoon."

"I bought a ticket on the first stage out as soon as we heard there had been an accident. I didn't know for certain that you were alive or dead until I got into Willow Shoals." His eyes were bleak at the memory of all the worry he'd suffered through. "For that alone, I should get a cup of hot coffee at least. Preferably with a good-sized shot of whiskey in it."

"I'm sorry about putting you through all this. I certainly didn't mean to pull you away from home so close to Christmas." He pointed down the hall with a crutch. "But we should be able to do something about the coffee if we can find . . ." He hesitated. How would Matthew react to seeing Annie? Even if it were Millie he could hear moving around in the kitchen, he wouldn't be able to keep Annie and Matthew apart indefinitely.

"There's something you should know before we go looking for that drink." He smiled, trying to reassure his friend.

But Matthew knew him too well. "What aren't you telling me, Isaac? After that stage ride, I'm in no mood to be lied to."

"You've met the woman who owns this boarding-house before."

"That doesn't seem likely considering I've never set foot in this town before today." Suspicion darkened his eyes. "There's only one woman I know of that . . . Oh, hell, it's Belle."

Isaac's eyebrows shot up in surprise. "How did you guess so quickly? It's been years since we even mentioned her name."

"He didn't have to. I'm right behind you." Annie swept into the room, her long skirts rustling across the floor. "Hello, Matthew. It's been a long time."

"Not long enough." The venom in his voice lashed out at her. He surged forward, his hands clenched in fists.

Isaac surprised them both by stepping in front of Annie, shielding her from his friend. "Matthew, not now. If not for her, I'd be dead."

His friend backed off, but only a little. "For that I'm grateful, but that doesn't change who she is and what she did."

Isaac kept his own temper lashed down. Conscious of the fact that they were not alone in the house, he kept his voice down to a harsh whisper. "No, it doesn't, but that was between the two of us. No one in Willow Shoals knows anything about her past. To them, she's Annie Dunbar. For now, it stays that way."

The muscles in Matthew's jaw worked as he tried to deal with it all. Isaac took pity on him. After all, he'd already had time to get used to having Annie back in his life. Matthew had been the one who helped pull Isaac back out of the whiskey bottle after Belle had deserted him. It might take more than a few minutes for him to accept her.

"I'll get the coffee." Annie backed away, keeping

a wary eye on Matthew as if she were afraid he might actually attack her.

"And the brandy." Isaac surprised them both by giving her a smile meant to reassure her. He wasn't sure that it worked, but she gave him a quick nod and hurried away.

Matthew stared at her retreating back. He shook his head and put his hand on Isaac's shoulder. "You really do have the worst damn luck of any man I know."

"Like I said, they tell me I would have died if it hadn't been for her. I guess there are worse things that could have happened." Although he didn't know what exactly. The pain in his leg was nothing compared to what she'd put him through.

He led the way back into the parlor. "I need to sit back down," he said, more to distract Matthew than because of any real problem with his leg. As he expected, his friend immediately offered his arm in support as he made his way back to the sofa.

Once they were seated, Matthew stared into the fire as they waited for Annie to return. There was a lot left to be said, but neither of them was anxious to have a discussion in front of her. At the sound of approaching footsteps, Matthew tensed and sat up straighter.

Only it wasn't Annie who stormed in and slammed a tray down on a table. Millie stood glaring down at Isaac with her hands on her hips. He'd never seen her angry, but there was no doubt that she was about to explode.

"Did you want something, Millie?"

She included Matthew in her glare. "Which one of you made her cry?"

Neither of them bothered to defend them-selves, nor did they offer her an explanation. As far as Isaac was concerned, it was up to Annie to tell Millie about their shared past if she wanted her to know. He sure as hell wasn't going be the one to speak up first.

"Well?"

He should have known Millie would be stubborn enough to demand an answer. Doing his best to ig-nore her, he reached for the nearest cup of coffee. Matthew did the same.

"Let me tell you something, Captain Chase. Annie Dunbar is nicer than I am. Believe me when I tell you that if you hurt her, I will personally throw you and your friends right back out in the snow." She sneered in the direction of his crutches. "Broken leg and all. She's my friend. You aren't."

Millie glared at them one last time before stomp-ing back out of the room, heading for the kitchen and Annie. Isaac sipped the coffee, wishing that Annie had laced it with brandy. He knew better than to press his luck, though. He'd drink the cof-fee and be glad to have it.

"Uh, who was that?" Matthew looked properly cowed. He might not like Annie, but he wasn't the type to feel good about making any woman cry.

"That, my friend, was Millie. She's another board-er, but she and Annie are as close as sisters." He looked at Matthew over the rim of his cup. "She's also the woman who has caught Joe's eye."

"You're kidding! She must work fast."

"Other way around. I think he must have taken one look at her and fallen flat on his face." He sipped at the coffee. "Actually, if I wasn't in danger of losing a hell of a first mate, I'd be happy for him."

"Not everyone wants to spend his entire life floating up and down the river."

"But I do." He always said that, but this time it didn't ring as true. He shoved that feeling back down in the dark part of his mind where he kept fears and worries. Life on the river was enough. It had to be. He had nothing else.

"You're afraid to stay on dry land."

"The *Caprice* is all the woman I need in my life." If she could be fixed. Damn, he hated the thought that she might be dying out there in the ice, but he kept that thought to himself. Although Matthew was his friend, he was also responsible to the bank he worked for.

"She's a beauty all right, but she's mighty poor company when you go to bed at night."

There wasn't much Isaac had ever been able to say to that. It was an old argument, one that neither of them had ever won. Matthew always tried to convince Isaac to find himself a good woman and settle down in one place. Isaac figured if he kept running long enough, he was safe from the kind of pain that Annie had caused him. He wasn't sure he'd be able to survive that kind of hurt a second time.

They drifted into silence

"Speaking of beds, is there a hotel in town?"

Isaac hadn't thought that far ahead, but Matthew would need a place to stay. If Annie was as upset as Millie indicated, she might refuse to let either of them stay another night under her roof. He pushed himself to his feet. Should he need to go in search of another room, he'd rather do it while the sun was still up.

"No hotel, but I'll go see if Annie will let you bunk in with Barton. I already share a room off the kitchen with Joe."

"Do you want me to come with you?" Matthew didn't look all that eager to move from the chair.

"No sense both of us risking injury." He was only half kidding. He figured that if Annie was all that upset, Millie might very well come after him with that cast-iron skillet he'd seen sitting on the stove.

He paused outside the kitchen, fully aware that the two women had probably heard him coming. Thanks to his crutches, he couldn't exactly sneak up on anybody. Gathering his courage, he took those last few steps forward. The scene in front of him was pretty much as he expected. Annie sat at the table, staring into a coffee cup, her eyes a little puffy-looking and red. Millie kept a wary eye on her as she kneaded bread dough. Her expression held a mixture of worry and frustration, and a whole lot of anger when she glanced over in his direction.

"Annie." There would be no soothing Millie until he made peace with her friend. "I hadn't had a chance to tell him. I'm sorry."

"Tell him what? What did that man need to know that made her cry?"

Both of them ignored Millie's question. If Annie had not explained anything to her, Isaac wasn't about to.

Annie swiped at her eyes with her sleeve. "I should have known he'd show up sooner or later. It was a bit of a shock to see him standing there." She kept her hands wrapped around the cup, her knuckles white with tension. "I suppose he needs a place to stay."

"He does. I know it's a lot to ask of you."

Millie slammed the dough down on the table. "I don't know what's going on between the three of you, but if having him here upsets Annie, I want him gone."

Annie reached out a hand to soothe her friend. "I'm all right, Millie. I appreciate your concern, but I run a boardinghouse. I'm bound to take in the occasional customer I'd just as soon not see cross my threshold. Matthew won't cause any problems." She looked to Isaac for confirmation.

"He won't stay long. The bank sent him to see what condition the *Caprice* is in because they hold the note. Once he has all the information, he'll be on the next available stage." He shrugged his shoulders. "Besides, I know he'll want to get back home to his wife and daughter."

That bit of information put a spark of interest in Annie's eyes. "A daughter? How old?"

"Cynthia is five and already a beauty." A smile tugged at his mouth. "She has Matthew on a short leash."

"You, too, I'd guess."

There was no use in denying it. "Ever since she wrapped those tiny little fingers around one of mine. I can't deny her anything." Except maybe his promise to be there for Christmas.

"Will Barton mind sharing with him?"

"Annie!" Millie wiped her hands on her apron and glared at Isaac again. "There is such a thing as being too nice."

"Isaac has already said that Matthew won't be here long, and the extra money won't hurt. I'll remind myself of that when I set one more plate at the table." She stood up, moving as if she had aged five years in the past hour.

The need to offer her some kind of comfort shocked him and then made him mad. It sure as hell wasn't his fault that her past was coming back to haunt her. Considering her previous lifestyle, it was amazing that someone else hadn't recognized her before this.

He backed up against the door frame to allow her room to pass without risking any contact with her. Before he could follow after her to tell Matthew he had a place to stay, Millie caught him by the arm.

"I don't know what's going on here, Captain Chase, and I really don't care. That woman is my best friend, and I won't stand by and let you or anybody else hurt her. Do you understand me?"

He understood all right, but he was in no mood to be lectured. "You might want to ask your friend who the villain was in all of this before you start hurling accusations. Now, if you'll excuse me, I have a friend waiting for me."

Millie caught up with him before he'd gone three steps. "I don't care what happened in the past, Captain Chase. All I know is that Annie Dunbar is a good woman and a good friend. Nothing you can say will change my opinion of her. The people in this town like and respect her. You're the outsider here, Captain Chase. Don't forget that."

He could have told her that she wasn't telling him anything new. He'd been on the outside looking in for a long time.

* * *

Dinner had been a quiet affair. Millie hadn't spoken more than a handful of words to her since Annie had offered Matthew a place to stay while he was in town. One would have thought that ham and beans were utterly fascinating from the way Isaac kept his eyes centered on his plate. The rest of the men had taken their cue from him and concentrated on shoveling the food in their mouths as fast as possible.

It would have been funny if she hadn't been so upset herself. Looking back, she regretted not telling Millie the truth the minute she'd recognized Isaac. Now her friend was justifiably upset about being kept in the dark. After dinner, Annie knew she needed to corner Millie and come clean about her past. Her stomach ached with the knot of tension that had been growing larger as the minutes on the clock ticked by.

Barton and Joe took turns looking at Isaac, Matthew, and then at each other. She wasn't sure if they knew any more than Millie did, but they weren't stupid. Something had obviously upset Millie. Joe would be concerned for that fact alone.

And she still needed to carry out her duties as hostess. "Would anyone care for some dessert?"

Her question hung in the air, as if she'd suddenly started speaking in tongues and no one could decipher her meaning. Looking around the table, she tried again, this time speaking a little slower and a little louder. "I asked if anyone would like dessert. I made an apple pie."

Barton was the first to respond. "I would like some, Miss Annie."

Joe nodded, his eyes never straying long from Millie. "Yes, ma'am."

Finally, Isaac stirred himself long enough to answer. "Apple pie sounds good to me, and I know it's one of Matthew's favorites."

"Well, now that we have that settled, I'll go see about serving it."

She picked up her own plate and reached for Barton's. He immediately jumped to his feet. "I'll help you clear the table, if that's all right."

"That would be nice."

Millie finally realized that she'd missed out on part of the conversation. When Barton picked up her empty plate, she looked up at him with confusion in her eyes.

"We're clearing the table, Miss Millie, to make room for the pie Miss Annie baked for dessert."

"I should help her." She started to rise, but Joe reached over to stop her. "Let Barton do it. He's been complaining about not having enough to do."

"Are you sure?"

"I'm sure." He kept his hand over hers until she reluctantly sat back down. "It won't hurt either of us to do some work around the place. It isn't as if we're regular boarders. I figure we're all more of an imposition than anything."

"You're no trouble, Joe," she assured him.

Annie suspected the slight emphasis in the way Millie said that was supposed to reassure Joe while at the same time making it clear that there were others at the table who clearly were an imposition. It warmed her heart to know that her friend stood ready to defend her despite being kept in the dark too long.

She carried an armload of dishes to the kitchen and then returned for more. Once she and Barton had the majority of the table cleared, she handed him the coffeepot to offer refills to anyone who wanted more while she cut the pie. She picked up the loaded tray and carried it back to the table. As always, the men seemed especially appreciative of her efforts.

"Miss Annie, I can't remember when I've had pie this good." Barton waved his fork in her direction. "You sure have a knack for it."

"Thank you, Barton." She didn't point out that he'd said the same thing a few days before. She appreciated his efforts to ease the tension.

No one seemed inclined to linger over their coffee. The pie disappeared quickly and, one by one, her guests excused themselves. Matthew followed Isaac into the parlor while Barton and Joe settled into playing cards at the table. Agatha gave everyone a gracious nod before making her way upstairs. That left Annie alone with Millie. She led the way to the kitchen with the rest of the dishes and braced herself.

"Millie, I know we need to talk, but not here. Upstairs would be better if you're willing to wait that long."

Some of the frustration eased in Millie's gaze. "I've waited this long. It won't hurt me to hang on for a few more minutes." Her tone, though, made it clear that she wasn't willing to compromise more than that.

For several minutes, they fell into familiar habits. Annie washed. Millie dried. Annie wiped down the table. Millie refilled the reservoir on the stove so they'd have hot water in the morning. Annie checked to make sure the doors were locked. Then Millie waited at the bottom of the steps for Annie to make good on her word.

With heavy steps, Annie headed for the privacy of her room with Millie right behind her. How would she tell her friend that she wasn't the decent woman that everyone thought she was? Or that Isaac wasn't the one who deserved Millie's contempt?

When she reached the door to the room, it took all the strength she could muster to open it and step through. She lit a lamp and turned up the wick, trying to cast out all the darkness from the one place that had been her sanctuary since moving to Willow Shoals. But despite the bright light, shadows lingered in the corners and in her mind.

"It can't be that bad, Annie." Millie knelt by the fireplace and stirred the coals into life. "We've all done things that we're none too proud of."

Despite her friend's attempts to reassure her, Annie couldn't feel the warmth of the fire or Millie's concern. "You might want to sit down. This could take awhile."

Millie took a seat on the bed and patted the spot next to her. "Only if you'll sit beside me."

Annie needed to pace or scream or anything that would make the telling easier. But for her friend's sake, she perched on the edge of the bed. "I don't know where to begin."

"I always figure that starting at the first and going on from there makes the most sense." Millie offered her an encouraging smile. "If it helps, I've already figured out that you and Captain Chase knew each other before you moved to Willow Shoals."

That much was true, but there were a lot of towns and a lot of years between her and the day she first met Isaac. Maybe Millie had the right of it, though.

"He was so handsome." She stared at the rug on the floor, not really seeing the colors that swirled through the braids that it was made from. Instead, she saw a young man, full of himself, swaggering through the doors of a saloon. "He hasn't changed all that much, except he used to smile more easily."

That might be her fault, too, but she hoped not. Surely her leaving hadn't caused that grim set to his mouth or those worry lines between his eyebrows.

"My full name is Annabelle." That seemed important for Millie to know. Perhaps she'd understand that the Belle that Isaac had known was still part of the Annie who sat next to her on the bed.

The story couldn't continue if she didn't describe her own part in the play. "I had just been hired to play piano in the saloon."

Millie drew a deep breath as she absorbed that bit of knowledge. "Had you always done that for a living?"

Annie answered the real question. "My pa was a gambler and a wanderer. My mother taught me how to read and how to play the piano. It's about the only real schooling I ever had because we never lit in any one place long enough for me to go to school. Whenever Pa's luck changed for the worse—and it always did—we would move on to the next town, the next saloon. He dealt cards and more often than not, he lost more money than he earned."

She thought of her mother and the way she'd faded away as the towns blurred into one long nightmare of losing games and skulking away in the night when they couldn't pay Pa's debts. Finally, after her mother died, her father had started dragging Annie to the saloons with him. Once people found out she could play the piano, she was the one who kept food on the table and a roof over their heads.

Ignoring the few tears on her cheeks and the matching ones on Millie's, she continued talking. "I guess you probably don't think much of my father, but he did his best by me. No one, no matter how drunk they were, ever laid a finger on me as long as my father was around. He made it clear that they were hiring a piano player and nothing else."

Her chin came up with what little pride she could muster. "I've played in some places that would turn your hair white, even some brothels." She shuddered at those memories and the nameless women who plied their trade in the shabby rooms overhead. "But I never worked upstairs. Not once. Not ever." Not even when Nick had tried to convince her to do otherwise.

Millie's arm had found its way around her shoulders. "Go on, Annie, get it all out."

It sounded as if Millie thought she was lancing a wound and needed to clear out the infection. Maybe that wasn't too far off the mark because once she managed to get started the words seemed to tumble out of her mouth.

"Anyway, I took a job in a small town along the river. My father had wanted to wander out farther west, but I was tired of living with my clothes packed in case we needed to leave in a hurry. I decided to try staying in one place for a while."

"As saloons go, it was clean and well run. A woman owned the place, and she saw to it that no one bothered me." Her throat was dry. She got up and poured herself a glass of water from the pitcher by the bed. "I'd been there a week, maybe two, when I saw Isaac and Nick for the first time." She smiled at the picture they'd made. "You've never seen two men more alike and more different. Both handsome as sin, but Nick was as dark as Isaac is fair."

She sat back down. "I don't know which one of them noticed me first, but pretty soon they had me surrounded, each one trying to outdo the other to get my attention. Rosie, the saloon owner, tried to run them off a couple of times, but they kept coming back. I think she finally realized that they were relatively harmless."

Despite herself, she smiled at the memory. "Both of them were so different from anyone I'd ever seen. The only men I had ever known were either gamblers or drunks or both. Nick liked to play cards more than Isaac, but mostly they were so full of themselves. Big ideas and big plans." Plans that had included her, made without asking her what she wanted.

"Isaac was more serious than Nick, but then he came from a good family. You know, the kind who went to church on Sundays and owned the house they lived in. Nick's background wasn't as bad as mine, but nowhere near as respectable as Isaac's."

Millie spoke for the first time in several minutes. "None of that matters, you know. It isn't what you're born with, Annie. The choices you make are more important than the things you can't help—like who your parents were or what your pa did for a living."

Maybe Millie was right, but then she didn't know the choices Annie had made. Her friend was loyal enough to think that Annie would have been the one who had been wronged. But that wasn't the case at all. She had made her own decisions, enlisted Nick's help, and Isaac was the one left behind, wondering what had happened.

"Most every night one or both of them would show up, maybe to play a few hands of cards or to drink a beer or two. Mostly, though, Isaac used those as excuses for hanging around the saloon so he could see me." Her eyes burned with the need to grieve, although she fought to hold back the tears. She didn't deserve the release that they might offer her. Regrets too numerous to name seeped into her soul, making her stomach ache with shame.

"You see, I never knew a man could love a woman enough to choose her over everything else in his life. Lord knows my father never loved my mother enough to change. He loved the excitement of the next turn of a card more than he cared about her—or me," she added after a few seconds. "He did his best to protect me in the saloons, but it would have never occurred to him that I shouldn't have been there in the first place."

"So what happened between you and Isaac?"

"He fell in love with me." She stared into the fading flames in the fireplace. More for something to do than because she noticed the cold, she knelt down to add another log to the fire. A few sparks flew up and burned out. "He should never have done that."

"Why not, Annie?"

She didn't have to look at Millie to know she was disgusted, but she didn't know why her friend felt that way. Maybe she'd finally realized that she hadn't really known Annie at all. She risked a peek over her shoulder. To her surprise, Millie had more tears sparkling in her eyes, but her expression looked sympathetic rather than angry.

She repeated her question. "Why not, Annie? Why shouldn't someone love you?"

Maybe Millie was asking for herself and not Isaac. "I had never even had a friend, much less a man who wanted more than a little fun in a saloon at night. I was like a kid with a new toy, having two such handsome men paying so much attention to me."

She made herself return to Millie's side. "Isaac started bringing me little gifts. Ribbons, flowers he picked, things like that. Nothing big, but the kind of things a man brings to a woman he's interested in. Only I didn't know about such things and didn't have anyone to tell me any different."

And Nick resented the way Isaac felt about her, another piece of the puzzle she hadn't understood. "Nick tried to outdo Isaac, pretending it was just another contest between them. I don't know what Isaac thought, but I was foolish enough to be flattered."

"But Nick wasn't in love with you."

"No, he sure enough wasn't. He'd grown up poor and evidently resented everything Isaac had. Certainly, he wanted some of it for himself. Knowing he couldn't take Isaac's family or his place in the community, he settled for taking the one thing he could—me."

This time Millie remained quiet, which hurt more than Annie could have imagined. Despite her reluctance to tell Millie the truth about her past, she maintained some little hope that her friend would accept her anyway. Waves of pain lapped at her heart, making her wish she could just disappear the way she had all those years ago. Well, if she was going to lose everything anyway, she wanted to—no, needed to—tell someone her story from start to finish.

"Isaac kept asking me to come home with him to meet his family." She picked at a loose thread on the quilt to keep her hands busy. "I found excuse after excuse to put him off. I could just imagine their reaction to having their son bring home a girl like me. They would have gotten the impression that he wanted to marry me. Besides, I didn't even own an appropriate dress."

"Did he propose?"

"I didn't give him a chance. I didn't give *us* a chance at all."

"You might as well tell me everything, Annie. I know there's more."

Maybe Millie wasn't thoroughly disgusted with her yet, but she would be. "I made another mistake. I trusted Nick. He told me what I wanted to hear, that Isaac wasn't serious about me. He said they had a running bet that sooner or later one of them would talk me into going upstairs at the saloon with him." She closed her eyes and let Nick's image fill her mind. "He even showed me the twenty-dollar gold piece that he carried in his pocket in case Isaac won.

"As much as I wanted to believe the worst of Isaac, it hurt so much to know he was only playing a game. When Nick offered to take me away, I agreed. How could I face Isaac, knowing that everything had been a lie?"

"Only it wasn't." Millie's arm came around her shoulder again. It felt like heaven. "Nick was the liar and the cheat."

"He was no worse than I was. After all, I had led them both on, taking their gifts and their attention, without ever giving anything back."

Sitting down was impossible. She left Millie's side to stand by the window and stare out into the cold darkness. "Nick had it all planned out. We'd leave Isaac a note telling him that we'd eloped. That way he wouldn't come after me, you see." She touched the glass, wishing the cold would numb more than the palm of her hand.

"Once I had time to think things through, I realized some ugly truths about myself. First, I'm a poor judge of character. Secondly, I'm a coward at heart. And third, I got what I deserved—a loveless marriage to a drunkard and wastrel."

In a blink of an eye, Millie was beside her. She took Annie by the shoulders and shook her gently.

"I will listen to your story, Annie, but I won't let anyone insult my closest friend, not even you. You weren't any of those awful things. What you were was a girl without anyone to guide you through those painful steps to womanhood. Of course you didn't know how to handle a man like Isaac or even Nick. And you were more comfortable with

Nick because you'd been raised by a man just like him. Your only mistake was in thinking you didn't deserve better."

She lifted Annie's chin with the side of her finger, forcing her to meet her gaze. "If you were such a weakling, you would have gone to work upstairs in that saloon. Instead, you made the best of a bad situation. I would guess that Isaac especially was drawn to an innocent girl who happened to play piano in a saloon. And even though he didn't deserve it, you were loyal to Nick while he was alive, weren't you?"

She didn't wait for an answer. "Of course you were. And when he died, you turned your life around. You left the girl Belle behind and became the woman you were meant to be. If you won't take my word for it, think about this: Your boarders don't stay here because you wash the sheets regularly. We all stay because of you."

Her friend's declaration of loyalty finally tore away the last of her defenses and the tears poured out.

CHAPTER TEN

Her eyes burned and her throat was raw, but her heart felt better than it had for years. Millie's shoulder was wet from Annie's tears, but she didn't seem to mind in the least. Finally, Millie stepped away long enough to rummage through Annie's things until she found a clean handkerchief. She pressed it into Annie's hand and then took one for herself.

The sight of them both blowing their noses and dabbing at their eyes set Annie off into a fit of the giggles. Millie joined in, evidently needing the same release that Annie did after such an outpouring of painful words and tears.

Her friend wagged a finger in her face. "Now, Annie Dunbar, I know there's more to the story, but it can wait until you get a good night's sleep. I'm not going anywhere, so don't lay awake fretting on what's going to happen next. Between the two of us, we can handle those men downstairs, no matter what they throw at us."

Annie surprised both of them by reaching out to give Millie a powerful hug. It felt so very good to have unburdened herself at last. And even more amazing, apparently it hadn't cost her the dearest friend she'd ever had in her life.

Millie turned back the covers on the bed. "Now you get yourself ready for bed and sleep as long as you can. I can and will make breakfast and there's men aplenty for taking care of any chores in the morning. Not one of them would mind hauling in wood or gathering the eggs, considering all you've done for them."

Annie doubted that Matthew and Isaac would care if she needed a few hours of extra sleep. Barton and Joe might even follow their captain's lead if he were to order them to let her fend for herself. But before she let herself slide back into a wallow of self-pity, she remembered Millie's kindness. No matter what the men thought, she had at least one person on her side.

And if Millie could accept where Annie had been and what she had done, perhaps other people could as well. It would be nice if Isaac could find it in his heart to forgive her, but maybe she didn't need his pardon for whatever crimes she had committed in his eyes. Matthew's opinion simply didn't matter. She'd only met him once or twice in the past. Who was he to sit in judgment of her?

She slipped on her favorite nightgown, worn soft and thin but comforting in the loneliness of her bed. As the night settled in around her, she thought about the one thing she hadn't told Millie and never would.

Nick had been the one to finally coax her into

his bed, but only after a circuit preacher said some words over them, not that she remembered a single thing the man had said. Her most vivid memory was the sick feeling in her stomach when she said "I do," knowing in her heart that she was standing beside the wrong man. She never told Nick that she pretended that he was Isaac each and every time he'd risen over her in the dark of night, but he'd known. Even as he grunted out his release, the accusation had been there in his eyes.

He'd never raised a hand to her, but he'd made her pay in a thousand ways. Public slights. Finding her work in the worst places. Flaunting his interest in other women, especially when he paid for their services out of the money she had earned. And Belle, to her everlasting shame, had let him get by with it because she'd deserved no less. But as Annie, she had long ago decided, she would never again let a man—any man, including the one who still made her heart race—walk all over her. Never. Not again. She was stronger than that.

A few more tears trickled down to dampen her pillow. She shuddered and sighed and finally slept.

He stared at the ceiling, wide awake but not ready to face the effort it took to get out of bed. He and Matthew had sat up until close to midnight talking about anything and everything, except the woman upstairs. He figured it was just as well. Matthew wasn't ready to hear anything good about Annie, and Isaac wasn't all that sure he wanted to be the one saying it anyway.

It was enough that both Barton and Joe had obviously fallen under her spell. Joe had an excuse; he was so obviously taken with Millie. Perhaps he felt that he had to accept Annie if he wanted to get close to her friend. If Millie thought well of Annie, Joe was prepared to give her the benefit of the doubt. And, of course, Annie had helped bring Joe back from the edge of death as well. That alone would make a man look upon the woman with favor.

Barton, however, was a different story. He wasn't easily fooled by the wiles and whims of the fairer sex because he'd had his own problems with women along the way. From what Isaac could see, his pilot liked both Millie and Annie quite a bit. He always seemed willing enough to leap to his feet and do their bidding without complaint.

It all made Isaac wish like hell he'd washed up on the shore of any other town than Willow Shoals. Things had been so blissfully uncomplicated until that damn chunk of ice had ripped a hole in his boat and a bigger one in his life. His first instinct when he'd recognized Belle had been to lash out, to cause her some of the same pain that she'd caused him.

But as the days went by, he was having a harder time seeing Belle in Annie. And that had him all tied up in knots, because he was also looking at her with more than a casual interest or gratitude for saving his life. No, all too often he found himself admiring her trim figure or remembering the soft feel of her dark hair. Her smile was enough to leave him hard and wanting.

When he was young and stupid, he used to ache with the need to kiss her. But he hadn't been the one to learn the taste of her mouth. Nick had stolen that honor, the lying son of a bitch. He'd pretended to be Isaac's best friend, and all the while he was planning on robbing him of everything that was important.

It had taken Isaac a long time to replace the money that Nick and Belle had stolen from him. The war years had delayed his plans even more. And now, when he was finally within spitting distance of success, it had all gone to hell again.

"Son of a bitch."

Joe lifted his head. "Something wrong?"

He hadn't realized he'd spoken out loud. "Sorry, Joe. I didn't mean to disturb you. Go back to sleep."

His friend blinked at him in the dimly lit room. "Are you sure you're all right?"

"As well as can be expected, considering I have a broken leg and a boat to match." He tried to reassure Joe with a smile, but his mouth wouldn't cooperate. "Don't worry. I'm just feeling restless. I'll get up so you can sleep."

He sat up and worked his legs into his pants. By the time he was finished he was breathing hard, but at least he hadn't had to ask for help. It was quite an accomplishment, all things considered. Once he reached the kitchen, he paused to decide what to do next. If he were careful, he might just be able to make coffee for himself.

It took a couple of trips to get enough wood to heat the stove. Then he had to fill the pot with water. Luckily he knew where Annie kept everything from watching her prepare meals. In only a few minutes the smell of hot coffee filled the air. He drew a deep breath of the soothing scent and reached for a cup. The sound of footsteps coming his way stayed his hand as his pulse surged.

He tried to tell himself that he was relieved to find out that it was Millie he'd heard. The more he avoided Annie, the less complicated his life would be. But even the coffee tasted a bit like disappointment.

"I hope you don't mind me helping myself." He set his cup down where he could reach it and then took a seat on the far side of the table to keep out of her way.

"I don't much care what you do, Captain Chase." She jerked an apron down off its peg and tied it around her waist. "Eggs or flapjacks?"

Now what had her all riled up? "I'm not particular. I don't want to be any trouble."

From the way she rolled her eyes, he suspected it was too late for that. "I can wait to eat until everybody else is up."

She was already up to her wrists in a pan of flour. "How noble of you." Her hands moved too quickly, sending a cloud of white flying through the air. She ignored the resulting mess and kept working the dough she'd put together.

He considered offering an apology for whatever he'd done to offend her but decided it wasn't worth the effort. No doubt she'd gotten all protective of Annie for some reason. Nothing he said would likely make any difference, especially if Annie had finally told Millie her own twisted version of their shared past. He could imagine how it went: poor little girl—so scared of a man who loved her that she robbed him of everything that mattered. Hell, he practically felt sorry for her himself.

"Thanks for starting the fire."

Millie's gratitude sounded a bit reluctant, but he'd

take it. No matter how she or Annie felt about him, he had nowhere else to go right now. It only made sense to try to get along.

"You're welcome."

"I'll fix you some eggs, if that sounds good. I don't hear anyone else stirring yet." She broke four into a skillet and started stirring them. In only a few minutes, she set a plate heaped with eggs and fresh biscuits down in front of him.

"Thanks, Millie. I do appreciate the hospitality that you've shown me and my men." That much was sincere.

"Thank Annie. It's her boardinghouse."

"I will." When hell froze over. He choked down the eggs more out of spite than any real desire to eat. When he'd eaten the last bite, he made his way to the parlor. Even without a fire, the room offered a warmer reception than the kitchen with Millie glaring at him.

About thirty minutes later, Barton and Matthew came down the stairs. Both men nodded in his direction but continued on to the kitchen. Evidently the promise of a hot breakfast was far more compelling than spending time with him. He didn't care. For the moment, he was happier alone than he would be answering the questions Matthew was bound to ask. The previous night he'd been there because he was Isaac's friend.

Today, he had a feeling that it would be the banker asking the hard questions, the ones Isaac had no answers to. He dreaded the moment his friend realized that the entire venture was in jeopardy. If the boat went down, the bank stood to lose a fair amount of money, even after the insurance paid off. They'd want to sell off the salvage to offset the difference. He closed his eyes and imagined the bastards tearing the *Caprice* apart, squeezing out the last drop of her lifeblood.

His stomach clenched and heaved at the idea.

A few minutes later, Matthew came in. From the grim set to his jaw, Isaac knew he'd guessed right. The banker was about to start the interrogation.

"How bad is it?" Matthew could always be depended upon to go right to the heart of the matter.

"Bad enough. Not a total loss, though. Most of the cargo is safely stowed here in town. The men have gotten their personal belongings off, and I sent most of them home by stage until we get the boat repaired. Barton has been overseeing the removal of anything that could be damaged if the water gets any higher inside the boat."

Matthew knelt down by the fireplace and stirred the fire to life while he digested Isaac's report. He'd have more questions as soon as he sifted through the information he already had. When he stood back up, Isaac braced himself.

"Is she worth the cost of fixing?"

How could he even ask? Isaac fought back the urge to explode, but his friend, even in his role as banker, didn't deserve the brunt of his fury. He waited until he'd drawn a few calming breaths before answering.

"So far, the *Caprice* only has the one hole in her side. She's taken on some water, but she's still afloat. Right now, the ice is holding her steady. But if it breaks up before we can start repairs, I don't know what will happen."

"I need to see her for myself."

"Get Barton to take you. He can show you everything." He slapped his injured leg in frustration. "I'd take you myself, but I'd only slow you down."

"You know the bank is going to want its money on time." Matthew turned toward the fire again, as if he couldn't bring himself to face his friend with what he was about to say. "If this hadn't happened, they would have been willing to extend your deadline a few months. But with the chance she might go down, they'll want to make sure they get paid."

"Are we talking about them or you, Matthew?" So he hadn't been able to keep all the anger under control after all.

"Damn it, Isaac, that's not fair and you know it." Matthew slammed his fist into his palm in frustration. "I'm your friend, no matter how this mess turns out."

"I'm sorry, Matthew. I can be a real son of a bitch when it comes to my boat." He closed his eyes against the pain. "I also know that if I hadn't been so damn greedy, none of this would have happened. I almost cost Joe his life, not to mention my own. The bank has every right to be nervous about their investment right now."

Since that was nothing but the bare-bones truth, Matthew only nodded and said, "I'll go talk to Barton."

"It looks bad."

Barton shrugged. The boat looked the same since

the ice hit her. Wounded, bleeding, but still holding her head up. He didn't really expect the banker to understand that a man didn't abandon a lady like the *Caprice* just because she'd come across some hard times. With a little care and even more luck, she'd be ready to face life on the river again.

"Isaac said you'd gotten everything of value off."

"The real value is the boat herself. But yes, we got the cargo and most of the furnishings stored in town."

"Have you been able to make arrangements to deliver the cargo by land?"

"Road conditions have been too bad. This snow has kept almost everyone tucked up tight inside. Once the weather breaks, though, I have a couple of wagons lined up to haul most of it the rest of the way. I'll be going along to make sure it gets where it's supposed to." Then he'd head right back to Willow Shoals to protect the boat from anyone who might want to do her further harm.

Including the man standing next to him.

"Is there anyone here in town who could give us an idea what the repairs will entail? I don't know a damn thing about fixing this kind of damage."

"You're not too concerned about that anyway, are you? I'd guess you and that bank of yours are more interested in getting your money than saving her."

"We have to protect our investment." If Matthew had any regrets about it, it didn't show.

And that attitude was one reason Barton lived on the boat as much as possible. He understood the treachery of the river, but men were a mystery to him. How could this man claim to be Isaac's friend and at the same time be planning on destroying the one thing that meant the world to him?

But the problem wasn't really his to worry about. He'd follow orders, do his best to protect the *Caprice* from greedy hands and small minds, and watch to see how it all played out. If the whole problem with the boat wasn't enough, the drama unfolding back at the boardinghouse had all the elements of a Shakespeare play. He wasn't sure if it was a comedy or a tragedy, but it sure as hell was entertaining.

Joe and Millie weren't at the core of the play, though. Those parts were reserved for Isaac and Annie, even if they didn't realize it. He wondered what had gone on in the past. Neither of them had admitted anything, but it was there in the way their eyes would meet and then slide on past. Eventually it would all come out; he'd bet on it.

"Can we go on board?"

Matthew had evidently seen as much as he could from the shore. He had his collar turned up against the wind and his hat shoved down on his head as far as it could go. Another sign he spent little time outside. It was cold, but not as bad as it had been the past few days.

"We can, but only if we're careful. So far we've been able to slip on and off without any real problems, but we need to keep an eye on the ice and the water levels to be safe."

He led the way down to the narrow plank that led from the landing out to the boiler deck. A couple of times he had to reach out to offer Matthew a steadying hand. The banker looked a bit nervous about traversing the short distance, but Barton didn't blame him. He'd seen firsthand what a quick dunk in the river in this weather could do to a man.

Once on board, he let Matthew find his own way around the decks. Every so often he would stop and take notes, but Barton wasn't close enough to see what he was writing down. Maybe the banker would tell Isaac what he was thinking. He hoped so. The captain had enough on his plate without playing guessing games with Matthew and the bank he represented.

"I've seen enough for now."

The banker left the boat with more confidence, perhaps because he was heading for the security of dry land. After a brisk walk, they reached the front door of Annie's boardinghouse. It felt surprisingly like coming home, a feeling Barton had rarely experienced in his life.

Millie had a pot of coffee on the stove. As soon as she saw Barton, she reached for a cup and filled it.

"Would you like one, too?" she asked Matthew and held up the pot.

"I'd love one, ma'am." Matthew accepted the steaming mug with obvious gratitude. Then he looked around. "Is Isaac asleep?"

Some of the friendliness disappeared from Millie's smile. "No, he followed Annie down to the church again." She set the pot down harder than necessary and turned her back to them.

Matthew looked at him for answers, but Barton didn't really have any. "I think I'll go take a nap upstairs. If the captain needs me when he returns, let me know."

* * *

This time the rehearsal included more than just Annie and the piano. If he'd realized that she wasn't going to be alone, maybe he would have remained back at the boardinghouse. As it was, there were children swarming all over the place, ranging in age from diapers to maybe fourteen or fifteen. Since Matthew's daughter was the only child he'd ever had much to do with, he wasn't the best judge of ages.

But the woman introduced to him as Mrs. Chesterfield had a real knack for marshaling her forces, organizing the various children into groups to sing or recite. The performances were far from perfect, but he could see the potential—and the need for more rehearsal. When he'd followed Annie into the church, he hadn't been expecting to see anyone else. His first reaction had been to retreat, but he was glad he hadn't. The whole affair had proved to be most entertaining.

Despite the off-key singing and misspoken words, he'd found himself humming along with the melody of the old familiar hymns. It had been years since he'd sat through a church service, fidgeting in the seat next to his mother. She'd done her best to instill a good Christian upbringing in him, although her success remained somewhat doubtful. It struck him as ironic that it was Annie who'd never set foot in a church when he'd first met her but was the one who belonged to a congregation now.

He studied her when she wasn't aware of it. Everything he saw led him to believe that her interest in helping at the church was sincere. When the pastor's wife led each group forward and explained what she needed from her, Annie nodded gravely and did her best to play exactly as the woman asked. The first few times through, there definitely were some rough spots. By the end of the rehearsal, though, he could see some real progress.

Belle's talent for the piano had been impressive. As Annie, she honed her skills with a real knack for bringing out the best in the singers she played for. Not only that, she made it look easy. He thought she acted a bit shy around the children, but he could feel the warmth of her smiles from across the room.

And wanted that heat for himself.

He had to be out of his mind to even think such a thing, but it had been Belle's essential innocence that had drawn his attention years ago. Her betrayal had ripped his heart into pieces, leaving him bleeding and wounded. Now, here she was, showing that same sweetness. Which one was the real woman—Belle, who had deserted him, or Annie, who played music for children in a church program? Hell, he couldn't tell.

Finally, the last group finished their singing and headed for the platter of cookies that a couple of the mothers had put together for the children to share after the rehearsal. Mrs. Chesterfield hung back to talk to Annie.

"Thank you for your patience, Mrs. Dunbar. I know you didn't expect the rehearsal to take so long, but we made real progress in putting the program together." The older woman reached out to lay a hand on Annie's shoulder. "God bless you for stepping in to take over playing for us."

Annie blushed and ducked her head, clearly embarrassed by the praise. "It's nothing, Mrs. Chesterfield. Anyone would have done it."

"Now, now, Mrs. Dunbar. Very few people have the gift you have with the piano, and even fewer have the patience to work with so many young children. If you and your gentleman friend would like to stay for some refreshments, please do. Otherwise, I think we're done for the day."

Annie glanced in his direction before answering. "I think that Captain Chase is too kind to say so, but I suspect he needs to get back to the house. His recent injury causes him to tire easily."

Mrs. Chesterfield looked stricken. "Oh, I didn't think. I'm so sorry that we selfishly kept the two of you so long."

Isaac suspected Annie was using his broken leg as an excuse to escape, but he didn't want to upset the older woman unnecessarily. He lurched to his feet. "Please don't let it concern you, Mrs. Chesterfield. Annie tends to worry too much. I'm fine." He smiled at her. "We probably should be going, but no harm was done."

He leaned against the pew to keep his balance while he pulled on his coat. Annie quickly gathered up her things and joined him at the door. Mrs. Chesterfield called out Annie's name just as they were about to leave.

She hurried across the room in such a way as to leave her almost breathless. "Mrs. Dunbar! I forgot to ask when you'd be available to rehearse again. Would tomorrow afternoon around two do?"

"That would be fine. I'll be here."

"Please come, too, Captain Chase, if you're of a mind to." She beamed at both of them. "I know my husband would enjoy your company. He spoke so kindly of you and how he enjoyed your conversation."

"I'm not sure about my plans at this point, ma'am, but I appreciate the invitation." He had liked the pastor, too, but the man saw too much with those world-weary eyes of his. His compassion and warmth made it too easy to want to confide in him. Right now Isaac had too many secrets that he wasn't ready to share with anyone.

Outside, the sun glinted brightly off the snow that still lay in thick piles around the town. Some folks had cleared paths to their houses and along the sidewalks, but their best efforts had little effect. The wind seemed determined to pile the snow in drifts to block their way. Despite how hard it was to walk, he supposed he should be grateful. His real problem with the *Caprice* would start when the temperatures started rising again.

"I hope you weren't too bored."

"I wasn't bored at all." That was true, although from the look Annie gave him, she didn't quite believe him. "It's true. I always did love listening to you play, especially when you get lost in the music."

Once again she seemed uncomfortable when he spoke of old times. "Annie, there's no use in pretending that we don't have a shared past, at least when we're alone."

"It was a long time ago." She kept her eyes firmly on the road in front of them. "We can't change what happened."

"That's true enough. But ignoring it doesn't make it go away." He wished he could drop his damn crutches without falling down. Right now, he wanted to haul her up short and force her to look at him.

He kept moving along at her side, doing his best to keep her from leaving him behind. There were questions he wanted answers to, ones that he'd been waiting a long time to ask her. Unfortunately, they were almost back to her house, leaving them no time to talk about anything important. And with the weather being so cold, he'd be a fool to stay outside a moment longer than necessary.

Silently, he followed her inside and wished there were a way to have some private time with her. Time where they could talk and he could satisfy his curiosity about the past and maybe even about how it would feel to kiss her. He'd missed his chance years ago; he didn't plan on making the same mistake again.

"Well, Millie, did you and Annie have a good talk last night?"

"Ouch!" Joe's unexpected question startled her, causing her knife to slip, nicking her finger. Rather than look at him, she kept her eyes firmly on the small droplet of blood that welled up from the tiny cut.

Before she could do anything about it, Joe reached over and took her hand in his. With infinite care he gently wiped away the blood and then kissed her finger, as if to make it feel all better. Her finger was fine. It was the rest of her that was a mess.

So much of her quiet life had been badly shaken up ever since the night the sheriff had asked for their help. Maybe they would have been better off in refusing to answer his summons, although she doubted either she or Annie could have lived with their consciences. No, they'd had no choice but to do as they had, but it was as if that knock at the door had set off an avalanche of changes that rolled over them faster than either of them could deal with.

Not the least of which was still cradling her hand as if it were precious to him.

"I didn't mean to startle you with my question." His warm fingers stroked her palm, sending a shiver of heat through her.

"That's all right. It didn't hurt." And she wasn't about to answer his question, but she didn't say so. She hadn't yet come to terms with all that Annie had told her. As a matter of principle, she wouldn't share her painful confidences with anyone, especially one of Isaac's friends.

"I don't want you to think that I was eavesdropping, Millie. Last night, though, I was on my way into the kitchen when I heard Annie say that the two of you needed to talk."

He reluctantly released her hand and leaned back in his chair. She missed his touch more than she liked. "We talked, but that will remain between the two of us."

Joe nodded, as if that was what he expected or at least he could accept her decision. "I only wanted to say that Annie looked better this morning than she has in days. Whatever the two of you discussed seems to have relieved her mind a lot." He smiled. "You, on the other hand, seem to have taken on some of her worry."

That was true enough. No wonder Annie had been fretting so much since Captain Chase had been laid out on her kitchen table. She must have taken one look at his face and thought her whole world was about to come to an end.

"I'm all right. I just have a lot things on my mind." She counted the potatoes she'd already pared and decided to add two more. Then she started on the carrots.

"And am I one of those things?"

She dropped a carrot, sending it rolling across the table into Joe's waiting hand. "I beg your pardon?" She snatched the wandering vegetable away from him.

"I just wondered what you thought of me. Am I one of the problems that's had you frowning all morning?"

She didn't know how to answer that. He did occupy a fair amount of her waking thoughts and most of her nightly dreams. Her cheeks warmed with the memory of some of those midnight fantasies. Keeping her eyes firmly on the pile of vegetables in front of her, she struggled to find the right words.

"I can't decide if you're a problem or not." She risked a quick peek in his direction. Rather than being offended by her indecisiveness, he seemed rather pleased. Why was that?

"Is there anything I can do to help you make up your mind?" There was a definite twinkle in his eyes.

She needed the kettle for the soup more than she needed an attractive man flirting with her. That much she knew for a fact. Before she could lift it down from the top shelf, a long arm snaked past her and grabbed it first. Instinctively, she turned around. And there was Joe, only inches away from her. He had already set the pot down on the table behind him, but he made no move to step back away from her. The temperature in the kitchen soared, but whether it was coming from the long length of his body so close to hers or from the sudden surge of tingly awareness that surged through her, she didn't know or care.

All that mattered was the slow descent of his lips to meet hers. She held her breath and waited for her world to change. He tasted her gently, without crowding her too much. When he tugged her closer, wrapping her in the safe cocoon of his arms, she went willingly.

For a precious few moments, everything felt simple and right. Then he released her and stepped back a short distance. All the questions came rushing back.

"Millie . . ." Joe frowned and started forward again.

She held out her hand to hold him back. "Joe, I need time to think about all of this."

"I don't want to rush you, Millie, but I'm not going to walk away either. I've never felt like this about anyone. You need to know that."

Could that be true? She'd known what it felt like to love and be loved; she wouldn't settle for less. His eyes met hers unflinchingly, letting her look her fill. What she saw there made her drop her hand; this time, she was the one to move closer and demand a kiss. He groaned as he plundered and coaxed her into accepting what he was offering, what he demanded. Finally, he eased back, letting sanity return.

He leaned his forehead against hers and smiled. "Lady, you bring me to my knees."

She allowed herself the privilege of caressing his

cheek. "You'll have to be patient with me, Joe. It hurt so much when Daniel died. I really didn't think I was ready to care about another man, not yet. But you've surprised me."

"As long as there's a chance you will come to care, I'll try to be patient." He gave her a quick kiss and stepped back again. "Now, can I do anything to help you with dinner?"

She was grateful for the sudden change in subjects. "You can set the table if you need to keep busy."

His grin was wicked. "What I need is something to keep my mind and my hands off of you." He took a stack of bowls from her and headed for the dining room.

She watched him disappear and started counting the minutes until he returned.

CHAPTER ELEVEN

"I'm not going to let you do that, Matthew, so you can just get that idea out of your head." Isaac prided himself on keeping his voice calm when inside he was screaming in fury. "She's not just a pile of wood and metal, ready to be sold off for scrap."

"You need to get your head out of the clouds, Isaac. Even if you manage to deliver the rest of the cargo, you won't have enough to bring in the equipment and labor to bring her up from the bottom."

"She was still afloat the last time I looked. I haven't heard anything from you or Barton to tell me that's changed at all."

Matthew gave him a look of pure disgust. "Be sensible, Isaac. The only thing holding her head above water is the ice. Once it breaks up, the *Caprice* will go down. It's only a matter of time." He stood over Isaac's chair glaring down at him. "Do you think I like telling you this? Hell, man, you're my best friend. The last thing I want to do is watch you lose everything."

Isaac was at a distinct disadvantage and he knew it. Normally, he was taller than Matthew by several inches. Right now, he'd give anything to be towering over his friend, hoping to intimidate him into seeing things Isaac's way. Unfortunately, he didn't cut much of an imposing figure sitting down with his leg propped up. It made him look weak and ineffective. Then there was the little problem of money.

He had none and Matthew did. Or at least the bank had enough to restore the *Caprice*, which is more than he could claim.

Silence thick as fog settled between them, neither able to see where the other stood. Matthew meant well, and Isaac knew his friend was in the rough position of being caught between duty to his employer and friendship. No matter which way he fell off the fence, one of them wasn't going to be happy.

"I'm sorry you're mixed up in this mess." That much was true, but the man had a wife and daughter to think about. He couldn't afford to do anything that might jeopardize their future.

Matthew was staring out of the window. "If you could come up with enough money for the repairs, I might be able to hold the bank off long enough for you to clean up this mess you're in." He sighed. "I don't suppose you have a secret source of money. You know, an investment I don't know about, like someone you loaned money to and can pay it back."

He started to shake his head but then stopped. The only people who owed him money hadn't actually borrowed it. No, they'd taken it with no warning and disappeared from his life. He tilted his head and considered the house that had been his home now for a week or more. If she owned this boarding-house, she had to have some money stashed away.

Or if it was all tied up in the building itself, she could take out a loan. He didn't care how Annie got it as long as she paid him back. Once he had some cash in hand, he'd be in a better position to bargain terms with Matthew and his banker friends.

"Let me see what I can come up with." There was no use in telling him what he had in mind. If Annie didn't have the money, it would only make him seem more desperate. "It may take me a couple of days to come up with a solution."

"That's about all I can give you, my friend. I need to get back home. I told Melissa and Cynthia that I'd only be gone for a short time. By the way, Cynthia is still expecting her Uncle Isaac to be there for her Christmas program. In fact, I think she'll be more upset about you not making it than she would be if I were to miss it." Matthew sat down, looking marginally more at ease now that Isaac had given him some hope of solving the problem of what to do about the *Caprice*.

"I don't think I'll make it back in time. Do you think a new doll will help her forgive me?" Maybe Annie would help him pick one out, if she was still speaking to him after he asked for his money back.

He hated like hell having to hound her for it, partly out of pride, partly out of a surprising reluctance to hurt her. He could only hope that she wouldn't cry or make a scene. He'd feel guilty about upsetting her when she'd been so decent to both him and his men, but the *Caprice* had to come first in his life. Too many people, himself included, depended on the boat to make a living.

"You need to move it a little to the left. Not that much—I said a little."

Annie shot him a dirty look over her shoulder. Too bad. She shouldn't have asked for his opinion if she didn't want it. "Now the loop on the other side is bigger."

She shifted everything back to the right. "How is that?"

"Better. Now raise it up half an inch or so." He didn't bother to hide his grin.

This time she hammered the nail without asking for any further advice. Then she stood back and studied the garland she'd strung along the front of the fireplace. She gave it a quick nod, obviously satisfied with the job she'd done.

"It looks festive, don't you think?" Annie was definitely pleased with herself.

"It does, now that it's straight," he teased.

"Oh, shut up, Isaac," she said without any real rancor. "You couldn't have done a better job, and you know it."

That much was true; it was amazing how a few pieces of greenery made such a difference in the house. Annie and Millie had tied the pine boughs they'd cut into long strands and then wound them around the banister on the staircase and everywhere else they could think of. Then they had added accents of red ribbon and strings of popcorn. Barton had found an excuse to leave for a few hours, claiming that Annie would likely decorate her boarders next, if she could get them to stand still long enough. She had giggled and tried to lasso him with a string of popcorn before he could get out of the door.

The whole house smelled of pine and Christmas cookies. It was Millie's turn to provide the refreshments for the next rehearsal at church, so she'd started baking as soon as they'd cleared away the breakfast dishes. The scent of molasses and cinnamon made Isaac's mouth water. He would have hung around in the kitchen, hoping to sample the cookies as they cooled, but he needed to talk to Annie.

So far, he hadn't mustered up the courage to ask her about the money. She was in such a good mood; he hated to spoil her fun. Even if she had the cash stashed safely in the bank, she wasn't going to be happy about handing it over to him. If he didn't say something soon, though, he'd miss out on his chance. She'd be leaving for the church as soon as they ate the midday meal. He wasn't sure she'd let him tag along behind her again.

Maybe his best chance would be on the way back from the church. For the length of time it took the two of them to walk home, he'd have her undivided attention. They could discuss the situation like two mature adults without involving anyone else in the matter.

It wasn't that he was afraid of Millie or even Miss Barker, but he thought Annie would like to keep some things about her life private. From the nasty looks he'd been getting from Millie, he suspected the two of them had finally had a long talk about Annie's past and how it had intertwined with his.

He'd love to know what she'd said. Obviously he was the villain in the story. How had Annie twisted the facts to have Millie come to that conclusion? He was probably better off not knowing.

Joe popped his head into the room. "Everything looks nice, Annie."

She beamed with pride as she gathered up the scraps and bits of stuff that lay scattered about the room. Once she had it all in the basket, she stood back to admire her work. "You don't think it's too much?"

Isaac knew enough of her childhood to know that it was unlikely she had much experience in how such things were done. Despite her insecurity, the room looked warm and inviting decked out with all its finery. But before he could tell her so, Joe beat him to it.

"Everything is perfect. You should be proud of your handiwork."

Her smile was bright enough to melt the snow outside. Joe grinned right back at her, making Isaac want to punch his first mate right in the nose. Wasn't it bad enough that the man was all calf-eyed at Millie all the time without him turning his charm on Annie as well?

There wasn't anything he could say now that wouldn't sound like an afterthought, although he was at a loss as to why it should matter to him. It wasn't as if he were courting her favor for anything. Everything between them was strictly a business proposition. He was paying for room and board for himself and his three friends. The money she owed him was a separate matter and would stay strictly between them.

But that didn't mean he wanted Joe monopolizing Annie's attention. "Was there something you wanted, Joe?"

His friend smacked his forehead with the palm of his hand. "I'm such an idiot. Millie sent me in here to fetch the two of you to eat. And Miss Barker." He immediately bounded up the stairs, leaving Annie and Isaac to follow as they would.

"How soon do we need to leave for the church?" He figured he'd include himself; if he waited for her to invite him along, he'd be gray-haired and toothless.

"I'm leaving right after we eat." She carried her basket into the kitchen. "It will be another long rehearsal."

"I've got nothing better to do." Besides, he wanted that chance to talk to her. He thought she was going to argue some more, but once again she surprised him with her generosity.

"I can imagine it is hard for you to watch your friends come and go while you sit and watch. I know you'd rather be out on the boat yourself instead of depending on everyone else to tell you what's going on." She set the basket in the corner. Then she smacked his hand when she realized he was reaching for a handful of Millie's fresh-baked cookies. "You can come with me as long as you promise to leave the cookies for the children."

"All of them?" He tried to sound outraged by the idea, but only succeeded in laughing. "How about most of them?"

"I wouldn't want you to lie in church. I guess I'll settle for 'most' of them and leave it up to Mrs. Chesterfield to hold you to your word."

"Fair enough." He punctuated his promise by sneaking one more cookie.

Even Millie laughed at that.

Annie was having fun. That in itself was a big surprise, but that everyone else seemed to be enjoying themselves because of her music was an unexpected pleasure. The rehearsal had gone smoothly. The little angels and the ten-year-old wise men had sung their parts with only a few mistakes. The entire congregation was in for a wonderful Christmas celebration.

And she was part of it all. It made her heart happy to know that. For the first time in her life, she felt those long missed roots starting to take hold in the rocky soil of this small Missouri town. Mrs. Chesterfield had made a point of inviting her to their house for dinner on the Saturday after next. The prospect excited her, even if she had been told to bring that nice Captain Chase with her.

She glanced in Isaac's direction. He was listening intently to a little girl, perhaps about five years old, as if her every word was a pearl of wisdom. Annie had to cover her mouth to keep from laughing out loud when the little blonde held her doll out for Isaac to take. Then her heart went slip-sliding when he accepted the precious gift and cuddled the well-loved rag doll to his shoulder while its owner went in search of another cookie or two.

Who knew he had it in him?

When she'd first met him ten years before, he'd been a puzzle to her. But then, thanks to her father's wandering ways, she'd had almost no experience with people who lived normal lives, the kind who stayed in one place for years at a time and raised their families to do the same.

His bright blue eyes, the color of a summer sky, used to look at her in ways that she hadn't understood until it was too late. There had been heat and hunger and something warm and utterly terrifying whenever he'd smiled down into her dark eyes. Even now, with so much time that had slipped past them, she could remember the nervous, almost giddy way she'd felt around him. The way he'd made her hope for things she had no name for.

And now, here they were, more in his old world than in hers, and at long last she felt as if she belonged there. He, on the other hand, was only counting the days until he could return to the real love of his life and disappear back down the river. This time he'd be the one leaving, taking her heart with him.

But then he'd always had it, even if she hadn't been smart enough to know it.

His little friend was back again, trading a sweet treat for the return of her doll. Isaac accepted the offering and then tugged on her braid and smiled. Annie was too far away to hear what he said to the little girl, but whatever it was had her giggling. As she skipped away, Isaac looked in Annie's direction, as if he'd felt her eyes on him all along.

Lord, what was she going to do about having him back in her life? He seemed in no hurry to turn away, letting her look her fill. From the unruly lock of hair that persisted in falling forward to the merest suggestion of a cleft in his chin, she liked what she saw. Maybe it was time to for her to risk finding out what there was about him that drew her as no other man had, either before or since. His eyes widened, as if he'd read her thoughts from across the room.

"Mrs. Dunbar, would you mind playing one more song for all of us?"

The pastor managed to startle her, so intent on Isaac that for a time she was unaware of anyone else in the room. She blushed, remembering where her thoughts had been headed—and in a church, of all places. With some effort, she managed to look up at Pastor Chesterfield. Somewhat belatedly, she made sense of his question.

"What would you like to hear?" Her fingers were already reaching for the keys.

"How about *Oh, Come, All Ye Faithful?*"

She immediately launched into the stately beauty of the hymn, letting the music soothe some of her edginess. Before she'd finished the first verse, almost everyone in the church had gathered near to listen and sing along if they knew the words. Isaac was one of the few who kept his distance. She knew he had the problem of his injured leg, but she suspected he was only using that as an excuse. If he actually joined the others, he might actually feel like a part of the group.

Which only went to show how far they'd come. Here she was, child of the saloons, leading the singing in a church. And there he sat, raised to be part of a community much like Willow Shoals. Perhaps there would never be any common ground between them. The thought made her sadder than she cared to think about.

She played four verses of the song and then immediately eased into another one. The pastor nodded at her approvingly while his wife joined him at his side. Without looking, he slipped his hand around his wife's shoulder, the two of them looking so comfortable, so right in each other's company. Annie suspected she was more than a little bit jealous.

When the last few notes died away, she was rewarded with a round of applause. It didn't matter to her in the least what Isaac thought of her performance, but she looked anyway. He was clapping right along with everyone else. His small nod of approval had her hands trembling. She busied herself with packing up the sheet music.

Mrs. Chesterfield stepped away from her husband long enough to thank Annie personally. "Mrs. Dunbar—Annie—I know I've said this before, but you don't know what a miraculous gift you have given us. This year's Christmas program will be the best ever because of you."

"There are a lot more people involved than just me, Mrs. Chesterfield." That much was true. "I'm only glad that I can contribute in some small way to the program."

"Now, my dear, you know better than to think you are a minor character in this." The pastor looked at her over the rims of his spectacles. "You have a real talent to share with those around you. I know that you aren't used to performing in front of so many people, but you'll get used to it. It just takes practice."

She had the practice, just not in front of the type of crowd that hung out in churches. The only saving grace was that Isaac was too far away to have heard the pastor's comments. She glanced toward where he'd been sitting only to realize that somewhere along the line, he'd moved. That's when she became aware of his presence right behind her.

At least he wasn't laughing or pointing out the pastor's error in front of everyone. She owed him for that.

"Annie, are you about ready to go?" Isaac stepped closer. "I'm afraid my leg is objecting to me doing so much."

"Oh, dear, Captain Chase." Mrs. Chesterfield's distress was sincere. "Perhaps we should send for a wagon to take you home."

"No, that's all right, ma'am. I'll be fine."

Annie suspected that he was faking part of his discomfort for her sake. She hated being beholden to him, but she appreciated the chance to escape before the pastor's praise did her in completely. She felt like such a fraud, letting these good people think that she was such an innocent. Perhaps someday she would find the courage to let them know the truth about her.

After all, Millie now knew almost everything there was to know. Yet she hadn't fallen over from the shock of finding out that Annie had more than a nodding acquaintance with saloons and brothels.

She gathered up her things and put on her coat. "I'll be here for the next rehearsal, Mrs. Chesterfield. Do you need Millie to send cookies again?"

"No, thank you, my dear. Several of the mothers have signed up to provide refreshments. We tried to spread that little chore around so no one has to do too much."

"All right then, we'll be going."

Along the way, various people stopped Annie to say good-bye or to ask Isaac about his boat and his men, so it took several more minutes to make it as far as the door. Once they were safely outside, she paused to thank her companion.

"I appreciate you getting me out of there." Someday she might feel comfortable in the face of so much attention in the church, but not yet.

"I can take only so much of such good cheer myself."

She watched as he made his way down the steps and then turned to wait for her. As soon as she was by his side, he started off down the street at a determined pace. Although she had no trouble keeping up with him, she suspected he was going too fast for his own comfort.

She slowed down and tugged on his sleeve. "This isn't a race, Isaac. And I'm pretty sure that no one is going to come charging out of the church to chase us out of town."

Rather than appearing relieved, his expression puzzled her. For some reason unknown to her, he looked down at her with what looked like both guilt and determination. "We need to talk."

The cookies she'd eaten suddenly felt like lead in her stomach. She wasn't going to like what he had to say. She knew it, just as she knew there was no way to stop him from talking. Why couldn't he wait until they reached the house?

The answer was obvious. The subject at hand was something he wanted to keep private from both his friends and hers. She wondered which one of them he was trying to protect. Most likely himself, but maybe not. He used to have a noble streak running a mile wide right through the heart of him. Maybe that hadn't changed.

He turned to face her but kept his gaze fixed on some point over her shoulder. So much for nobility. She definitely wasn't going to like this, but she wasn't going to cower or try to slink away from whatever unpleasantness he was about to dump in her lap.

"So talk, Isaac. It's cold out here." She kept her chin up and was proud of how calm she sounded. Let him do his worst.

Then he did.

"Look, Annie. I figure I owe you some for taking us in and nursing me back to health." He paused as if waiting for her to acknowledge his generosity.

"Go on." She crossed her arms over her chest and waited for him to continue.

"Matthew knows about us and what happened, but Barton and Joe don't, at least not for sure."

She supposed she should be grateful that he hadn't told everyone who would listen. Honesty forced her to admit that she'd done some talking of her own. "I had to tell Millie, but she had already figured out some of it on her own."

"I knew something had changed. When I got up this morning, she kept giving me dirty looks." He arched an eyebrow, as if waiting for her to explain how that came to be.

Millie's hostile attitude toward Isaac surprised her because she'd made a point of letting Millie know that she had been the one who'd done wrong. "I can't imagine why she should be mad at you, but I'll talk to her again."

He shrugged off her concern. "She's your friend, Annie. Of course she's going to take your side in things. That's what friends do."

"Is that why Matthew acts as he does toward me? I hardly knew the man, so I can't remember doing anything to make him dislike me so." She shivered. The wind was coming up again. She hoped Isaac would come to the point soon. "He's leaving soon, so I'm not concerned about his opinion of me or the way I've lived my life. Now, can we go home?"

"Not yet." He shuffled his feet a bit before finally looking her straight in the eye. "I know you've worked hard to make a good life for yourself here in Willow Shoals, Annie. You never deserved spending your life in saloons and the like. I'm proud of what you've accomplished."

That was all well and good, but why couldn't he have told her that someplace warm? There had to be more to it, something she wouldn't like. He was just adding sugar to sweeten the taste of whatever came next. The wind whipped down the street, cutting her straight to the bone. She stomped her feet, trying to jar some feeling back into them.

Isaac seemed to take no notice of the worsening weather. "If it weren't for the *Caprice*, I wouldn't even bring this up. I'd love to wait for the ice to thaw and then disappear from your life."

Like you did from mine. Although he didn't say that part out loud, she heard it anyway.

Finally, the words poured out of him. "It's like this. Matthew can hold the bank off for a while longer if I can come up with enough money to start repairs. Without it, they'll likely collect on the insurance and let the vultures in to tear the *Caprice* to pieces for what they can get for salvage."

There was real grief in his eyes. "I can't . . . I won't let that happen."

She understood that. She'd struggled long and hard to make a life for herself, just as he had. Neither of them would let someone else take it away without a fight.

"Are you asking me to let you stay until the boat is fixed?" She couldn't imagine what else he might want. She found out soon enough.

"No, that's not it, Annie." He looked up at the sky, as if searching for divine guidance. Finally, he shifted his crutches to one side and grabbed her by the arm. With a curse muttered under his breath, he dragged her between two nearby buildings, perhaps to provide them some privacy from curious eyes. More likely, he wanted out of the wind. She stumbled along beside him, trying to maintain some dignity if anyone was indeed watching them.

Once they reached the alley, he turned those angry, angry eyes on her and just spit it out. "I need the money back, Annie. I'm sorry, but I need it now."

Her knees shivered, this time from weakness rather than the cold. She reached out to him for support but jerked her hand back when she realized what she was doing. At that moment, Isaac Chase was the last person she'd ask for any kind of help. "I don't understand, Isaac. What money?"

How could she have thought his eyes ever held the warmth of summer when they were the color of shattered ice? She took a step back and then turned to walk away. Obviously the man had lost all good sense.

He stopped her with words. "I need the money you and Nick stole from me when the two of you ran off together, Annie. Don't pretend you don't know all about it. The two of you must have had a hell of a good time laughing at my expense." He stomped toward her. "I still can't believe that I was fool enough to trust either one of you."

She prayed that the ground would open up and swallow her whole or that lightning would strike or for anything else that would end this nightmare. She'd always known there was something that Nick hadn't told her, something that had pleased him. A secret he had never shared with her.

"I don't know anything about your money. When I left town, all I had was a battered old trunk packed with the same stuff I had when I arrived. Nick didn't have much more than his saddlebags full of clothes."

His hand gripped her arm hard enough to leave bruises. "Don't lie to me now, Annie. Not now. It's too important."

She jerked free of his grasp, ignoring the ache in her arm and the worse one in her heart. "I'm not lying, Isaac. I can assure you that if we'd had any money, we wouldn't have stayed in such awful places. As it was, we were half-starved by the time I found work again."

But another memory surfaced. After being broke for so long, Nick suddenly had enough money to stake him in a poker game. Where had that come from? It sure hadn't been from her wages because she hadn't had time to earn that much yet. No doubt it had been another lie from the man who had sworn before a man of God to love and honor her.

But then, she knew she hadn't exactly been honest with him, either.

And together they had both betrayed Isaac in yet another way. She wondered which had hurt him more—her leaving him without a word or the money that had disappeared at the same time. She wished her conscience would allow her to disavow the debt, but Nick had been her husband. She had paid off all the other money he had owed people, and this was no different. Most of the other debts had come as a surprise to her as well.

"I don't have much. I'll have to make payments." Just when she was finally starting to be able to put some away toward the future. She still remembered the pride she'd felt when she'd made that first deposit in her very own bank account.

"Son of a bitch." The curse was a harsh whisper, probably not meant for her ears. "He didn't tell you, did he? Nick took it and then let me think it was your idea."

"Does it matter?" She wanted to comfort him in some way, to wipe away the pain. "I made my own mistakes, Isaac. But you're right: I was a coward, but never a thief."

"I should have known that about you, Annie. All these years wasted blaming you for something you never did." His shoulders slumped in defeat as he leaned against one of the buildings for support. "It was Nick all along."

She could have reminded him that even though she was honest, she wasn't completely innocent. But then she'd spent far longer in Nick's company than Isaac had. After all, they had lived as man and wife, a far more intimate arrangement than mere friendship. She'd been fooled by Nick's handsome face and black soul, too. And all of them had suffered greatly.

"Sometimes I think he hated both of us, Isaac. I don't know why he felt that way about you, though. You'd done nothing to deserve such treatment from him."

Isaac's eyes drifted shut for a minute or two. "I think he was jealous of me, although I didn't see it at the time. He was always talking about how easy I'd had it, growing up as I did. My family wasn't rich, not by any standard, but we always had enough to eat and decent clothes to wear. I don't know how much Nick ever told you about his past, but it wasn't pretty."

"He told me, but he still had it better than I did in many ways. At least he wasn't dragged from one hellhole to another, never knowing from one night to the next where he'd sleep."

Isaac ran his fingers through his hair, clearly frustrated. "I know, but he didn't see it that way. Looking back, I realize that he resented having to work so hard for everything he wanted. But, damn it all, if he had stuck with a real job, he might have made a success of himself. He was smart enough." He pushed away from the wall. "But that's not how he ended up, is it?"

She'd made a habit of protecting Nick's memory, but Isaac already knew or at least suspected the worst. "No, it's not. You know how it is with cards. Some days the right ones come your way; other days, you don't see a winning hand at all. He was always sure that his luck would turn. It just never did."

She rubbed her hands up and down her arms,

trying to stave off the cold. If they were going to talk this out, she'd prefer to do it here, away from the others. "He took to cheating. Most people didn't look past that handsome face of his to see the weakness behind it. They trusted him, so he got by with his tricks for longer than you would have expected."

She stared up at the faint yellow circle of the winter sun. "Then he ran into the wrong man."

Somehow Isaac's arms had found their way around her, wrapping her in warm security against the rough cloth of his coat. The scents of bay rum and damp wool filled her senses, making her all too aware of the man who offered the comfort of his embrace. She tried to ignore the powerful stirrings of long dead feelings.

"That's when he died." There was no need to go into detail. How Nick had screamed as his lifeblood poured out on the saloon floor, just one more stain mixed in with tobacco juice and spilled whiskey. How he had looked at her with such loathing as the light faded in his eyes. How she hadn't been able to cry for the boy she'd known or the cold man he'd become.

"We all made poor choices, Annie." Isaac's voice rumbled through his chest as his hand patted her on the back as if she were a small child rather than a full-grown woman.

She didn't feel like a little girl, not in this man's arms. He still frightened her, not because of his anger, but because of the power he had over her, even after all this time. No one else, Nick included, had ever made her want as much as Isaac did.

When she tried to step back, to give herself some breathing room, he stopped her, using nothing more than a gentle caress that started at her waist and moved slowly up to cup the back of her head. It dawned on her that he intended to kiss her, and she was going to let him.

Not because it was the right thing to do, but because at that moment, it was the only thing to do.

The strength of him surrounded her, making her ache and setting her very skin on fire with the pleasure of his embrace. Lord of mercy, his kiss was sweet, so very sweet. He tried to be gentle with her, coaxing her at first and then just that quickly, the kiss became so much more as he demanded as much as she could give and more. The frustration of their thick coats and clothing held them apart, making her want to burrow through layers to the man she'd wanted for so long.

"Hey, Ma, look at that!"

A horrified gasp was followed by the sound of footsteps in full retreat. Rather than push her away, Isaac pulled her closer even though he stopped kissing her to chuckle. "I guess this isn't the best place for this sort of thing."

His good humor about the situation kept her from being quite so embarrassed at being caught like two spooning sweethearts. She could only hope that she had been too wrapped up in Isaac's arms to be easily recognized. "I should say not."

"Shall we leave by the back door?" he asked, giving a gallant little bow and gesturing toward the far end of the narrow passage between the buildings. He even went so far as to offer her his arm, somehow balancing with both crutches under one arm.

"Don't be silly, Isaac. I can walk on my own." She

eyed him up and down. "I'm not sure I can say the same about you, especially on snow and ice."

"Well, never let it be said that I didn't try to act the gentleman." He readjusted his crutches and nodded for her to go ahead of him.

It felt strange to be walking through town having just kissed a man from her past. She still wasn't sure how it had come to pass that Isaac had started off accusing her of being a thief and ended up kissing her as if his life depended on it. It most assuredly had not solved any of their problems.

For the rest of the short journey back to the house, they walked in silence, neither one knowing what to say. Once inside the house, they separated, he to the parlor to join his friends, and she in search of Millie to start the evening meal.

She worried that her friend would somehow notice that something momentous had happened to her on the way home from church, but Millie seemed distracted herself. For once they worked side by side in complete silence.

CHAPTER TWELVE

Isaac glared down at the envelope that Annie had just dropped on the table in front of him. He'd been going over the figures Matthew and Barton had come up with concerning the cargo and the repairs when she came into the room.

"What is this?" he asked, although he had a sick feeling he already knew.

"It's a down payment on what I owe. You never said how much Nick took, so I'll have to work out terms when you come up with a final figure. I think we'd both be happier if we drew up a contract of some kind."

He kept his eyes firmly on the table as he tried to think of something to say that wasn't obscene or an explosion of bad temper. Despite his anger, his hand had almost reached for the money. Had he come to this, that he'd take money from a widow who hadn't known her bastard of a husband was a thief as well as a cheat?

He shoved it back toward her, putting some distance between him and temptation. After another morning of futile discussions with Matthew, he was feeling pretty damn desperate. "Put that back in the bank or under your mattress or wherever you kept it." He slowly raised his eyes. "I don't want your money, Annie."

Her sharp intake of breath warned him that her temper wasn't under much better control than his. "Maybe you don't, but you need it, and I owe it." She shoved it back.

He was lucky that she had chosen to deliver the cash when he was alone. Matthew would have already snapped it up and started counting it. Well, this was one transaction his friend the banker was going to know nothing about.

"Nick owed it, but he's dead. The debt died with him." He picked up his pen and tried to concentrate on a column of numbers. At that moment, he couldn't have added two cents together and come up with the right answer. But if he kept up the pretense of working long enough, perhaps she would give up and leave. The envelope came sliding back across the table. He continued to ignore both it and her. Finally, she walked out.

The money stayed.

He calmly finished adding up the numbers. The total made him sick. Once again, his eyes strayed to the envelope. He wondered how much she'd managed to scrape together, not that he was going take one damn penny from her. Not after yesterday. Not after the kiss. Not after he'd held her in his arms.

From what little she'd told him, she had paid

dearly for her poor judgment, perhaps causing herself more pain than he had suffered. Starting over and building a new life for himself had made him a stronger man. Her own struggles had done the same for Annie. It had taken a lot of gumption on her part because there were so few viable options open to women. And she obviously had her pride, wanting to pay off Nick's debts just because he'd been her husband.

Well, to hell with her pride. He snapped up the envelope and his crutches and headed for the kitchen. She must have heard him coming, not that he could exactly sneak up on anybody thumping along as he did, because the back door slammed shut just as he crossed the threshold. Joe and Millie were staring at the door in astonishment.

As soon as Millie spied him, though, she nodded as if suddenly everything made sense. "That's your doing, isn't it?"

He didn't know whether to laugh or curse. He did a little of both. "Yes, Millie. Most women take one look at me and run for the nearest henhouse. I'm surprised you're not fleeing in utter horror right along with her." He tossed the envelope on the table. "When she gets tired of her feathered friends, give that to her. Tell her . . ." He paused, wanting to protect Annie's privacy but wanting a message delivered anyway. "Tell her it was a nice thought."

Then he went in his room and closed the door.

He had stretched out on the bed but he hadn't expected to fall asleep. The sounds of the door opening and someone moving around in the room gradually penetrated his dreams enough to wake him. He half expected to find Annie trying to hide the envelope somewhere in his things, but instead it was Joe.

"What did she say?"

Joe looked up from the stack of freshly ironed shirts he was putting away. "Nothing. In fact I think she left it laying right where you set it down." He put Isaac's own shirts in a neat pile on the table. "I don't suppose you'd like to tell me what's in it."

"You suppose right." He sat up and rubbed his eyes clear of his restless dreams. "What time is it?"

"We ate about an hour ago. I wanted to wake you up, but Annie said to let you sleep. She did set a plate on the stove to keep warm for you." He sat down on the other bed. "If you've got a minute, I'd like to talk to you." He stared at the floor, shifting his feet from side to side as if he couldn't quite get comfortable. "I guess there's nothing for it but to say it straight. I'm going to stay here in Willow Shoals and look for work."

Isaac looked up. One glance at his friend's worried expression had him smiling. "If it makes it easier, I've already talked to Barton. We're going to promote the second mate to take your place." He hated like hell to lose Joe, but it had to happen sometime.

"You know it's not because of what happened, don't you? I mean falling overboard had nothing to do with my decision." Then he gave Isaac a wry grin. "Well, maybe a little, but that's not the real reason at all."

"Of course not. You'd never quit over a minor mishap like that." He smiled to let his friend know he was kidding. "Millie, now there's a good reason to be looking to make a few changes."

"I never expected this to happen to me, Isaac." Joe shook his head. "Maybe it's because of everything that's gone on, what with both of us almost dying that night or something. But I swear, I took one look at Millie and nothing was the same."

"It can happen." He'd felt the same way ten years before when he'd walked into that saloon and saw Belle for the first time. In some ways, it had happened again over the past couple of weeks, even though Annie was so different from the woman he'd known before.

"Then you believe me." There was no missing the surprise in Joe's voice and eyes. "I'm planning on asking Millie to marry me. Maybe not right away, because she's sort of skittish right now. She doesn't think she's ready to build a life with another man." He dropped his voice in an attempt to make sure that his words didn't carry into the next room. "It's hell being jealous of a dead man, especially one I suspect I would have liked."

Again, Isaac knew how he felt, except that he had stopped liking Nick a long time ago. But the jealousy, that part was the same.

"Once the cargo is delivered, I'll make sure you get your share of the profits right away. You'll be needing all the money you can get now that you're going to have a family to look after."

"If she'll have me." He stared at the door, as if he could see straight through the thin wood to the woman he loved.

"Millie doesn't strike me as a fool, Joe. She'll have you all right and be damned glad about it."

"There's the problem of my nightmares, although they haven't been as bad since coming here." For a brief moment, his eyes looked haunted. "I told her about what I did in the war, but not about the dreams. I'll have to, though. It wouldn't be fair to her otherwise."

There had been more than a few nights that Joe had walked the decks, trying to outdistance the ghosts who had haunted him since the war. A talent for sharpshooting did not make for happy memories, but Isaac thought for sure that Millie was strong enough to handle the problem. And her loving heart would likely work wonders in healing his friend's wounded soul.

"I'm happy for you, Joe."

He meant it. He really did. And he was jealous as hell.

"I'm leaving tomorrow morning on the stage." Matthew set down his coffee cup and picked up a stack of papers. "I have all the information you've given me to take back to the bank."

"It's not much, I know." He half expected Matthew to refuse to present his case to his superiors. All in all, it looked pretty hopeless even to him.

"You haven't thought of anything else that might help, have you?" He was already shoving the documents into an envelope. "No secret accounts, no sudden gold strikes?"

His attempt to lighten a dark moment was pretty pathetic, but Isaac appreciated that he had at least tried. "It meant a lot to me that you came."

"I'm your friend, Isaac. No matter what happens, try to remember that."

Matthew's normally cheerful countenance looked strained. This hadn't been easy for him, either. It had to be hard for a man like Matthew who went out of his way to help people, especially those he cared about. If he did his job as he should, it was likely that he was going to be the one who stripped Isaac of the one thing in his life he'd worked so hard to attain.

"It will work out, Matthew," he lied. "I'm sure that something will turn up before it's too late."

"Well, I hope it does before the ice breaks up too much. If you're going to repair her, it'll have to be before the river lets go of her." He wasn't telling Isaac anything he didn't already know. Evidently he thought it was time to change the subject. "So where is everyone else?"

"Barton is upstairs. He said he had to leave at first light with the wagons if he hoped to get upriver by dark tomorrow night. He'd like to get there and back in three days, no more than four. Miss Barker retired for the night, saying she had a slight headache. Joe is playing chess in the kitchen with Millie." That accounted for everyone but Annie. He hadn't seen her since she hid in the chicken coop. He wondered if she was still there or if she'd found a better hiding place.

"Well, I hate to leave you all alone, but I need to get to bed. It's going to be a long, cold ride in that damn stagecoach." Matthew stood up and stretched. "I'll be glad to get back home, though. I hate to be away any length of time."

"I know you do. I'll try to see you off in the morning. But in case I don't make it for some reason, give Melissa and Cynthia my love." Damn, he'd forgotten all about buying a doll for Matthew's daughter. Now he'd have to send it by mail and hope it got there in time for Christmas. "Tell Cynthia that I'm sorry I won't be there to hear her."

"You could always come on the stage with me. There's not much for you to do here."

He really meant that it would be easier on Isaac to be away when the ice destroyed his lady. "I can't leave as long as the *Caprice* is here." He'd stay until the problem was resolved one way or the other. He owed it to himself to keep trying to save her.

"Take care of yourself, Matthew."

His friend looked as if he wanted to say something more, but in the end he stopped by Isaac's chair long enough to squeeze his shoulder and then disappeared up the stairs.

It was almost a relief to be left alone to stare into the fire in desperate solitude. He was far more used to being surrounded by the constant noise of life on the river. The paddle wheel was never quiet except when the boat was tied up at a landing. Someone was always moving around in the pilothouse keeping watch on their course. And of course, the passengers often stayed up until the wee hours of the morning playing poker or smoking cigars out by the railing.

Life on shore was a much lonelier proposition. He had rooms at a hotel that acted as a poor substitute for the captain's quarters he had on board. In fact, he would have lived on the boat all the time, but sometimes business required that he stay ashore.

He looked around Annie's parlor. She had done

a nice job of making this boardinghouse feel warm and friendly. The furniture wasn't new and wasn't fancy, but it was comfortable and cozy to come home to. The place was clean and the food both plentiful and good. Hell, if the place had a noisy wheel cranking night and day, it would be almost as good a place to live as the *Caprice*.

That was a hell of a thing for an avowed steamboat man to admit.

He gradually realized he was no longer alone. Annie stood behind him, hovering at the edge of the room. He kept his eyes on the flames in the fireplace, content to watch them dance and dart as he waited for her to make up her mind to come in or go up to bed. Finally, he decided to tweak her nose a bit.

"What's the matter, Annie? Did you get tired of living with the chickens?"

"Shut up, Isaac." Her words were tart but held no real heat.

"Come on in and sit down. I'll share my quilt if you ask nice." He patted the spot beside him on the sofa. "I'd promise to behave, but I'm not sure that's true."

"I'll risk it. For one thing, I know I can outrun you."

She sat down, leaving no more than a hand's width between them. He offered her the edge of the quilt. She pulled it over her and let their shared warmth and silence settle between them. He was tempted to put his arm around her shoulders and close that irritating gap she'd left, but he didn't want to risk running her off.

She broke the brief silence. "Why didn't you take the money, Isaac? You asked for it."

Her eyes remained focused on the fire. He turned to watch the shadows and light dance across her face. "Because you weren't the one who took it."

"You only have my word for that."

"For some reason, that's good enough for me." And to his surprise, it was. She'd betrayed him on one level, but she'd never denied that. It hurt, it made him furious, but it was the truth. Maybe he should lie to himself and claim that she owed him even if she hadn't been the one to benefit from the missing cash. But as much as he wanted to punish her for leaving him, even if it meant taking her last penny, he had to live with his own conscience. There had been many dark nights when that would have seemed like a dream come true. And if he'd run into Belle playing rowdy music in a saloon, maybe he would have still thought about it.

But Annie was no longer Belle, and he wasn't enough of a son of a bitch to do it to a woman like her. Besides, in many ways, he'd actually come through the experience stronger than before. Without the fight to prove himself, he probably would have settled in his hometown and shoveled shit out of the stable or worked stocking shelves at the mercantile for a living. Instead, he'd built a life for himself that he was damned proud of.

And if he lost everything, he would cuss a little— or rather a lot—and then start digging himself out of the hole he was in. He'd done it before and succeeded. He would do so again.

But tonight, he would let Matthew be the one to do all the fretting about Isaac's future. Instead, he would enjoy the warmth of the fire with a beautiful woman at his side. Come sunup tomorrow would be soon enough to worry about his future again.

"Can I get you anything?" Annie was already throwing off her side of the quilt. "I'm going to fix myself a cup of tea."

"Actually, that sounds good." He tucked the blanket back down around his legs to keep in the warmth—her warmth—until she returned. "Any chance that there are any of Millie's cookies left to go with it?"

"I know where her secret hiding place is." Annie winked at him and left in a swirl of skirts and the scent of lavender.

He wondered how she felt about their kiss. Hell, he didn't know how he felt about it himself, except that it had sent a rush of heat burning through him that had kept him warm for hours afterward. Even now, his body was hungering for more; the rest of him, though, was feeling a little more skittish. Now that Belle had changed into Annie, she wasn't the type of woman a man trifled with. But damn, he wanted to do a lot more than trifle with her. Images filled his mind of tangled limbs and hot, soul-scorching kisses. Of course there was the little matter of his broken leg, but he was sure they could work around it.

A rattle of china announced Annie's return, jarring him out of his reverie. He was glad for the quilt that hid his body's response to her. He watched as she set a tray down on a small table and pulled it closer to sit between them. After pouring two cups, she added a double serving of sugar to his before handing it to him. He grinned when he saw the stack of cookies.

"Will we be in trouble with Millie? She might have been saving them for Joe."

Not that he cared. He reached for a handful.

"You might have to worry some, but she thinks I don't eat enough." Annie settled back on the sofa and sipped at her tea.

"I'll claim you ate them all. I can see it now." He opened his eyes wide and innocent. "Why, Miss Millie, I swear I've never seen such a little bit of a woman devour so much! I tried to tell her those cookies were being saved for a special occasion."

Annie laughed at his antics but slapped at his hand when he tried to snag another one off the plate. "She'll never believe you. I've never eaten more than three cookies at a time as long as she's known me."

After only one bite of the spicy cookie, he had decided he would willingly risk Millie's wrath. She could do her worst to him; it was worth every crumb. He'd even fight Joe over the rest that were still stashed somewhere in the kitchen.

"I hear Matthew is leaving in the morning and so is Barton." She looked at him over the rim of her cup. "Is that good news?"

He didn't want to talk about it, but she had a right to know what her guests were doing. After all, she had meals to plan for. "Matthew wants to get home to his wife and daughter. And he needs to find out what the bank is willing to do about the mess I'm in. Barton offered to go along with the wagons I hired to deliver most of the cargo. He hopes to be back in three days, four at the most."

"You'll feel better about things when that's taken care of."

"Maybe." There wasn't much else he could say. He wasn't going to feel good about much of anything for a while. At least until he knew the fate of the boat.

"I'm sorry that all this has happened to you, Isaac. You didn't deserve it." She reached out to touch his arm, her dark eyes warm with sympathy. "I want to do whatever I can to help. If you won't take the money as payment of a debt, will you take it as a loan? It's not all that much, but it would be a start."

"No!" The word came out sharper than he meant for it to, startling her into spilling some of her tea. He dug into his pocket for his handkerchief and did his best to blot it up. "Did it scald you?"

She shook her head. Maybe the tea hadn't burned her, but his snarl of a response had. It was there in her eyes, making him feel like a brute. She immediately set down her cup and moved as if to leave.

When he took her arm and tried to tug her back down beside him, though, she let him. That didn't mean she was in a hurry to forgive his outburst.

"I'm sorry, Annie. I'm frustrated and I'm angry. Most of the time I can keep a lid on my temper, but sometimes I lash out without thinking." When she didn't try to yank her arm free, he let go. "At this point, I don't even know if more money will help the *Caprice*. It all depends on what happens when the ice breaks up. Until then, it's anybody's guess what it will take to repair her."

The corner of Annie's mouth kicked up in a smile. "You men all talk about that boat as if it were a living, breathing woman."

He didn't try to deny it. "All boats are feminine.

The *Caprice* sure enough has her moods. Some days she's all grace and beauty as she moves through the water. Other times, she has to be coaxed into it. There's real strength in her. A lesser boat would have gone down the other night, but she hung on until she got us to safety."

"Except for you and Joe," she reminded him. It seemed that all the women in his life were fickle. Herself included.

"That was our own damn fault. Ask Joe; he'll tell you that if he'd been more careful, he wouldn't have gone overboard in the first place. If he hadn't, I wouldn't have had to dive in after him."

He sounded indignant, as if she had insulted his ladylove. She was tempted to point out that the boat's paddle wheel had almost killed him, but there was no use in testing his temper any more. Fighting wasn't what she had in mind when she had given in to the impulse to sit with him rather than going on up to her room alone.

On the other hand, she wasn't sure at all what she'd had in mind. Certainly, she didn't want him to kiss her again. Absolutely not. Never again. It had taken her hours to calm down after the last time. He might have laughed at her for hiding with the chickens, but she'd needed some time away from him and everyone else to convince herself that she had no desire for a repeat performance.

But she did. Even now, she was tempting fate by sitting so close to him. Despite the chill in the room, she was comfortable, almost hot. She fingered the quilt that covered both of them. It was thick and soft, but it had never kept her this toasty warm be-

fore. Had the quick embrace meant anything at all
to him?

"Annie?"

There was a huskiness to his voice that hadn't
been there before. It made her all edgy, as if she
couldn't sit still a minute longer. She managed to
croak out an answer. "Yes?"

"I've been thinking about what happened ear-
licr."

Her throat closed, making it difficult to breathe
and impossible to talk. Or to protest the way his
arm snaked around her shoulder to pull her across
that small zone of safety she'd left between them.
Instead of fighting him, she let the moment carry
her away, right into his arms. It felt like coming
home.

This kiss was no mere flirtation. It was deadly serious and about the most exciting thing that had
ever happened to her. He had problems, and so
did she, but for the moment, nothing else existed
except the two of them.

He touched; she sighed. He explored; she followed his lead. The old quilt kept them wrapped
in a world that contained just two people, both needing a little touching, a little loving, and a lot of each
other. His lips brushed across hers, finally settling
firmly centered over hers when she shyly invited
him in.

"Lord of mercy, Annie," he murmured. He
cupped his hand along the curve of her jaw and
caressed her cheek with the pad of his thumb. "I
wish we . . ." His voice trailed off as he kissed her
again. He tasted of molasses and a spicy flavor that
was all man and made her ache for so much more.

She gave in to the temptation to run her fingers through his hair, its highlights burnished red and gold by the firelight. What had he been wishing for? It didn't matter. At that moment, there wasn't anything she could have wanted more than she wanted to be in this man's arms, tasting his kisses, feeling the heat of his hands as they learned how the gentle curve of her body fit so well along the strength of his.

She didn't know whether she pushed him down on the sofa or if he laid back and tumbled her down on top of him. Either way, she found herself looking down into his laughing eyes. When he winced a bit when she landed on his bad leg, she tried to scramble off, but he shifted her slightly to one side and held her there.

"Don't move."

"But your leg, Isaac." She could barely talk, her lips felt swollen and her breath was shallow and rapid.

His answering chuckle could be felt the length of her body, sending new sparks of desire shooting through her. "Honey, believe me. I'm not feeling any pain right now. At least not in my leg." Then he tugged her mouth down to his. "Kiss me, Annie, and I'll be fine."

She did as he asked, only too glad to give in to his demands. His hands roamed up and down her back and then down lower to cup her backside. He settled her over the pressing evidence of his hot desire. He thrust up against her, sending jolts of hot wanting through her.

The quilt had long since slid down to the floor, but neither of them noticed the cold. Isaac was too busy trying to loosen the buttons on the front of Annie's dress. Finally, she put her hands on his chest and pushed herself up to grant him better access. The new angle created new pressure against him at the juncture of her thighs. She threw her head back and whimpered with the sheer wonder of it all.

Then he had her dress open and her chemise untied. "Lovely, Annie, just lovely." He filled his hands with her breasts and gently kneaded them. It helped, but she wanted, needed, so much more. Then he was suckling, first one then the other, tenderly and then with increasing strength.

"Isaac!" His wicked hands had already moved on, tugging her skirt up to her waist. Then his fingers slipped past the waistband of her drawers to learn the curves of her bottom.

"Annie, I want to take you, but I can't with my leg." He punctuated his words with a trail of kisses along the valley between her breasts. "I need to be inside you, honey. Help mc."

He'd found the core of her, testing her readiness for what had to come next. She thought she knew what he wanted, but she wasn't sure how to go about it. Her experience with Nick hadn't taught her much about all the ways it could be between a man and a woman.

"Tell me what to do."

"Lift up."

When she did as he asked, he reached for the buttons on his pants. She tried to help, but her fingers fumbled too much. He brushed them aside with a ragged laugh. Then he stopped and looked up at her, his eyes wild and hot.

"I want to know that you want this, Annie, before we go any farther. I have almost enough control to stop now, but just barely."

And he would if it killed him, if that's what she wanted. Hell, he'd waited almost ten years to kiss her. He could wait awhile longer to bed her. But, damn, surrounded by the scent of her and the taste of her sweet breasts still on his tongue, he wanted it all.

Her eyes looked away. "I've never . . . not this way."

"It's easy, honey. So easy." He helped her slip off her drawers, leaving nothing between them but the slip-sliding heat that was starting to build again. He kissed her again, enjoying the crush of her breasts against his chest. He rocked her a bit, so that he was poised at the opening of her body. Then he lifted her up and over, letting her take her time taking him deep inside her.

He thought he'd die as she slowly, so damned slowly, eased down until he was buried in her damp heat. Then he guided her up and down, until she figured out the rhythm for herself. He had always figured her for a quick learner.

And then all coherent thought fled him, possibly forever, the way his mind lost contact with everything except the growing pressure to explode with screaming pleasure.

"Annie, that's it, that's it," he encouraged her.

Even in the dim light of the fading fire, he was entranced by her beauty. He pulled the pins from her hair, sending it cascading down her back in dark chocolate waves. If the moment could have lasted for an eternity, he would have been content.

But the pleasure was too intense for mere mortals. No longer in control, he urged her higher and faster until the night shattered around them. He yanked Annie down to kiss her, muffling her pleasured moans and his own, until the need to keen out their satisfaction faded into the quiet of the night. He managed to drag the quilt back up off the floor to partially cover them both.

Annie lay sprawled in a boneless heap across him, their bodies still connected. She was so quiet that at first he thought she'd fallen asleep just that quickly. Instead, she was already thinking beyond the moment.

"Isaac, has it always been like that for you?" she whispered.

"I think it would have killed me years ago if that were the case." Then he pressed a gentle kiss against her damp forehead. The moment demanded honesty. "Annie, it's never been like that before. Not once. Not ever."

"I didn't know." Her voice faded, leaving the rest of her thought unspoken.

What didn't she know? That a woman deserved the same satisfaction that a man demanded? He didn't ask. The last thing he wanted was the spectre of Nick hovering over them, not now of all times.

He tucked her head down against his shoulder, amazed at how perfectly she fit against him. He knew they couldn't stay this way for long. With five other people in the house, they risked discovery with each passing moment. He didn't want to be the one to bring up the subject for fear she'd think he wanted to hurry her off now that he'd gotten under her skirts.

That was the farthest thing from his mind, but

he knew women could be pretty touchy at such a time. Evidently, though, her mind was running along the same lines because she stirred a bit.

"I'd better go, Isaac. Millie might get worried if she doesn't hear me go up to my room soon." Her eyes were wide, dark pools as she looked down at him.

He pulled her down for one last, lingering kiss. "I don't want to let you go. I've thought about this moment for so long, I'm afraid it's all a dream."

"Me, too."

She kissed him one last time before trying to extricate herself from the tangle of quilt and twisted clothing. With care, she managed to make it to her feet without jarring his leg again, for which he was grateful. Even though she had been the one who'd done all the real work, his leg ached from all the exertion.

"Do you need any help?" It hadn't taken her long at all to get herself decently covered again.

He already missed the sweet feel of her skin sliding over his. He also hated feeling so damn helpless all the time, but he wasn't going to let that ruin his good mood. "I think I can manage on my own, but maybe you'd better stick close by to make sure."

Annie nodded. "I'll just take the dishes back to the kitchen. I'll check on you on my way back through."

He appreciated her understanding. Some women would have wanted to hover or, worse yet, cling to him because of what had just happened between them. Annie allowed him some sense of privacy but without abandoning him completely.

The longer he was around her, the more he realized how special she had become to him. Again. It had taken him years to get her out of his system the last time. How would he manage to do it again now that he knew the sweetness of her touch, her kiss, her body? The thought scared him clean through and through, making him feel sick deep inside. Once she left the room, he hurried to push himself up off the sofa. In his haste to do for himself, his hands fumbled a bit with the buttons on his trousers. Finally, though, he got the job done and was buttoning up his shirt when he heard her coming back his way.

"Is everything all right?" she asked, meaning could he get himself off to bed without help.

"Everything is fine, Annie." He meant he could reach his room, but the truth was nothing was fine. He wondered if it ever would be.

She looked at him with questions in her eyes, but she didn't ask them. Instead, she started up the stairs, leaving him to fend for himself. He tried to tell himself that was what he wanted. After all, he'd been doing so for a damn long time. But the house felt extra cold and a whole lot lonelier as he limped his way back to the room he shared with Joe.

Making love to Annie was the best thing he'd ever done—and possibly the worst mistake he'd ever made.

CHAPTER
THIRTEEN

By the time Annie finally awoke, the sun had already climbed a fair way up into the sky. She felt groggy and thickheaded, probably from tossing and turning for a good portion of the night. By the time she dragged herself downstairs, she felt like she'd already wasted most of the morning. On her way past the parlor she checked the clock, only to find out that she'd been right about the time.

On any other day, she would have fussed at Millie long and hard for letting her sleep in so late. But considering the turmoil she was feeling, it had probably been a blessing. She wasn't sure she was up to facing Isaac across the breakfast table, not until she'd had some time to come to terms with the abrupt change in their relationship.

It took her a little longer to realize how quiet the house was. That worried her more than she cared to admit. It didn't take long to track Joe and Millie down in the kitchen. From the looks of things, breakfast had been over for some time. Annie tried to act as if it were perfectly normal for her to come strolling into the kitchen at mid-morning as she poured herself a cup of coffee. She made a face when she sipped it, never having been fond of the bitter taste of coffee that had set too long.

Careful to sound only mildly curious, she asked, "Where is everybody?"

She hated to ask the question, fearing the answer, but the house had an empty feel to it that had been missing since before the night the *Caprice* had run aground. When Millie immediately focused her attention on scrubbing a spot off the table and Joe found the henhouse out the kitchen window to be fascinating, she knew she'd been right to worry.

"Millie?"

Finally her friend dragged her attention away from the already immaculate table long enough to answer. "They've all gone."

Annie had known that Barton had planned on leaving before first light and that Matthew had booked a ticket for the early stage, but that didn't account for Isaac's apparent absence. Keeping her eyes firmly away from his bedroom door, she sat down at the table and continued to drink her coffee.

"Would you like some bacon and eggs?" Millie's smile was too bright to be believable.

"Some bread and butter will hold me until later." Why were the two of them acting as if they were walking on thin ice? It was as if they were tiptoeing around something that they both knew and didn't want to have to tell her.

Rather than let them stew about it, she went right for the heart of the matter. "Where is Isaac?"

"He left with Matthew." Millie wrung out her cleaning rag, slapped it down on the counter, and started scrubbing again. "Said he has business to tend to."

Up until then, Joe had remained quiet, obviously not wanting to draw attention to himself as the sole remaining male in the household. Annie figured she wouldn't get anything positive out of Millie, so she tried him. "Joe, do you know anything about his sudden change in plans?"

His eyes flicked to Millie and back to Annie as he considered his answer. "Well, I know he and Matthew were both worried about what the bank would have to say about everything."

"We've known that all along." She held out her cup to Millie in a silent request for more coffee. Her stomach would probably revolt, but she needed something to keep her hands occupied. "I'm just surprised that he left without letting me . . . I mean all of us know what his plans were."

"All I can think of is that Matthew thought of something that required Isaac's personal attention." Joe's smile was halfhearted at best.

Millie mumbled something under her breath as she rinsed out her rag again. If anything, she managed to make even more noise with her efforts to clean. Annie and Joe were both careful to ignore her for the moment.

"I know he'll be back, Annie."

The sympathy in Joe's voice was almost her undoing. The last thing she wanted from Isaac or any of his friends was pity. She was rather proud of the calm demeanor she presented.

"Of course he will."

Millie joined in. "Well, he can't very well come walking back through that door any old time he wants to, Joe. Annie has other tenants to consider, you know. She can't keep that room empty for his convenience."

"I sleep there, too, Millie. Am I in the way?"

Joe knew full well he wasn't, but for some reason Annie appreciated his comment. Although the news that Isaac had left with Matthew surprised her, she wasn't angry about it, at least not exactly. She was more concerned and confused.

And she and Isaac had caused each other enough pain in the past because of wrong assumptions and misunderstandings. She of all people couldn't say much about someone who might have panicked a bit when a relationship had turned too serious. No, no matter what his reasons were, she wasn't going to jump to any conclusions without talking to him first. She owed him that much.

Amazingly, once she decided that was how she was going to proceed, her stomach settled.

She realized that she'd missed out on part of the conversation between Millie and Joe. Joe looked frustrated while Millie was still slamming things around, letting the noise express her bad mood. It was time to take charge of the situation.

"Joe, you are welcome here as long as you want to stay, even after Isaac gets the boat repaired." She smiled at him, wanting him to know the invitation was sincere. "And I'm sure Isaac knows I have a business to run here, but as long as you don't mind sharing a room with him, then there's no real problem."

Turning her attention back to Millie, she asked,

"Do we having anything special going on today? I have a rehearsal this afternoon at two."

"I need to buy a few things at the store. I'll wait until later, though, so I can pick up the mail at the same time." She stepped out on the back porch and slung the dirty wash water out onto the snow. When she came back in, she went on. "I thought I'd spend some time working on some candy bags. We're going to need more if we're going to give them to all the children Christmas Eve."

Annie was relieved to see her friend's mood improve. She appreciated Millie's concern, but whatever problems Annie had with Isaac were strictly her own concern. In fact, if Joe hadn't been sitting there, she would have told Millie that directly. If Millie was going to make a go of it with Joe, she was going to have to learn to get along with Isaac. After all, the two men had known each other for years. It wouldn't be fair to make Joe choose between his friend and the woman he loved.

"Well, I'd better go make beds and dust a bit." Between the rehearsals at church and the extra work because of the men, she'd fallen behind in her routine chores. She wasn't sure either of the other two in the kitchen noticed when she left. But despite Millie's uncertain mood, Annie was sure Joe could handle it. He didn't strike her as a man who would be easily deterred from reaching his goal.

And it was pretty obvious he had a few specific goals in mind when it came to Millie. One of which was probably pretty similar to the experience Isaac and Annie had shared the night before on the parlor sofa. When she thought about how reckless the two of them had been, she blushed. Not that she regretted a minute of the time she'd spent in his arms.

Looking back, she realized Nick had known that although he'd managed to take Annie away from Isaac, he would never have her heart. To get even, he had made a point of making her feel like less than a woman. He'd told her often enough what a cold fish she was, both in bed and out of it. Maybe she did deserve some of his comments, but she'd always hoped that things would be a little better with the right man.

She just hadn't expected that man to be Isaac. And the experience had been so much more than just a little better. It was as if she'd never before been bedded. That thought brought a reluctant smile to her face as she started up the stairs with her dust cloth and a broom. She was hardly a virgin, but just as Isaac had been her first love, in one sense, he had also been her first real lover.

What had happened in the bed she'd shared with Nick had had very little to do with love and a lot to do with control. When he failed to make her love him, then he'd settled for forcing her to do his will. She had retaliated by refusing to respond to him, whether he approached her with gentleness or the fits of temper he was more prone to.

She was not particularly proud of her own behavior during those years. There was no excuse for his.

So rather than getting overly upset over Isaac's rather rapid departure after the unexpected events of the previous evening, she would reserve judgment until she saw him again. Both of them had pretty powerful emotions to work through. Maybe he needed the time apart to think clearly. Satisfied with her reasoning, she found herself humming a song as she climbed the stairs.

Miss Barker opened the door to her room as Annie was passing by. "Oh, Annie, I was hoping to see you."

Annie turned and came back down the steps. "Is there something you need, Agatha?" It still felt strange to call the older woman by her first name.

"Well, yes. You know Christmas is almost upon us."

Annie counted off the days in her mind. "It is, isn't it? Not even a week away. That doesn't seem possible. Why, wasn't it only a few days ago that we celebrated Thanksgiving?" Where had the time gone?

"Well, I was wondering if you knew if all three of your gentlemen boarders will still be here to celebrate with us? I'd hate to not have a gift for them, seeing as they are so far from home."

"That's mighty nice of you to think of that, Agatha. I suspect that Joe is planning on being here indefinitely. Barton will be back in a day or two, and I believe he'll stay on until the problem with the *Caprice* is resolved one way or the other." What should she say about Isaac? She couldn't very well say that he'd run off after canoodling with her on the parlor sofa. Finally, she settled for part of the truth. "I don't know what Captain Chase's plans are."

Agatha's expression was a little too knowing for her comfort. What had the older woman seen or heard to put that look in her eyes?

"Don't you fret about Captain Isaac, my dear. I may not have ever been married myself, but that doesn't mean I don't know a little about men. The way that man looks at you is enough to make a woman swoon." She pretended to fan herself with the flat of her hand, a wicked twinkle lighting her eyes. "I think I'll just plan on all three of them being here. You just wait and see, my dear. We'll have a Christmas like you've never seen before."

"I'm looking forward to it."

As she continued on her way upstairs, she realized that to her surprise, that was true. In the past, Christmas had come and gone with little notice, but not this year. Perhaps it was because she now had a sense of really belonging in Willow Shoals, with real friends, not just a handful of boarders who came and went as the mood hit them. She suspected that helping with the church program had broken through that last barrier that had made her feel like an outsider.

All things considered, the problem had been with her, not with the rest of the congregation. The minister and his wife had always gone out of their way to be friendly. Maybe it was time for her to talk to Pastor Chesterfield about her past. She had a strong suspicion he would understand. Once he knew, she wouldn't feel like she was hiding behind a thin veneer of respectability.

Feeling better than she had in a long time, she made quick work of straightening her own room. Next she stripped the sheets in Barton's room and replaced them with clean ones. On an impulse, she tucked some dried lavender under the sheets to give his bedding a summer-fresh scent. After dusting the furniture, she gathered up his dirty laundry and bundled it up with the sheets. There should be time to have it all washed and pressed before he returned. She normally charged extra for such services, but it was almost Christmas. Besides, he had done a fair amount of extra chores around the house since he'd been staying there. It was a fair trade.

By the time she'd finished giving the upper two floors a quick going-over, Millie had left to run her errands and Joe was nowhere to be found. It didn't surprise her to find out that he'd accompanied Millie to the store. Annie took advantage of his absence to give his room some attention. At first she kept her eyes carefully averted from the bed that Isaac had been occupying.

But once she'd changed Joe's sheets, she had no choice but to do the same for Isaac's. That's when she noticed something that sent a flutter of excitement through her. Some, maybe even most, of Isaac's personal belongings were still scattered around the room. She peeked under the bed and found a few boxes shoved back out of the way. It looked like the stuff they'd carried off the boat. She wasn't nosy enough to go through them, but she knew for certain that they didn't belong to her or Millie. That was all that mattered.

It wasn't exactly proof that Isaac hadn't completely abandoned her, but it was a far cry better than thinking he'd turned tail and run for good. He'd be back sometime. She might not know when, but he'd be back. She allowed herself a quick dance step up and down the narrow space between the two beds.

It wouldn't be prudent to read more meaning into the situation than just the basic facts that he'd left with the intention of returning at some point. She wouldn't even say anything to Millie unless she happened to say something herself. Besides, certainly Joe would eventually notice, if he hadn't already. Maybe that's why he'd seemed so unconcerned about Isaac's sudden absence.

Feeling better than she had in hours, she hummed and sang her way through the rest of her housework until it was time to leave for the church.

"Millie, wait up."

Joe was getting damn sick and tired of apologizing for his friend's decision to up and leave without a word. It was hardly his fault that Isaac could be an inconsiderate bastard. Maybe he had good reason to bolt for the door. Annie's eyes had the same haunted look to them this morning.

Isaac still hadn't told Joe anything about his past encounter with Annie. Maybe he'd said something to Barton, but Joe doubted it. Whatever it was involved some pretty powerful memories and feelings. And he was willing to bet it wasn't all one-sided. Annie's disappointment had been pretty damn easy to see when she'd realized that he'd gone. Maybe she had some good reasons to be upset, but she'd actually seemed to take the news calmly.

That was more than he could say about the irate lady who insisted on walking at least two steps ahead of him all the way to their destination. Once inside the dry-goods store, she'd treated him like a pack animal, letting him carry the few items that she'd insisted she couldn't live without a moment longer. Once she handed the store owner enough money to pay for her purchases, she'd turned on her heel and marched back out, leaving Joe to follow as he would. She'd even left her basket on the counter for him to carry for her.

He didn't mind that, but he did mind paying for crimes he'd yet to commit. If she didn't slow down and talk to him, he'd show her a whole new meaning of stubborn. Damn it, what was wrong with her?

He checked his watch. If he remembered correctly, Annie was due to be at the church for the next couple of hours. He wasn't sure what Miss Barker's plans were for the day, but she rarely ventured out of her room except for meals. Rather than confront Millie out in public, he'd bide his time. He slowed his pace and let her continue to outdistance him.

Maybe he'd even stop at the saloon and have a shot of whiskey. That idea sounded so good, he veered off at the next corner and took a roundabout route back to his new destination. If Millie happened to glance back to check on his whereabouts, she'd have no idea what had happened to him. He didn't want to worry her—much, anyway—but he didn't want her to take his good nature for granted, either.

He felt a little foolish carrying a woman's basket into a saloon, but no one seemed to notice. There were few enough customers this early in the day anyway. He headed straight for the bar and tossed down a couple of coins.

"Whiskey please." He added another coin. "Make it the good stuff."

The bartender poured him a generous helping in a fairly clean glass and shoved it across the scarred surface of the bar. "That will warm you up some."

"I hope so." Joe knew better than to drink it too fast. Even the so-called good stuff could burn right through a man's gut if he weren't careful. He sipped at it, enjoying the slow spread of heat that started in his stomach and moved outward. He didn't linger over it too long, though. He had business to see to and wanted some degree of privacy to carry it out.

While he leaned against the bar, he considered the possibilities. He had every intention of claiming his woman, once and for all. Millie had her doubts about him and his intention to settle in Willow Shoals. Having Isaac take off so suddenly had only fed into her fears. Unless he missed his guess, that accounted for her prickly mood and short temper.

But he wasn't Isaac, and if the two of them were going to make a go of things, she had to quit comparing him to other men, her dead husband included.

Most of the heat he was feeling had nothing at all to do with the whiskey. Yep, he had some damn fine plans for the next hour or so. He closed his eyes and imagined Millie's response when he laid her down and made sure she knew exactly who was bedding her. He wouldn't have waited this damn long to lay claim to her, but the house had been too damn crowded.

Anxious to be about his business, he set the empty glass down on the bar and walked back out into the biting cold sunshine. It didn't take him long to walk the few blocks back to the house. He caught a movement at the edge of the front window. She was watching for him but didn't want him to know it. He managed to hide his grin.

She was nowhere in sight when he stepped through the door and set down her basket. He hung up his coat and tried rubbing some warmth back into his hands. It wouldn't do to put icy fingers on Millie's smooth skin.

The sound of footsteps on the staircase caught his attention. Miss Barker was just coming down. He was pleased to take note she was bundled up to go outside.

"Good afternoon, Miss Barker. Where are you off to this chilly afternoon?"

"A friend invited me over to do some sewing together. Would you please let Annie or Millie know that I won't be returning until well after the evening meal?"

"I'd be glad to, ma'am." He opened the door for her. "Do you know where Millie might be?"

Miss Barker gave him a rather knowing look. "Why, I do believe I heard her go up to her room just as you came in. Until later, Joe."

He took the steps two at a time, not bothering to try to muffle the noise he was making. He wanted Millie to know he was coming. Outside her door, he took a deep breath, knowing that he was about to cross a threshold that meant far more than simply going through a door.

He knocked loudly. She kept him waiting a full minute before answering his summons. The door opened a crack.

"Is there something you needed, Mr. Cutter?"

Oh, yeah, he needed all right. "Let me in, Millie."

He pushed on the door with enough pressure to

let her know he was serious about it. She resisted him briefly and then threw the door open wide.

"Are you in the habit of forcing your way into a lady's room?"

He pushed past her. "No, as a matter of fact, I'm not."

"Then what do you want?" She backed away, keeping a wary distance between them.

It was time to lay his cards on the table. "You, Millie. I want you." He didn't want to corner her. This had to be a mutual decision if it was going to work.

"Millie, I'm not your husband, and I'm not Isaac either. I can't promise I won't up and die on you, but as long as I draw breath, I'll be here for you. You have my word on that." He reached out to touch her sweet, worried face. "I don't know how to convince you that I mean that other than to say it over and over again until you believe me."

She rubbed her face against the rough texture of his hand. "I want to believe you, Joe. But all this scares me. It's all so sudden."

"I've been looking for you my whole life, sweetheart. It doesn't feel sudden to me." He was close enough now to fill his senses with the scent of her. "I want you so damned much."

Then just that quickly she was in his arms, kissing him as if he were her lifeline. When he eased them both back onto her bed, he knew he'd found peace at last.

The stagecoach driver took direct aim at every damn pothole in the road. Isaac had been flung from one side of the seat to the other so often, he was surprised he hadn't worn the seat of his pants clean through. What had he been thinking of when he'd decided to go back to face the bank with Matthew?

He knew the answer to that. He hadn't been thinking at all. Instead, he'd fled Willow Shoals in an all-out panic. He wasn't proud of his actions, but at least he was being honest with himself about what he was doing. Never in his whole life had he felt more like a coward than he did at that moment.

How long would it have taken him to write a simple note? Minutes at worst. Instead, he'd thrown a couple of changes of clothing into his valise, grabbed his shaving gear and headed out into the bleak early hours of the morning to make his escape.

And Matthew, damn him, had the effrontery to be sleeping through the lurching and jostling of this never-ending hell of a ride. At least there were only the two of them in the coach. He needed most of the seat to prop up his leg, not that he'd yet found a way to brace himself in one position.

A steady stream of muffled curses from the driver was the only proof he had that someone was still at the reins. Otherwise, he would have sworn they were tearing across country totally at the mercy of the gods. It had been years since he'd traveled by coach, and if there was a God in heaven, it would be years before he had to do so again once he made the return trip to Willow Shoals.

He had to go back.

His beloved *Caprice* was still a prisoner of the river.

His personal belongings were still tucked under the bed in his room.

And Annie was there.

He leaned back and closed his eyes. The sweet memories of making love with her carried him away from the constant discomfort of the coach. Who knew that a woman's skin could taste so sweet or that her body could be such a perfect fit to a man's? If he never knew such an amazing experience again in his life, he would die a contented man.

Would she understand what had driven him out of her house, out of her town? Maybe if she did, she would be kind enough to explain it to him. All he knew was that he'd found it all but impossible to sleep after he'd made his way to his bed after they had . . . There were no words to describe what they'd shared.

Had they just managed to scratch an itch that had been plaguing them both for too damn many years? He hoped not. He wasn't sure he'd survive anything better than what they'd shared, especially considering how restricted his own participation had been. Normally, he took some pride in his ability to make a woman feel both treasured and pleasured. The small play on words made him smile. But last night, it had been all Annie.

How had he ever been stupid enough to think he'd gotten over her?

"Those are some serious damn thoughts you're having." Matthew had pushed his hat back up from shading his eyes. He stretched out his arms and sat up straighter. "Somehow, though, I suspect that it isn't the *Caprice* that has you all twisted up in knots."

"Go to hell, Matthew." His friend always did see more than was good for either one of them. "No matter what I'm thinking, it's none of your business."

"Belle has changed. Even I can see that." Matthew kept his eyes carefully focused on the limited view out the window. "Of course, I never knew her all that well, but Annie is nothing at all like I expected." Did Matthew realize he was talking about her as if she were two different women? Maybe that wasn't too far off the mark.

Either way, however, Isaac wanted his friend to go back to sleep. As long as he was awake, he'd keep pushing in that sneaky, never ask a direct question way of his until he knew every detail of Isaac's life.

He glanced toward Isaac before he resumed talking. "I had an interesting discussion with her friend Millie. Seems Annie bought the boarding-house with a small amount of cash and has done most of the work fixing it up herself. From what her friend says, the previous owners had all but ruined the place. Even that piano in the parlor was destined for the trash heap until Annie got her hands on it." There was a hint of pure admiration in his voice. "She pays her bills on time and keeps her boarders happy. The only reason she had room for you and your men was that a couple of the women who live there left town until after the first of the year."

He wasn't telling Isaac anything he didn't already know, even if he'd been too damn stubborn to notice at first. The story about the piano shouldn't have surprised either of them. After all, it was Belle's gift for music that had kept her steadily employed all those years ago.

"I'm glad for her." And he was. Somewhere along the line, his anger had faded into something else. It wasn't exactly friendship; but he was afraid to think what would happen if it were something more. "She had a rough time of it growing up."

Isaac hesitated before saying more, but Matthew would keep anything he said to himself. As a banker, he'd had years of practice being discreet. "You know, her father was a gambler and not a very good one. He wore his wife out, dragging her and Annie from town to town, chasing down a winning hand. From what Annie told me, she's seen the inside of more saloons than you and me combined. When her pa's luck turned bad and stayed that way, she started playing piano for enough money to keep them fed."

"You never told me that before."

Was there a note of censure in that comment? If so, he probably deserved it. But once she'd left him, he hadn't wanted anyone to feel any sympathy except for him. Besides, at that point, what had it really mattered?

The rocking of the coach slowed appreciably. Isaac maneuvered his weary body to get a better look out the window. "Looks like we're coming into town." The knot in his stomach tightened as they passed by Matthew's bank.

"What do you think they'll say?" He hated to put his friend on the spot, but he needed to know what he was going to be facing.

"We're almost home, Isaac. Let's get a good night's sleep under our belts before we start working out our strategy." Matthew looked as worried as Isaac felt.

"*Our* strategy?" It was Isaac's boat, after all.

Matthew's employer might stand to lose some money. Isaac's whole livelihood and that of his men were on the line.

"Hell, yes, *our* strategy. Did you think I was going to leave you out on that wobbly limb all by yourself?" Matthew slammed his hand down on the seat, clearly offended by Isaac's insinuation. "Do you think the president of the bank was thrilled to have me take off upriver with no notice? Hell, Isaac, I'll be damn lucky if he doesn't have me back working as a teller or sweeping the place out at night."

Matthew glared at him from across their cramped quarters. No, Isaac hadn't thought what effect all of this could have on his friend. Wasn't it bad enough that his normal crew were all in limbo about their futures without adding Matthew and his small family to the list?

"I'm sorry, Matthew," he said, meaning it. The last thing he'd meant to do was cause everyone all these problems. Weariness washed over him in waves. What was he going to do if he took them all down with him if he couldn't save his boat and their jobs?

"Like I said, let's worry about it tomorrow. Stay at my house tonight and we'll talk everything over at breakfast."

He had been planning on staying in his usual room at the hotel, but it might be easier for him at Matthew's, if for no other reason than he wouldn't have to maneuver up and down so many stairs. He always enjoyed spending time with Matthew's wife, and his daughter would provide a welcome distraction from everything else.

"That sounds good to me as long as Melissa won't object to having an unexpected guest."

"She'll be glad to see that you're all in one piece." He glanced down at Isaac's leg. "Or mostly in one piece. And Cynthia always loves it when her favorite uncle comes to visit. So for tonight, we'll just pretend the bank doesn't exist and your boat is tied up safe and sound."

"For tonight, then, we'll pretend."

Annie found one excuse after another to linger after Mrs. Chesterfield declared the rehearsal to be over. So far, no one seemed to find it odd that she had rearranged her sheet music three times over. Then she'd moved the piano a foot to the left, only to push it back to the right a few minutes later. Finally, when enough people had left, she gave up all pretense of being busy and approached the pastor directly.

"Pastor Chesterfield, can I talk to you for a few minutes?" To hide her nervousness, she kept her hands down at her sides, clenching the dark blue fabric of her skirt.

"Of course, Mrs. Dunbar." He wiped more than a few cookie crumbs off the front of his coat, looking rather guilty as he did so. He whispered, "I do hope my wife has lost track of how many cookies I've eaten. She worries, you know." Then he picked up another two and slipped them into a pocket.

Annie smiled when he winked at her, including her in his conspiracy. "They'd be easier to resist if she wasn't such a great cook. I had several myself."

"Would you like to talk in my office?"

She hesitated. If they were seen going into his private office, people were bound to be curious what was so important that it required such privacy. On the other hand, there were enough people still lingering in the sanctuary that someone was bound to overhear their conversation.

"I think that would be best." She'd rather leave folks guessing than knowing the truth, at least until after she had a chance to discuss her past and problems with the minister.

He led the way to his office and offered her a chair to sit in. He sat down in the other chair in front of the desk. She appreciated his efforts to make her feel at ease.

He gave her clenched hands and white knuckles a glance and raised his eyebrows. "Now what has you so worried, Annie?" His use of her first name pleased her.

She'd worried that she'd find it difficult to tell him about the lie she'd been living. However, his sympathetic eyes and calm demeanor broke through her natural reserve and the words came tumbling out. Other than to hand her a clean handkerchief to dab her eyes with, he remained quiet until she slowed down enough to catch her breath.

"And I heard about the boardinghouse being up for sale and came here to look at it." She studied her hands in her lap. "It was in such terrible shape, but if it hadn't been, I would never have been able to afford it."

She gathered up enough gumption to drag her eyes up to face the censure she fully expected to see written on his face. Instead, his mouth was curved up in a gentle smile.

"Well, it's certainly not in terrible condition now, Annie. I've heard your boarders talk often enough about what a wonderful establishment you run. You have provided an excellent home for those ladies."

He reached across the short distance that separated them to take her chilly hands in his warm ones. "Now, as far as the rest of it, I can understand why you were worried. It's true that some of our more . . . uh . . . shall we say, conservative members might need a bit of time to get used to knowing your prior profession. But if you were worried about my opinion, you needn't have been concerned. I, of all people, am not in any position to judge anyone on their past actions."

The real anguish in his voice almost started the tears flowing again. Whatever he was thinking about had hurt him deeply. She found herself wanting to offer him the comfort she had come seeking for herself.

With some effort, he pulled himself back to the present. "We can talk more about your former profession, if you really feel it's necessary." He leaned back in his chair and peered at her from over his spectacles. "However, I suspect that there's more that has you upset than what you've told me. Something to do with Captain Chase, perhaps?"

She'd always suspected that there was a sharp intelligence behind the parson's affable smile and warm eyes. What had he seen or heard that had led him to that conclusion? Not that it mattered. She had promised herself to tell the pastor the worst there was to know about her, and Isaac was certainly part of that.

She'd come this far; it was time to lay all of her

cards on the table. "I knew him . . . you know, before."

"And?" the minister prompted when she stopped speaking.

"And I'd never known anyone like him in my life. When he showed signs of getting too serious, it scared me. Maybe I had more of my father in me than I cared to admit, because rather than face the problem I left town without telling him why."

"You don't strike me as a coward, Annie, but you were young. Don't judge yourself so harshly."

"It would be different if I'd taken off on my own, but I didn't. Nick—my late husband—was supposed to be Isaac's closest friend. Instead, when he figured out that I was planning on leaving town, he convinced me that I should let him go along. You know, to keep me safe."

"I take it that he didn't turn out to be much of a friend to Captain Chase or to you, either."

"No, he wasn't. I think my only real attraction to him was something he could have that Isaac couldn't. I don't think either of us ever really knew Nick Dunbar." The weight that had been pressing down on her for days seemed to be easing up. "I'm not blaming everything on Nick, though. If I hadn't been willing to go, he wouldn't have forced me. And I knew I didn't love him when I married him. He never forgave me for that, and I guess I never did either."

"Let me pour us some tea, Annie. Confession always seems to be thirsty work."

He left the room for only a minute or two before returning with a tray laden with two cups, a teapot, and a few more of the cookies. It made her smile. After he'd poured them each a cup, he took his seat and offered her first choice of the sweets. When he didn't immediately reach for a cookie for himself, she knew he had something serious to tell her.

"Annie, I know that folks, especially young ones, like to think that everyone should marry for love. And maybe that is the best way to go about it. But the truth is, more people than you know marry for other reasons—some of them good, some not. You may not have married Nick Dunbar out of love, but you did your best by him."

"How do you know that?"

"Because I figure you stuck by him, no matter how bad things got. I'm not wrong about that, am I?"

It was the second time in a week that someone had thrown her guilt back in her face, as if she'd been thinking wrong all this time. Millie's opinion had been colored by her friendship with Annie, or so she'd thought. But Pastor Chesterfield was supposed to represent the Lord's way of looking at things.

"I stuck by him." And she had. "But I still ran out on Isaac."

"Had he asked you to marry him?"

"Not exactly."

Pastor Chesterfield tilted his head to one side and gave her a quizzical look. "Then what did he do that sent you running for the hills?" He sounded curious more than anything.

"He wanted me to meet his family. His mother, of all people." She hoped that her reason didn't sound as stupid to the minister as it suddenly did to her. No luck. He chuckled and shook his head.

"Annie, did you try to tell him how much that scared you? That you had no experience dealing with what folks like to call decent women?" When she didn't immediately answer, he clucked his tongue and rolled his eyes toward the ceiling. "Lord, save me from the desperation of the young."

Then he smiled at her. "Annie, you've done things you regret. You've made mistakes. But Isaac isn't innocent in all of this, either. Did he come looking for you?"

"I don't know. If he did, he never said so." She frowned. Where was this all leading?

"I can't imagine that it would have taken him all this time to find you if he'd been looking all that hard. Maybe, just maybe, you two weren't supposed to find each other until now." His eyes closed for a few seconds. "I believe the Lord leads us all in the path He wants us to follow. He wanted you here, playing for His people as they celebrate the birth of His Son. And because you have changed your life around, He has brought Isaac back into your life so that the two of you can find the happiness that escaped you before."

He rose to his feet. "I hope you feel better about things, Annie. I'm always here for you, if you need to talk some more."

"Thank you, Pastor." She smiled and followed him to the front door of the church. She walked home in silence, her mind a whirl of confusing thoughts.

Stunned was too mild a word for the way she felt. The man's logic was relentless and bewildering. But he'd given her so much to think about. Maybe she was supposed to be in Willow Shoals.

And maybe her gift of music was the key to feeling like an accepted member of the community. And maybe at long last she could find a way to atone for the heartache she had caused Isaac.

He had turned down her offer of money. There had to be something else she could do. When Barton returned, she would sit down with him and Joe and see what ideas they could come up with.

CHAPTER FOURTEEN

The creak of the tread on the floor below sent Millie into a dither. She didn't know whether to burrow under the covers and hide or make a grab for her clothes. Joe's arm tightened around her, holding her closer to his warmth, trying without words to reassure her.

"It's just Annie," he whispered close to her ear.

"I know, but we're . . . you and I just . . ."

He hushed her with a kiss. "Yes, we did just. And I'd like to again, but somehow I don't think you're going to want to right now."

Oh, she did, she did and told him so. "But I'm still getting used to this . . ." She glanced down the length of the bed. Despite the blankets they'd pulled over them, it was easy to see how entwined the two of them were. "Getting used to the idea of *us*, Joe. I know Annie will understand and likely even approve."

"But?"

"But you're only the second man I've ever . . . um . . . well, only the second man I've shared a bed with. That's not to say that I have any regrets." She raised up long enough to offer Joe a kiss as proof of her sincerity. "This is all new territory for me, and I'm not sure what it all means." Would he understand how confused she was without getting his feelings hurt? Or did it all seem so much more important to her than it did to him?

He shifted to be able to look her right in the face. "Millie, I don't know how to convince you how much you've come to mean to me. I won't tell you that I've never known other women, but there haven't been all that many. And none of them, not even one, has ever made me feel this way before."

He cupped her face with his work-roughened hand. "I have something to say that you may not be ready to hear, but I'm going to say it because I need to. Millie, I love you."

Her heart caught in her throat. There was nothing in his expression that gave lie to his words. Dare she believe him? Before she could say a word, though, he placed his finger across her lips.

"I'm not asking you for any promises until you're ready to give them. I've already told Isaac and Barton that I won't be returning to the boat. I figure I need to stick close by if I'm ever going to convince you to marry me." Then he settled back on the pillow.

Had he just proposed? She wasn't sure. It sounded as if he planned to sometime, but maybe not quite yet. Would he think her brazen if she asked him to clarify his intentions? Or should she tell Joe to get dressed so the two of them could try to slip back downstairs without being seen?

A chuckle rumbled deep in Joe's chest. "Millie, there are more thoughts darting around in that mind of yours than lightning bugs on a summer night. Tell me what you're thinking."

Before she could decide what she should say, the one thing she really wanted to know popped out. "Did you just propose to me?"

"I did, if you're going to say yes. Otherwise, I was just giving you fair warning that I plan on doing so when I'm more sure of your answer."

"Now that's hedging your bets, Joe." She poked him in the ribs. "Now which is it?"

The warmth and laughter didn't fade from his eyes, but his mouth turned all serious. "Marry me, Millie. Please."

"I knew from the first that marrying Daniel was the right thing for me to do." And she had. Their love had been gentle and strong. "Being with you feels different, Joe, but no less right. If you still want me after everything gets set to rights around here—the boat, Annie, Captain Chase, everything— why, then I'd be honored to be your wife."

"That's a deal I'm going to hold you to, Millie mine." He kissed her long and hard. "Now, we'd better see about getting some clothes on before someone comes looking for us."

He sat up on the edge of the bed with his back to her, giving her some semblance of privacy as he pulled on his pants and shirt. She appreciated the consideration. After she quickly braided her hair, he stood behind her and rested his head on top of hers and looked at her reflection in the mirror.

"Do you want to tell people that we're engaged or wait for a while? I'll leave it up to you." He smiled. "I can tell you this much—it won't come as a surprise to Barton or Isaac. As I said, I've already told them I was going to stay in Willow Shoals even if they get the *Caprice* repaired. They figured out why on their own."

She was still getting used to the idea herself. She would need to tell Annie soon, but there were bound to be a lot of questions that she and Joe weren't ready to answer. Like, where were they going to live? What kind of job would Joe find here in town?

"I want to tell everyone as soon as we can, but let's wait a few days. Can you give me until after Christmas?"

"Are you sure you aren't having second thoughts?"

She spun into his arms. "No second thoughts; no third ones, either." Still feeling a bit shy, she burrowed into the warmth of his chest. "I love you, Joe. You're not going to get away from me anytime soon."

"I wouldn't even try." He stepped back. "I'd better get out of here, though. Annie might not mind me spending an afternoon in your room, but Miss Barker might have a different take on the matter."

She appreciated his concern for her reputation. A widow didn't have to be quite as careful about what people thought of her as a single woman, but she didn't want folks to get the idea that she was fast. She and Joe would have to be discreet until they decided to have Pastor Chesterfield marry them.

"I'll need to make a new dress." The idea pleased her.

"Well, I'd better go then, before you try to use me as a pin cushion."

She beat him to the door. After listening to make

sure all was quiet, she opened the door and peered out into the hall. "It's all clear for now."

He planted a quick kiss on her mouth as he eased past her into the hall. She watched as he disappeared down the stairs in his stocking feet and carrying his boots in his hand. He even took care to avoid the squeaky step. Bless his heart, he was surely a Christmas present like no other she'd ever received.

She felt a little guilty savoring the joy he brought her when her best friend had yet to resolve her problems. Glancing up at Annie's doorway, she could only pray that the season of miracles had a few in store for Annie and Isaac, too.

"We're sorry, Captain Chase, but we can't give you a definitive answer until we know the extent of the damage to your ship."

The damn fool didn't know enough to know boats worked the rivers. Ships went to sea. How could he sit in judgment on Isaac's future? "My boat, Mr. Powell, is a quality vessel. With the proper repairs, she should be able to earn a profit for all of us for years to come."

The man steepled his fingers and looked over them at Isaac. "I understand your reluctance to admit defeat, Captain, but can you guarantee that repairs can be effected at a reasonable cost and that the boat will be seaworthy once they are completed?"

He hated talking to men who'd spent their whole lives counting money and worrying over columns of figures. Unfortunately, they were the ones who usually controlled the purse strings for the rest of the world.

"I will make sure that the repairs are done correctly and for the best price. Once the ice breaks up, the *Caprice* will return to service along the White River."

Several of the other men seated around the table shifted in their seats. They'd been stuck in this airless room for the better part of an hour and were no closer to resolving the matter than they had been when they walked in. Matthew caught his eye and shrugged just enough to let Isaac know that he had no idea what decision the committee would come to.

That they hadn't already rejected Isaac's request for a delay in his loan payment was probably due to Matthew's influence. If not for his friendship, Isaac didn't know what he would have done.

Mr. Powell gave up considering his fingers long enough to meet Isaac's gaze. After a few seconds, he nodded rather abruptly and stood up. Isaac's stomach plummeted to the floor, certain his future was looking pretty damned bleak.

Either way, he needed to be going. The stagecoach that went through to Willow Shoals was due to leave in a little over two hours. He was going to be on it, even if he had to walk out of here without a dime in his pocket or a decision about the future of the *Caprice*.

"I'll tell you this much, Captain Chase. Matthew here has assured us that you are a man of your word. I will give you until after Christmas to get us a proper estimate for repairs and a detailed plan of how you will manage to make your next payment if—and I do mean if, Captain—we agree to the delay." He paused to light up a cigar. "You will, of course, have to come up with the repair money yourself. The bank must behave in a responsible manner in this. We will not pour additional funds into the White River."

He gave Isaac a few seconds to consider his words before adding, "A wise man would take the insurance money, pay off the debt, and start over in a less chancy business."

"Then I guess I'm not particularly wise."

A cloud of acrid smoke drifted Isaac's way. Unexpectedly, Mr. Powell grinned. "Perhaps not, Captain. But I suspect you are determined, and sometimes that is enough."

He left the room with the others trailing after him like so many baby ducks. Matthew stayed behind with Isaac. The two of them waited until the others were out of sight before speaking.

"Did he just say that I might get my way because I'm too bullheaded to realize when I'm defeated?"

Matthew grinned. "Something like that. The others have some say in the matter, but if Powell decides you've got a chance of success, they'll follow his lead."

"Wish I had one of his cigars."

"Why? He's too cheap to smoke good ones. Most of the time, we keep the windows open even in the cold to get rid of the smell."

"For luck, my friend. For luck." He reached for his crutches. "Now, we've got plans to make and not much time. Do you want to talk over lunch?"

"Are you buying?" Matthew settled his hat on his head and tugged on his gloves.

"Today's your lucky day." As he followed Matthew out the door, he added, "Let's just hope it's mine, as well."

* * *

The return trip to Willow Shoals seemed destined to never end. It had been bad enough when he at least had Matthew for company, but the trip back was far worse. The worst thing was that there wasn't room in the crowded interior of the coach to arrange his leg in any sort of comfortable position. And at least a couple of his companions had evidently given up bathing for the winter.

If the temperature outside wouldn't freeze a man straight through, he would have considered trying to ride up top with the driver. He could just see Barton and Joe unloading him at the stage station in town like a block of ice. Of course, Annie could thaw him with just one kiss.

That is, if she hadn't written him off completely for running off without a word after their wonderful night on the sofa. He could offer up a whole wagonload of excuses but not one of them meant a damn thing except for one.

He'd awakened scared and hit the floor running. Well, limping as fast as his crutches could carry him.

Maybe it had been worth it. He suspected that had he not been there to confront Mr. Powell and the others in person, he would have received a telegram from Matthew telling him that they wanted his *Caprice* sold for scrap. As it was, he'd gotten a little reprieve. Not a guarantee, but at least a chance to find another alternative.

For now, though, there was nothing he could do but try to catch some sleep. The stage was scheduled to reach town sometime after first light. He had a lot to accomplish and a dwindling limit of time left in which to finish it. Mr. Powell had sent word through Matthew that Isaac needed to have a plan ready for their approval by the first of the year.

Christmas was only two days away, so he had little more than a week left before he would have to give up the fight to save his livelihood. The strange thing was that he no longer felt panic at the thought of having to find a way to make a living on dry land. It wouldn't be his first choice, but he could live with it.

He settled back into the corner and let his eyes drift shut, even though he wasn't particularly sleepy. Annie's sweet face filled his mind as it had far too often the past few days. Maybe she was the reason he wasn't as afraid of the future as he had been. If he told her that, would she take off and hide in the chicken coop again?

He smiled and started counting the hours and minutes until he could find out for sure.

"He might not make it back for Christmas, Millie, but he's coming back."

Annie adjusted the bow on the package she'd just wrapped.

"I wish I had your confidence in the situation." Millie picked up the pouch of tobacco they had bought for Barton and covered it with brown paper. "Tell me again why you're so sure he'll come back to Willow Shoals."

Annie ticked off all the important points on her fingers. "His friends are here. His boat is here. His personal belongings are still scattered all over his room." And if those weren't enough, she was in Willow Shoals. He'd come back to her.

He had to. She wouldn't have it any other way.

"Think he'll like the shirt?" It was exactly the right color to bring out the bright blue color of his eyes. She'd even caught herself hugging it a few times when no one was looking.

"He'll like anything you give him." Millie tied a knot in the ribbon on Barton's package. "Put your finger here."

Annie dutifully put her finger on the ribbon, holding it tight until Millie could get it secured with a second knot. While Annie waited, she decided her friend had been right, although unwittingly. Isaac had liked what she'd given him the other night on the sofa. Almost as much as she had.

She'd already wrapped the small gifts she'd gotten Joe and Agatha. Millie's package was hidden in Annie's room—a new nightgown with a pretty lace collar. She even had a couple tucked away for Kate and Patience for when they returned. What would the two ladies think about everything that had happened since they'd left? Knowing the two of them, they'd be mad that they'd missed out on the excitement.

"Did you tell Joe that I wanted him and Barton to stick around after dinner so we can talk?"

"I told both of them myself."

Millie gave Annie a curious look, probably hoping for some hint about what was going on. She ignored the unspoken question, not because of any great need for secrecy, but because she was still trying to organize her thoughts into some semblance of order. She had something she wanted to bring up for discussion before Isaac returned.

"Let's put the presents under the tree now."

Just as she had hoped, the ploy worked. Millie snatched the shirt out of Annie's hand. "It's not even Christmas Eve yet, Annie. Not until then."

"But . . ."

"No, you wanted a traditional Christmas, and that's what we're going to have. Presents can be put out on Christmas Eve, but we're supposed to open them Christmas morning." She tucked the packages into the back corner of the pantry where the men were unlikely to run across them.

Annie let her friend think she'd won the small skirmish. Actually, she was really excited about all the little touches of Christmas that had made their way into her house. The garlands, the strings of popcorn, and even the small tree that Barton had surprised them with the day before.

All of it traditional, the sort of thing that people had done for years. And all of it new to her, and therefore so very precious.

Now if the one person who would make it all complete would manage to show up, she'd be perfectly happy.

As soon as they cleared away the clutter, Annie called the others down to eat. She wasn't feeling very hungry herself, but Joe and Barton had both put in a couple of hard days. They'd need their strength once they started repairs on the boat.

Caprice.

She wondered if Isaac had chosen that name or if the boat had been called that before he'd bought her. Either way, it was a fine piece of irony. He probably knew that the name meant a whim or un-expected change. That certainly fit their circum-stances. But the term was also a name for a lively piece of music. Considering how they'd met, the name was doubly appropriate.

And she planned to do whatever she could to save his ladylove for him, even if it meant that he'd walk back on board and disappear downriver, tak-ing her heart with him.

But it was Christmas, the season of miracles. It would be enough of one if they could save his boat, but maybe there were a few others left to go around. One for Millie and Joe. One for the congregation that the program would bring the whole town to-gether for a night of worship and joy.

And, please God, one for her and Isaac.

"Agatha, you're welcome to stay, but this discus-sion is really intended for Captain Chase's friends." She softened the words with a smile, not wanting to hurt the older woman's feelings.

"I would hope that I fit into that category, Annie. After all, I helped the night the captain and these other gentlemen arrived on your doorstep." She settled back in her chair, daring anyone else to suggest she should leave.

Barton spoke up in her defense. "We would never have made it through that night without your help, Miss Barker."

She rewarded him with a bright smile. "Well, I don't know about that, Barton, but I'd like to think I played my own part."

Annie opened a drawer and pulled out an enve-lope. From the looks on their faces, Millie and Joe both recognized it immediately, even though they didn't know what it contained. She laid the envelope beside the page of notes she'd written and sat down at the table. The others quieted immediately, recognizing her unspoken request that the impromptu meeting come to order.

"We all know that Isaac—Captain Chase—stands to lose the *Caprice* if he doesn't come up with the money for repairs. Even now, the bank may have already said something of the sort to him." She looked around the table.

Looking decidedly grimmer than they had a few minutes before, Barton and Joe both nodded. Millie took her cue from them and did the same.

"I assume that you've come up with a plan to rescue Captain Chase yet again?" Miss Barker looked at her with raised eyebrows and an encouraging smile.

Would the older woman never cease surprising her?

"That's exactly right, Agatha." She fiddled with her notes, wishing she were better at business discussions. "As Isaac's friends—and mine, I hope— you deserve to know the truth. I doubt that it will come as a surprise to any of you that he and I knew each other years ago."

She drew a deep breath and launched right into their shared past. It wasn't as difficult to talk about; maybe it got easier with practice. She didn't go into as much detail as she had with Millie or Pastor Chesterfield, but she needed to give the others enough information to understand why it was so important for her to try to help Isaac.

As she'd hoped, neither of the two men looked particularly surprised. Agatha looked remarkably pleased about something. "I admire a person who has managed to overcome such adversity, Annie. You and Captain Chase should both be proud of all you have accomplished."

"Thank you, Agatha. I appreciate your support." She shuffled her papers a bit before continuing. This was the tricky part. "Knowing Isaac as you all do, you know he can be bullheaded and has enough pride for a dozen men."

Joe grinned. "That's him all right."

"And you also know he needs money to begin repairs to the *Caprice,* money he doesn't have. Not if he's going to make the necessary payments on the boat as well."

"I didn't realize the situation was that bad." Agatha shook her head. "That poor man. And I bet he's the type to shoulder all the worry himself."

"True enough." Annie picked up the envelope. "I don't have a lot of money to spare, but I have some. Enough to maybe get repairs under way, at least. I offered it to Isaac before he left, but he refused to take it." They didn't need to know the exact circumstances of that discussion.

Barton sat across from her, puffing away on his pipe. "What exactly do you have in mind, Annie? I can't imagine him changing his thinking anytime soon. He won't take kindly to charity from any of us."

"I know. But he might be open to a business proposition if we handle it right."

Everyone leaned forward, as if she had finally captured their attention. She spread out her papers. "This is the way I see it. Isaac owns the *Caprice,* except for what he owes the bank. He also needs to pay for the repairs, but the bank likely won't want to either wait for their payment or loan him some additional money to pay for the work that needs to be done." She looked at the two men. "That pretty much sums up the situation, doesn't it?"

"It sure does." Joe frowned. "I know Matthew tried real hard to pull off some kind of miracle. If it were up to him, I think he'd help Isaac any way he could, but the bank owners really have his hands tied."

"So if the bank won't help and Isaac won't take charity, where does that leave him—or us?" There was new tension in the way Barton gripped his pipe. "That boat doesn't deserve to be torn to pieces because some man in a suit doesn't understand how special she is."

"I agree with you. And even if she did," Annie went on, conscious that she was starting to think of the *Caprice* as more than just the metal and wood that made up her parts, "Isaac deserves better."

"So what are you thinking, Annie?" Millie had finally entered into the discussion.

"I'm thinking that what Isaac needs is a new business partner." She looked around the table, meeting each person's gaze head on. "Or several partners, if any of you are willing."

The silence was heavy, the way it felt right before a storm broke. She waited as they considered her words. As the seconds ticked by on the clock, she began to have second and third thoughts about her idea. It had all made such good sense to her. However, if his best friends thought it was crazy, she didn't know what she'd do next.

Finally, Barton spoke. "I'd be glad to throw some cash into the pot." He paused to relight his pipe. "I sort of like the idea of being part owner of a boat, even if it's only for a short time."

Joe's eyes went to Millie first before he looked back at Annie. "I'm currently unemployed, but Isaac is welcome to my share of the profits if it will help keep the *Caprice* off the bottom of the river."

Agatha came next. "I will have a draft drawn off my account immediately. I'm always on the lookout for a good investment."

That left Millie. "I've got a little put by. I don't know much about steamboats and investments, but I do know about friendship. Let me know when you need it." She looked toward Joe for approval. His pleased smile set her to blushing.

Annie felt better than she had, well, since the other night on the sofa. She hoped the others assumed the sudden flush of color to her face was due to their enthusiastic support of her plan. She decided to let them chat among themselves for a few minutes before bringing their attention back to her. It was all well and good that they were willing to help. The hard part was going to be getting Isaac to let them.

He should have known that nothing would go right. He'd been waiting for half an hour with no sign of either Joe or Barton. Where the hell were they? He stomped back inside the stage office to where the clerk sat behind a desk. After Isaac stared at him for a bit, he finally looked up from the book he was reading.

"Next stage don't leave for two days." He went back to reading.

Isaac leaned forward on his crutches and glared at the lazy bastard. "I don't give a damn about the next stage. I want to know if you've heard anything about the telegraph lines being down between here and Hart's Ferry?"

"They were yesterday. I ain't heard no different today."

Isaac wanted to find the broken wire and use it to strangle the surly fool. He didn't bother to thank the man. Back out on the sidewalk, he knew there wasn't much use in waiting any longer. It was obvious that his telegram hadn't gotten through to Willow Shoals. No one was expecting him and no one was coming to get him. He didn't mind walking, except Annie lived clean on the other end of town. He turned up his collar, pulled his hat down solid on his head, and headed across town.

The whole trip had been badly planned from the beginning. Of course, he hadn't really planned it at all. Because he had gone, Mr. Powell and the others had agreed to a short reprieve, but he wasn't sure that they'd really done him any favors. If, in the end, they were going to force him to give up the *Caprice* and that seemed damned likely—a clean break might have been easier to bear.

Instead, here he was with his thoughts going round and round in circles, trying to figure out if he had a chance in hell of coming up with the money or if he should just give up. Maybe all the jostling he'd suffered through on the stagecoach had scrambled his thoughts, but he wasn't as upset about the possibility of losing as he might have been.

Faced with the reality of giving up life on the river, he should have been screaming mad. Instead, he'd been more concerned about getting back to Willow Shoals for an entirely different reason: Annie.

He stuck to the sidewalk as long as he could, because the snow had either been packed down or shoveled off completely. Once he reached the end of it, though, he had to take to the street. The wind had piled up drifts that often as not forced him to walk around them. His meandering route through town seemed to take him twice the time getting back to the boardinghouse as it had leaving it only a few days before.

But other than the wear and tear on his leg, he didn't really mind. Another outcome of his rushed trip downriver was that he'd come to the realization that the town of Hart's Ferry held very little attraction for him. He had a few good friends there, such as Matthew and his family, but other than that he had no real ties to the town.

But he liked Willow Shoals and the people he'd met there. Well, except for the stage office clerk, but every town was entitled to one or two bad ones. His surliness was more than offset by the warm friendliness of Pastor Chesterfield and his wife, the sheriff, and all the others who had risked their own lives to save his.

A man could do far worse than to call a bunch like them friends and neighbors.

Then there was Millie, loyal to a fault, and Miss Barker. From what he'd heard, he'd also like Annie's regular boarders, the two spinsters who were expected to return after the first of the year.

He was still a boatman at heart. But once he got the *Caprice* back into service, he might very well operate her out of Willow Shoals. And if she was beyond repair, well, there had to be other opportunities in a growing town.

The boardinghouse was just coming into sight. As early as it was, he was relieved to see some light coming from the windows. With luck, the coffee would be hot and maybe Annie would consider making him some breakfast. He hadn't eaten anything but beans since leaving Hart's Ferry the day before.

Rather than bang on the front door, which was probably locked, he made his way around to the back of the house and knocked twice on the door. Before he could knock a third time, the door opened a crack. Then Annie swung it open wide and stood out of the way to let him inside.

"Did you walk all the way back?"

"Damn near. I take it my telegram asking Barton or Joe to meet me never made it."

"You take it right. Barton just got back yesterday, but I know Joe didn't say he'd heard anything from you. Now why don't you sit down before you fall over? I've seen better-looking corpses."

She helped him off with his coat and held out a chair for him to sit in, fussing over him without making him feel totally helpless. The warmth of the kitchen gradually seeped into him, aided by the big cup of coffee she plunked down on the table in front of him. Although she hadn't said anything more to him, her silence seemed to be more because she was cooking than out of anger.

He allowed himself the small pleasure of watching her bustle about the room, putting breakfast on the table for everyone in the house. Himself included, he was relieved to notice when she set a plate down in front of him.

While they were still alone, he wished he could think of a tactful way to bring up their last evening together and the reasons behind his abrupt departure. He wrapped his hands around the cup, glad to have something warm to hold onto while he tried to come up with an idea.

Before he managed to figure it out, the door behind him opened and Joe came out blinking sleepily.

"I thought I heard you. Welcome back." He grabbed his coat and headed out the back door, probably heading for the privy.

The blast of cold air from the door set off another set of chills through Isaac. He sipped at the coffee, fighting off the cold from the inside out. Joe didn't seem overly surprised to see him, so evidently it had been expected that Isaac would return to Willow Shoals.

Millie was the next one to join them. She merely nodded in his direction and reached for her apron. While Annie fried the bacon, Millie kept an eye on the cornbread. On the whole, he found their behavior a bit puzzling. He'd half expected Annie to come after him with her cast-iron skillet. If not her, then certainly he'd thought Millie would be upset about the way he'd disappeared with no warning.

"Here's your breakfast, Isaac. After you've finished eating, why don't you go lie down for a while? Judging by those dark circles under your eyes, I'd wager you haven't slept much these past few days." Annie smiled as she refilled his coffee. "You can tell us all about your trip when you've got some sleep under your belt."

Before he realized what was happening, the two women had shooed him out of the kitchen and into his room. He would have argued about their bossy treatment, but the minute he sat down on the bed, he decided they had the right of it. He barely managed to shuck off his boots and pants before crawling under the blankets.

As he closed his eyes, he drew great pleasure from the feel of clean sheets and the scent of lavender. No matter what else happened, it felt damn good to be fussed over and welcomed back.

"When should we tell him?" Millie held her voice to a low whisper; her eyes kept straying toward the door to the room Isaac shared with Joe. "Tonight at dinner?"

Annie had been giving the matter some serious thought. She didn't want Isaac to continue to worry about things any longer than necessary. However, she wanted to make the announcement something really special. With Christmas Eve only a day away, she had enough to worry about with the last-minute rehearsals and the actual performance.

She thought perhaps the best way to broach the subject was as a combined Christmas gift from all of them. There would be presents aplenty for all of them under the small tree in the corner of the parlor. Surely that stubborn man in the next room would accept the offer of help in the spirit in which it was given.

Millie was still waiting for her answer. "Christmas morning, I think."

Her friend considered the matter and then nodded. "That would be perfect, I think. He'll have to understand, don't you think?"

"I hope so. I just don't want him to think that we're ganging up on him." She dried the last of the dishes and put them away. "I'd better be going. I want to have time to go through the music one last time by myself before all the others show up for the rehearsal."

"I'm so happy you decided to do this for the church and everybody. I know you only agreed because it was me who asked."

"I'm glad you did. I've been enjoying myself."

"I know. I can tell." Millie wiped her hands on her apron and followed Annie to the front door. "I've been tempted to come along to watch, but I decided I would rather wait and see it for the first time tomorrow night. I know the program will be extra special this year."

"Is that because you like the way I play piano or because Joe will have an excuse to sit next to you?"

"Annie! Keep your voice down!"

Millie looked more guilty than shocked, which made Annie giggle. "Who are you worried about hearing me? Joe knows full well he spent the other afternoon upstairs in your room."

"How did you know? I mean, we . . . uh . . ." Millie seemed unable to do more than stammer and blush.

Annie took pity on her flustered friend and hugged her. "If he's responsible for putting that sparkle in your eyes, then I'm all for it. And your secret is safe with me."

"He's asked me to marry him. I told him I would."
Millie looked totally bewildered by the prospect.

Annie took Millie's shaky hands in hers. "Aren't
you happy about it?"

"Yes . . . yes, I am. I'm feeling a bit confused because it's all happened so fast. I know I keep saying
that." She glanced back toward the kitchen, listening for the return of Joe and Barton. "He's promised
to give me some time. I'm afraid if I take too long,
he'll be the one to realize he's made a mistake."

Annie understood only too well Millie's dilemma.
The difference was that when she'd been confronted
by the same uncertainties years ago, she'd
turned coward and disappeared. Millie was made
of stronger stuff.

"Neither of you is making a mistake. Joe's a good
man and a smart one. He knows that with you, he's
found something worth hanging on to with both
hands." She wrapped her scarf around her head
and neck, preparing to face the cold outside.

"I'll be back in three hours or so. Mrs. Chesterfield said we'd be rehearsing for an hour and a half,
but she tends to be a bit of an optimist." Annie patted Millie on the shoulder. "Try not to fret so much,
Millie. I have a feeling that things are going to turn
out fine."

"For Joe and me or for you and Isaac?"

Annie winced. The trouble with knowing someone as well as she knew Millie was that she could
read Annie just as easily. "We'll have to wait and
see if there are enough Christmas miracles to go
around."

CHAPTER FIFTEEN

Isaac dragged himself out of his bed feeling stiff and groggy. He sat on the edge of the bed to pull on his boots, wondering why the house seemed so quiet. The other bed in the room was empty and a glance out the window made him guess that it was early afternoon. Good. That left plenty of time for him to make a trip down to the river to look at the *Caprice*.

If he was going to lose her, he wanted some time to say good-bye.

Reaching for his crutches, he pushed himself up to his feet and edged his way over to the washstand in the corner. He managed to balance without his crutches, freeing his hands to splash water on his face. The chill did a lot toward clearing his mind of the last vestiges of sleep.

He shrugged on a clean shirt and ran a comb through his hair. Leaning forward, he studied his face in the small mirror on the wall. He needed a shave, but otherwise he looked better than he would have expected, considering everything. There were a few lines around his mouth and eyes that hadn't been there a few years ago, but he didn't care. A man didn't command the respect of a rough crew on a steamboat by looking like a wet-nosed kid.

Of course, come the first of the year, he wouldn't have a crew left to command. Shoving that thought back down where it came from, he picked up his crutches and went in search of better company than his own thoughts. The kitchen was empty, so he headed for the parlor. Luck was with him. Barton and Joe were both there.

"Captain! Glad to see you made it back in one piece." Barton got up off the sofa to make room for Isaac. He waited until he was settled comfortably before taking another seat in a nearby chair. "What did that bunch at the bank have to say for themselves?"

No use trying to sugarcoat the news. "Well, they didn't say yes or no. The best they'd agree to was to wait until after the first of the year to make a final decision." He stretched out his legs, enjoying the warmth from the fireplace. "To give the bank president credit, though, he was the one who said they'd wait. I think if it were up to the others, we'd already be chopping up the boat for kindling."

If he sounded bitter, so be it. Although he knew there were other alternatives to living on the river, he didn't have to pretend to like it. "How did your trip go?"

"I delivered the goods and got paid. The owners were relieved to have lost so little of their order. In fact, they said to tell you that they were looking forward to doing business with you again." He started fiddling with his pipe. "I put the money in the account you opened here in town."

Joe had remained quiet to this point. "I'm glad you came back."

He wondered if Joe and Barton had been concerned that he might not return at all. Since he hadn't explained why he'd left in the first place, he wouldn't have blamed them for wondering. His reasons were his own, but he hadn't meant to worry his friends any more than was necessary.

He told them so. "I decided at the last minute to ride along with Matthew. I didn't want to make him face his bosses at the bank alone." That was true, although it hadn't been the real cause for his abrupt departure.

"Do you think we could make a trip down to the river this afternoon? I'd like to see how she's doing for myself." There was no need to explain which she he was talking about. Only one female in his life was held captive by the ice.

"Should be able to. Let me go see about a wagon." Joe seemed glad for something to do.

Isaac pulled out his wallet. "Take what you need to rent one at the stable. We shouldn't be gone all that long, if the stable owner needs it back for someone else."

"Good enough. Tell Millie where I've gone." He grabbed his coat and disappeared out the door.

Isaac shook his head. "He's got it bad, hasn't he?"

Barton tamped the tobacco in his pipe. "I'd guess he figures he's got it good. She's a nice woman and will make him a good wife."

"It's gone that far already?" Isaac pushed and prodded at his feelings on the subject. He wasn't sure, but he suspected he was a little jealous.

"I'd be surprised if he hasn't hustled her in front of the preacher by the end of next month. He seems right anxious to stake his claim."

"Lucky bastard."

Barton got up to add another log or two to the fire. "Miss Annie is a nice woman, too. A man would have to be some kind of fool not to notice that."

This time there was no doubt about how he felt. Jealousy with a side helping of anger stirred in his gut. "You been looking at her for yourself?"

"And if I were?" His friend didn't seem overly concerned with how Isaac felt about it.

He had no real claim on her, despite what they had shared the other night on the very sofa he was sitting on. There was no way in hell he would share that with Barton. What could he say? That he'd loved her with a boy's heart and quite possibly loved her with a man's? He couldn't say the words even though it was the truth.

Evidently, his silence was enough of a statement. Barton sat back down in his chair with a satisfied smirk on his face. "Looks like Joe won't be the only one looking for work in Willow Shoals."

"Go to hell, Barton."

"I probably will but . . ."

Before he could finish his sentence, the front door opened again. It was too soon for Joe to be back, so Isaac wasn't surprised to see that it was Annie returning. He let his eyes drink their fill of her while she hung up her coat, unaware of his scrutiny.

Once again, Barton was the first to speak. "Welcome back. How did the rehearsal go?"

"Just fine. I'll be a nervous wreck by tomorrow night, but today went well." She crossed the room to stand near the fireplace. Glancing back over her shoulder, she asked, "Did you get enough sleep, Isaac?"

He shifted his position, making room for her on the sofa. "Enough to get through the day. Why don't you come over and sit for a spell? I'm sure this sofa will hold both of us." He winked at her, careful not to let Barton see him.

Two spots of color stained her cheeks as she sat down, putting as much space between them as she could. Judging by the look she gave him, he'd pay for his sass later. He didn't care. It was enough to know that she wasn't immune to him or the memory of what they had shared. For a handful of minutes, the three of them sat in companionable silence.

"We'd better start bundling you up, Captain. Joe could be back with the wagon anytime now." Barton stood up and tapped the last of his tobacco out into the fireplace.

Annie looked at Isaac in alarm. "Are you leaving again?"

A small smile tugged at his mouth. So she was worried about that, was she? Good. "No, we're going to take a short trip down to the river so I can check on the *Caprice* myself."

And to start saying good-bye to his former life. It grieved him something considerable, but he'd never been one to lie to himself.

"Can Millie and I come along? I've never seen

the boat, even from a distance." Then the excitement died in her eyes. "There might not be room in the wagon for two extra people."

"We'll manage." This time Isaac managed to get in the first word. "You won't be seeing her at her best, but I'd be glad to have your company."

"I'll go tell Millie." Annie practically ran from the room in her haste. "Don't leave without us."

"We won't."

He let Barton help him on with his coat. Rather than let the women see him be lifted up into the wagon, he decided to be outside waiting when Joe returned. That would give him some chance of already being seated when Annie and Millie came out. It probably didn't mean anything to either of them, but he hated any sign of weakness on his part. He had no idea why it was so important to him, but it was.

Joe was just coming into sight. Isaac was glad to see that he'd brought a wagon with two seats. Millie could sit up front with Joe while Annie joined him in the back. Barton could sit wherever he damn well felt like as long as it wasn't by Annie.

Barton took Isaac's crutches and laid them in the back of the wagon. Then he and Joe shoved and lifted Isaac up to the backseat. He'd no more than scooted across to the other side then the women came rushing outside.

Annie was still pulling on her gloves when she stepped out into the biting cold. The sun had done little to warm up the temperature, but at least the day was bright and clear. She waited at the bottom of the steps while Joe handed Millie up to the front seat. Barton stepped forward and offered Annie his assistance climbing up onto the seat next to Isaac. When she was settled, he climbed up into the back of the wagon.

"Will it be safe to go on board?" Millie laid her hand on Joe's arm. He covered it with one of his and left it there.

"We'll see when we get there. If she hasn't shifted too much, it should be safe enough. Just watch your step because the gangplank is icy and so are the decks." Joe gave her an encouraging smile. "I'll be right beside you the whole way."

Annie realized that Isaac's hand had somehow found its way to hers. "I'd like to say that I'll be able to help keep you steady once we're onboard, but I'm afraid I'd be more of a hindrance than a help." His smile warmed her.

"I'll be fine on my own." That didn't mean she wanted to pull her hand free of his. The small contact pleased her.

And she would be fine, but she planned to stick close by his side for the duration of their visit, knowing that it was important for her to understand what the boat really meant to him. She smiled at her own silliness. How could she possibly be jealous of the *Caprice*? But in some strange way, she was. The boat had brought Isaac back into her life, but it could just as easily carry him away again.

In fact, that was the logical outcome if her plan to help him actually worked. Maybe she'd stand a better chance of keeping him in her life if she had simply put her money back into the bank when he first refused it. But she wanted Isaac to be happy. If that meant helping him leave, so be it.

The whole ride lasted less than fifteen minutes. Before allowing Barton to help her down, she stood up in the wagon and studied the boat that sat trapped in the river. Although it was listing to one side, the boat looked far more intact than she had expected. For anyone to be considering the *Caprice* to be a total loss seemed ludicrous from where she stood, but then she didn't know much at all about the boats that plied their trade along the rivers in the area.

"She's beautiful." She looked down at Isaac and smiled. "I can see why you think the *Caprice* is so special."

"She is that."

It hurt to see such sadness in his expression. He didn't say another word as he awkwardly lowered himself to the ground. Annie accepted Barton's help down but then she immediately went around the wagon to stand beside Isaac.

"You'll have to tell me all about her." She looped her arm through his, offering him what support she could.

Millie and Joe followed Barton on down to the gangplank, leaving the two of them alone on the slope. He seemed to need the silence, so she stood quietly beside him until he stirred, taking a few steps down toward the river.

Annie walked along behind him, trying to stay out of his way. He had enough to handle just keeping his balance on the uneven ground. Barton stood waiting to help both of them across the narrow planks that led out to the cargo deck. She watched as Isaac made his way across, stubbornly refusing to let Barton support him until he reached the dubious safety of the icy deck.

Annie had no such reluctance to hang onto the pilot with both hands as he led her onboard the *Caprice*. "I'll be up top if either of you need me."

"Thanks, Barton." Isaac's gratitude was a bit strained, but at least he'd acknowledged his friend's efforts.

Annie offered him an encouraging smile. "Show me around."

"There's not all that much to see."

"Liar! You know you think every square inch of this ship is . . ."

He cut her off. "The first thing you need to learn is that she's a boat, not a ship. Ships sail the oceans. Boats work on the rivers." His frown didn't look all that serious. "The *Caprice* is a steamboat, my steamboat."

Annie held up her hands in surrender. "Excuse my mistake, Captain Chase. As I was saying, you know you think every square inch of this *boat* is special."

"She is that and could be again, if those vultures at the bank weren't circling overhead."

"She's not a lost cause yet." She tugged on his arm. "Now show me around before we all freeze out here."

And so he gave her a tour, starting at the bow and working their way back to the stern. He even managed to climb the stairs that led up to the upper decks, finally coming to the pilothouse. He stopped to knock on the door before entering.

"Why do you have to knock when you know Barton is the only one in there?"

"Because he's the pilot."

Before she could ask him to explain further, Barton opened the door. "Come on in. I was just studying the ice upriver."

It felt good to be in out of the wind, but the small room was not much warmer than standing outside. The two stared out the windows and conferred on what they thought about the river and how long it would stay frozen solid. Mostly they grumbled without really accomplishing anything.

"I've seen enough here. I think Annie might like to go below and see the salon." Isaac opened the door for her and then followed her down the passageway to the passenger areas on the lower decks.

The rooms were compact. Although most of the furnishings had been removed by Isaac's crew before they left town, it was easy to see the boat had been designed with the passengers' comfort in mind. She told him so.

"The rooms are lovely. I'll bet you fell in love with the boat the minute you laid eyes on her."

He laughed and shook his head. "You should have seen her. No one had done a thing to maintain her since before the war. I almost wore myself out scraping and painting and rebuilding. I wouldn't be exaggerating to say that I've put my life's blood into her." His words trailed off, his eyes fixed on something only he could see.

"After you left, I was lost for a long time." He glanced down at her. "I don't mean to rehash the past. But it's hard for anyone to understand what the *Caprice* meant to me when I found her. When I signed the papers on her, it felt as if I had a purpose in my life for the first time in years. Fixing her up damn near killed me, but I don't regret a single minute I spent working on her."

She understood far better than he knew. "That's kind of funny, don't you think?"

"What is?"

"That both of us found our path in life by buying something that needed all our energy and heart to restore it. My boardinghouse and your boat."

"You still have your boardinghouse." His blue eyes took on a hard edge. "It's not going anywhere soon."

"And you still have the *Caprice.*"

And he'd continue to own her if it was the last thing Annie did. If there was going to be any kind of future for the two of them, she wanted it to be because he chose to share his life with her. If he lost the boat, he might very well stay in Willow Shoals. But in her heart, she'd always wonder what he would have chosen to do if the circumstances had been different.

"Look at her, Annie." He pointed down at the railing that dipped almost into the frozen ice. "She's crippled, maybe beyond repair even if I had the money."

The grief in his voice cut straight through her. She put her arms around his waist and pulled him close. "Remember, Captain Isaac Chase, it's almost Christmas. There's no telling what can happen."

His eyes softened a bit. "All right, if you insist. For now, she's still mine."

Then he kissed her, driving away their worries about the future and the cold of a December day.

CHAPTER SIXTEEN

Would the sun never go down? Annie stared out the window at the still bright day and fidgeted.

She and Millie and even Agatha had spent the entire day in the kitchen. Annie stood surrounded by the products of their labors: spicy cookies, apple pies, and fresh bread that filled the house with the scents of Christmas. They'd prepared a quick dinner for later since Annie was due at the church as soon as they finished eating. But for now, Millie and Agatha were taking a much-deserved rest. She only wished she could settle down enough to do the same.

The men had even volunteered to pitch in with the cleanup of the kitchen, since they planned on being the main recipients of all the goodies the women had concocted. Later on, they would escort Millie and Agatha down to the church. There wasn't one of them who was willing to miss the Christmas program celebrating that most special night of the year.

"You'd better sit a spell, Annie. You have a long evening stretching out in front of you." Isaac pulled out the chair next to him. "Come on. You've already worn a groove in the floor between the window and the clock in the parlor."

He was right, but she wasn't sure she could actually stay seated. A swarm of nerves had taken up residence in her stomach. Although this was far from her first public performance, it had been years since she'd played for a group of people. And she suspected her previous audiences, mellowed by whiskey and beer, had been less demanding.

"You'll do fine, Annie." Isaac touched her shoulder briefly. She immediately missed the warmth of his hand.

"I figure I'll be fine once I get there and have the music in front of me. But until then, I keep thinking about all the things that could go wrong." His hand was back. She laid her cheek against it and drew comfort from his support.

"Have I mentioned how proud I am of you?" He leaned closer. "You've made a good life for yourself here in Willow Shoals."

"Considering everything, you haven't done so badly yourself. I especially like your friends." She grinned. "Even Matthew, but don't tell him that."

"They're all good men." His fingers played with a strand of her hair that had worked its way loose. "We've had a good run together." It hurt to hear the sad resignation in his voice.

"What's it like, living out there?" She gestured in the direction of the river.

"It can be right peaceful, when there's enough

water." His eyes took on a dreamy look. "I especially like standing out on the bow in the evening. The sound of the paddle wheel turning. Voices drifting over from the saloon while Barton yells out directions to the engineer below. Folks line up along the shore to wave at us, as if seeing the *Caprice* chugging by is something real special in their day."

She could picture him in her mind, the wind blowing his hair, the sun shining brightly off its golden color. "And do you wave back?"

"Most of the time. Barton blows the whistle for them, too. Kids get real pleasure out of that."

She searched for questions to keep him talking, wanting this insight into his life, into the man himself. "Do you carry mostly cargo?"

"Yes, but we take a few passengers, too. We didn't this time, more out of dumb luck than anything. I hadn't planned to make this trip, but the chance came up for this new route and I needed the money one more successful run would bring in." His hand curled around the nape of her neck, tugging her closer. "That didn't exactly go as planned."

She leaned into him, wanting this moment, needing his touch and comfort. And it seemed as if he needed the same from her. "I'm sorry about what happened, but I'm not sorry that it brought you back into my life."

Trailing her fingertips along the edge of his stubborn jaw, she traced the outline of his lips. "Kiss me, Isaac."

"My pleasure, Annabelle."

This time her name sounded like a caress in the quiet of the room. She let him lift her onto his lap, giving both more of what they were needing—comfort mixed with a generous serving of heat and need.

Their hands wandered a bit as their tongues danced and teased. She moaned, giving in to the sheer joy of the moment. When kissing was both too much and not enough, she pulled away. He let her go with obvious reluctance. A touch of wry humor sparkled in his eyes.

"Do you think the kitchen table is as sturdy as your sofa in the parlor?" He waggled his eyebrows in a parody of a seductive look.

"I'd say the wood is as hard as your head, but beyond that I don't know." She giggled as he tried to pull her back into the trap of his arms. She wasn't sure whether she was too quick for him or if he let her go. Either way, it was time for her to get ready. She planned to be dressed before dinner, so she could leave for the church as soon as they were finished eating.

He frowned when her smile died. "What's wrong, Annie?"

"I've got to go upstairs and change clothes."

"Need any help with buttons?"

She laughed and waved good-bye on her way out of the room. This lighthearted, teasing Isaac was a nice surprise. It brought back memories of the good times they'd shared when they were both younger and more foolish. She could learn to like bantering with him. Even more, she found herself craving more of his touch. She was leaving herself wide open to hurt if he should decide to leave once his boat was fixed.

But no matter how bad it might be, she was tired

of merely existing, afraid to experience life because she might have regrets. After all, no one made it through life without them. She'd missed out on love once. She wouldn't do so again, even if it didn't last any longer than the spring thaw.

The church was filling up quickly, making Isaac glad that Millie had talked them into arriving early. He'd chosen his seat based on the best view of the piano. He was sure all the children would be adorable in their costumes, but he wanted to watch Annie.

He thought about going up to wish her luck, but she was like a butterfly flitting from place to place to place. On his best days, he would have had a hard time catching up with her. With crutches, he'd have been following in her wake without making any progress.

Finally, the pastor moved to the front of the church, immediately drawing everyone's attention to him. "I would ask everyone to join me in prayer."

Bowing his head felt awkward to Isaac, but he did so out of respect. The prayer was short, asking for the Lord's help in getting through the evening. The pastor went on to remind everyone that it was the season of giving and miracles. Coming from any other preacher Isaac had ever met, the words would have held little meaning to him. But there was something about Pastor Chesterfield's simple faith that drew him.

Maybe Annie was right about not giving up hope. With that thought, he leaned back and let the beauty of the words and the children and the woman at the piano ease his weary soul.

It felt strange to be outside at night walking down Main Street and singing Christmas carols. The folks, mostly strangers to him, deliberately slowed their pace to let him keep up as they made their way to their various homes. The boardinghouse was only a short distance down the street, and he was surprised how much he wished it were farther away.

Annie was striding along beside him, almost floating on the night air with excitement. Millie and Joe were off to his left, his arm wrapped tight around her shoulders, declaring to one and all that she was his. Barton was belting out the latest song in a surprisingly good baritone. Had Christmas ever been this much fun when he was growing up?

Not that he remembered. Maybe it was the company that made it so special this time.

They'd reached the front steps of Annie's house. Everyone paused in their journeys to finish singing the last chorus of *Joy to the World*. Then Annie and the others made their way inside, accompanied by the fading echoes of "Merry Christmas" and "God Bless."

With coats hung up and the fire tended, they all gathered in the parlor. It felt good to be with friends on a night like this one. By unspoken agreement, they had let Isaac have the sofa. Annie sat down nearby, but not close enough by his reckoning. But he had no hold on her, not yet anyway, and he didn't want to presume, especially in front of everyone.

"Annie, you were wonderful!"

He meant it, too. The music had transformed a small-town Christmas pageant into something almost unearthly in its beauty. People would be talking about the performance for weeks to come. She looked pleased with herself and rightly so.

"I was so nervous starting out, but then the music spoke for itself." She leaned back against the sofa and smiled toward the fire. "I'm so wound up, I don't think I'll ever be able to sleep tonight."

She wasn't the only one, judging by everyone's obvious reluctance to be the first to leave the gathering.

"I left some cider on to heat when we left. Would anyone like a cup?" Millie stood up, ready to fetch the spicy concoction. She smiled when every hand in the room shot up. "I'll be right back."

Barton was leaning against the mantel, as always fiddling with his pipe. "Seems to me that since it's nigh onto midnight, we ought to consider opening some presents."

They all looked toward Annie, obviously wanting her approval, perhaps because it was her house after all. She bit her lip as she considered the sudden change in plans. After giving Isaac a strange look, she nodded.

Immediately, everyone disappeared, no doubt to pull gifts out of their hiding places. He did the same, not that he'd been especially clever with his choice of spots. On his way to his room, he stopped to tell Millie what all the excitement was about.

"I'll finish pouring the cider and be right out. I have a few things to gather up myself."

Joe was already in their shared room, bundling

up several small packages. "Do you need any help with carrying yours?"

"No, I should be fine." He tugged a couple of sacks out from under his bed. He'd already tied them together so he could carry them over his shoulder and still manage his crutches.

He was rather pleased to find that he wasn't the last one to return with his treasures. Barton was arranging his offerings under the tree and performed the same service for Isaac. The two of them took cups of Millie's cider and settled in to wait for the others.

"This is a good night to be alive." Barton smiled contentedly at the fire. "Good friends, good gifts, and good intentions."

Before Isaac could ask him what he meant by that last remark, the others came streaming in, laughing and excited. The few packages tucked under the small tree soon grew into a mound of gifts decked out with ribbons and bows.

Annie came in lugging a bucket of water. "I wanted to light the candles."

Joe took it from her hands and set it by the tree. "Go ahead. I'll stick close by just in case." No one took the chance of fire lightly.

"Thank you, Joe."

As he stood guard, Annie and Agatha lit all the candles on the tree. Soon their flickering light bathed the room in a warm glow.

"Who wants to hand out presents?"

"Being the oldest person here, I think I should have that privilege." Agatha rose to her feet and began handing out the packages to each person in the room. As she did so, she admonished, "Please wait until they are all distributed before opening them. We would all like to share in your excitement."

Isaac enjoyed watching as his friends shook and poked at each package that Agatha delivered. He was pleasantly surprised by the number of gifts that had his name on them. Finally, Agatha sat back down and arranged her own presents to her liking.

Then one by one, at her signal, they each chose a package to open. Millie seemed pleased by the tea he had bought her. Agatha exclaimed over the writing paper she'd received from someone else. Joe and Barton had gone in together to buy him a new log for the *Caprice*. He appreciated the gesture even if he'd never have a chance to write in it. He shoved that sad thought back out of his mind. This was a night for joy, not regrets.

Annie picked up a package. When she read the label, she smiled at him and then began to unwrap it. It would have been impossible to disguise the contents, but that didn't keep her face from lighting up in surprise when the last of the paper fell away.

"Music," she sighed, her fingers trailing over the words and notes. "You bought me music."

"I hope I picked out some you'll like." The store in Hart's Ferry hadn't had a huge selection, but he'd chosen carefully. "There's a couple of waltzes and a sonata or two."

She immediately set everything aside to scoot closer and kiss him. Right on the mouth. Right in front of everybody. It was the best gift of the night as far as he was concerned.

After the last present had been opened and admired, everyone grew quiet and looked at Annie.

The increased tension in the room puzzled him. What was wrong?

Slowly, she crossed the room. She stopped in front of the tree and wiped her hands on her skirt as if a sudden fit of the nerves had left them damp. Joe gave her an encouraging smile from his station next to the tree. Her shoulders rose as she drew a deep breath. From where he sat, Isaac couldn't see what she was picking up, but gauging from everyone else's intent expressions, he was the only one in the dark.

In the space of a heartbeat, he suddenly wished that he'd pleaded exhaustion and gone on to bed. Surely whatever had Annie's eyes looking so worried could have waited until morning.

"Isaac, we saved this one for last." She held out a large envelope in her trembling hand. "It's from all of us."

No one spoke and no one moved as they waited in heavy silence for him to accept her offering. He wasn't sure if the sound pulsing in his head was his heart or the clock on the mantle counting off the seconds until he could figure out what he was supposed to do next.

Barton cleared up that little mystery for him. "Open it, Isaac. I promise it won't bite."

He wished Annie would sit down rather than hovering in front of him looking as if she were on the verge of bolting from the room. His own hands were none too steady as he cut the top of the envelope with the letter opener that had magically appeared in front of him. He thought perhaps Agatha had brought it to him, but he wasn't sure.

A stack of two or three sheets of papers slid out

of the envelope, the rasp of paper on paper sounding unnaturally loud in the too quiet room. His eyes skimmed over the front page and then the second before returning to the beginning to linger over each word. As their meaning sank in, the blood in his veins ran hot, then cold. He didn't know what to say or do.

He didn't want charity. Every damn one of the people in the room knew that. He also didn't want to lose the *Caprice* just because he was too damn broke or too damn proud to accept help. The sheets of writing floated to his lap to sit there, waiting along with Annie and the others for him to speak.

Words weren't easy to come by when a man had just been handed back the life he'd thought he had lost. So he said exactly what he thought about their conspiracy to get past his pride and right to his heart. He said it simply and truthfully. And he said it straight to the woman he'd loved and lost and loved again.

He stood up, leaning on his crutches and giving them all his best wobbly smile, he managed to say, "Thank you."

The tension burst apart and disappeared in a flash of smiles and pats on the back and babbling statements about how proud they were to be part owners of a steamboat as fine as the *Caprice*. The whole time, Annie stood watching him, tears sparkling in her eyes. Then, when he was busy hugging Agatha, Annie disappeared.

It took a few minutes for everyone else to notice, but by then Isaac was already climbing the three flights of stairs to her room on the top floor.

The rest of them could sort themselves out on their own. He barely paused long enough to knock before he opened the door and pushed his way into Annie's room. He found her sitting on the edge of the bed crying, just as he knew she would be. He just wasn't sure why.

"Annie?"

"Go away." She turned away from him when he sat down next to her.

He ignored that the same way he ignored the tears. "What's wrong? Did I do something to upset you?" He obviously had, but again he had no idea what had gone wrong.

"No, it's not you." She managed to look him in the face, tears streaming down to drip off her cheeks. "You did everything right. You looked at what we did, what we offered, and instead of getting all huffy about it, you said thank you."

"What was I supposed to say? That was a very generous thing you all did. I would have never thought of taking on some temporary business partners until I get my boat back out on the river." He used the side of his thumb to wipe away her tears. Then he kissed her damp cheek. "It was all your idea, wasn't it?"

She nodded. "I knew you wouldn't take just my money. It had to be all of us to make it work."

Smart woman that she was, she had the right of it. A man had his pride, after all. Not that he was going to admit it and risk setting her off again. In the distance, he could hear the clock chiming out the midnight hour.

Christmas with all of its promises had finally arrived. And as she had told him only a few days before, maybe there were enough miracles to go around. He desperately needed one more.

"Annie, I've been a fool, but I'd like to think that I've changed since I was that boy you ran away from years ago." He risked an arm around her shoulders, pulling her closer.

"I was a coward back then, Isaac. I should have trusted you." Her hand lifted up to caress his face.

"You've built a wonderful home here in Willow Shoals." He glanced around her cozy room, tucked up under the eaves of the house. "It's a big place. I was wondering if you might have room for another permanent boarder once your regular ladies return."

She looked puzzled, but at least she wasn't crying anymore. "Joe has already asked to stay on. Of course, he plans on marrying Millie, so I don't know how long they'll live here. Either way, the other bed in that room—your bed—will always be there for you."

It was time to risk everything on a single throw of the dice. "I don't want to sleep in Joe's room, Annie. You see, I want to sleep in yours. And I'll be wanting some special privileges." Before she could protest, he hushed her with a single touch of his finger to her lips. "I want a husband's privileges, because I want a wife. And Annie, I want her to be you."

"But the *Caprice* . . ."

He finished the statement for her. "Because of you, she'll be fine, but she's not enough for me. Not anymore. I'd like to still captain her on a few runs each year. But now that Barton is going to be one of my partners, I figure I can trust him to handle her the rest of the time."

He held her close to his heart. "Please, Annie, don't hold it against me because I didn't know how to handle what happened the other night. What we shared was just so damn good that it scared me. I thought I'd never find anything like it again."

"What changed your mind?" She snuggled closer, giving him hope.

"I realized I didn't have to go looking for what was already right there in front of me. I love you, Annabelle Dunbar. Can you love me back?"

She surprised him by giggling. "You know, I so wanted to be mad when you left that morning, but I couldn't pull it off. Since I ran the last time, I figured I owed you one."

Then she kissed him with the kind of kiss that melts a man's soul. And when she was done, she smiled. "I'd be honored to be your wife, Captain Isaac Chase. I'll miss you when you're out on the river, but as long as I know you're coming back to me, I'll be fine."

Happier than he had felt for years, he decided once again to go for broke. While he kept his hands busy pulling the pins from her hair, letting it tumble down around her shoulders, he asked, "Think Pastor Chesterfield would be interested in celebrating Christmas with an unexpected wedding?"

Her smile lit up the room more brightly than all the candles on the tree. "I think we might be able to talk him into it. If not, I'm willing to wait—but no more than a day or two." She slid up onto his lap. "Tell me, though, how would you like to pass the time until we can ask him?"

Once again, the right words were hard for him to come by. Instead, he took great pleasure in showing her exactly what he had in mind.

Complete Your Collection Today
Janelle Taylor

Put a Little Romance in Your Life with
Georgina Gentry

Available Wherever Books Are Sold!

Visit our website at **www.kensingtonbooks.com**.